"A Caffeine Conundrum is a we [text obscured by barcode] dash of romance and a whole latte—I mean lot of—fun. I look forward to more adventures with Tandy and Marissa."

Christy Barritt—Publishers Weekly Bestselling Author of the Lantern Beach and Squeaky Clean Mystery series.

"A Caffeine Conundrum surprised me with a twist I didn't see coming."

Sandra Orchard—Award-winning author of Port Aster Secrets and Serena Jones Mysteries

A Caffeine Conundrum

A Caffeine Conundrum

Book One in the CafFUNated Mysteries

By

Angela Ruth Strong

A Caffeine Conundrum
Published by Mountain Brook Ink
White Salmon, WA U.S.A.

The website addresses shown in this book are not intended in any way to be or imply an endorsement on the part of Mountain Brook Ink, nor do we vouch for their content.

This story is a work of fiction. All characters and events are the product of the author's imagination. Any resemblance to any person, living or dead, is coincidental.

The author is represented by and this book is published in association with the literary agency of WordServe Literary Group, Ltd.,
www.wordserveliterary.com

Scripture quotations are taken from the King James Version of the Bible. Public domain.

ISBN 978-1-943959-47-1

The Team: Miralee Ferrell, Nikki Wright, Cindy Jackson
Cover Design: Indie Cover Design, Lynnette Bonner Designer

Mountain Brook Ink is an inspirational publisher offering fiction you can believe in.
Printed in the United States of America

DEDICATION

To Heather, Lisa, and Becky of *Team Love on the Run*, my partners in writing crime.

ACKNOWLEDGMENTS

As a fellow reader who grew up on Nancy Drew, I'm excited to share my very first cozy mystery with you. In the past I've written quirky romance and suspense, but now I get to mix my puns with peril, my jokes with jeopardy, and my anecdotes with danger. What could be more fun?

I'd first like to thank my editor, Miralee Ferrell, for believing in me and suggesting the idea of a cozy mystery series set in a coffee shop or tea house. Without her business sense and direction, all these great stories I get to tell would be nothing more than daydreams.

Next, I want to thank my mom who started The Daily Joy Tea House and is not only an inspiration for my story but for the pursuit of my dreams.

On the coffee side is my best friend, Charla, who I tried to get to start a coffee review vlog, but her hair was messed up the day I filmed her, so she never posted the clip. Now I just use her coffee knowledge for my own pursuits. (It helps that I'm a writer and not a vlogger because my hair rarely looks good.)

Heather Woodhaven and Kimberly Rose Johnson were my "mystery consultants extraordinaire." Good luck solving the crime faster than they did.

My dad has been known to drop in on our writing group at the local coffee shop to say hi, though with all his enthusiasm for life, he really doesn't need caffeine. I am thankful for his enthusiasm.

Thanks to Jim Strong who bought me a coffee pot when I was a single mom. He's the reason I enjoy writing heroes so much.

I'm thankful my girlies, Caitlin and Lauren, both love going to the tea house with me and wearing big hats and drinking with our pinkies up.

I'm thankful for my son, Jordan, who doesn't do tea or coffee, but he does do pizza and plotting.

I'd also like to thank The Journey Church where another one of Pastor Mike's sermons helped me tie up my story with a big red Christmas bow.

And, of course, you. I love that I get to share this book with you.

Chapter One

HIDDEN TREASURES WOULD SOON BELONG TO her. Marissa held her red knit beanie on her head and sighed in satisfaction as she looked up at the sign over the small town antique shop on a corner in downtown Grace Springs. She'd only been into the other antique shop in town, so it made sense that this one was going out of business. It would become a better teahouse anyway, allowing her to carry on Grandmother Ettabell's tradition of bringing beauty and elegance to the world. Her previous attempts hadn't worked out so well, but she'd put the past behind her and...

Her ankle snagged some kind of band or strap, throwing her stride off balance. Her hands splayed to catch her if she fell, which experience told her she would, though she still looked down in an attempt to find her footing.

Instead she found a black leash. Attached to a furry varmint. The dog yapped and dove between her legs, entangling her even more.

Marissa twisted, bent her knees, and plopped onto cold, stone steps. If only she'd been this graceful when stumbling off the stage at the Miss Ohio pageant last summer.

A dark-haired woman, supposedly in control of the leash, wore what looked like yesterday's eyeliner, a high ponytail, hoop earrings, and a little leather backpack in place of a purse. One fine eyebrow arched in cynicism. "You okay?"

Marissa stiffened for two reasons. First because the stranger could at least pretend to care. And second because her accident was really the other woman's fault. "You need to watch where your dog is going," she said before she could sugarcoat her words with the artificial sweetener ladies in her family were so well-known for serving.

The dog owner lazily untangled the leash, dropping it low enough for Marissa to step over like they were playing a game of jump rope. "Cocoa wasn't going anywhere. The two of us were just standing here. I expected you to stop or go around us."

"Oh." Warmth burned Marissa's cheeks. She ducked her face, pretending to look at the fluffy little dog. He was kind of cute. A Pomeranian perhaps. Marissa would have expected this woman dressed in black to own an attack dog. "Sorry, Cocoa."

Cocoa's owner extended a hand to help her up. "I take it you're heading into the antique shop?"

Marissa eyed the black leather glove warily. She didn't want to accidentally pull the other woman down on top of her, but to salvage her pride, she accepted the offer by clasping hands. "Yes, thank you." She carefully shifted her weight forward to stand. Her tailbone only stung a little. At least her knee-length wool coat had softened the landing.

The other woman released their connection and led Cocoa to the side of the stairs. "I'll get out of your way."

Marissa gave a weak smile, though she should be used to jokes like this. She always did her best to play along. "Well, nice meeting you. Maybe we'll run into each other again sometime."

Lips smirked, but green eyes lightened in a brief flash of humor. "I wouldn't be surprised."

The other woman couldn't just leave it alone, could she? Marissa hoped she never had to deal with this snarky pet lover again. "Watch your dog, and we won't. Who wants a

2

dog that little anyway?"

One of the owner's shoulders lifted lazily. "Who doesn't?"

"Normal people." Marissa brushed off her rear, pivoted on the toe of her high-heeled boot, and returned to the task at hand. Hopefully she'd gotten all the clumsiness out of her system, but just in case, she'd be careful in the store. Some of the antiques were sure to be both expensive and fragile. She gave her image a once over in the glass door to be certain she was presentable before ushering herself inside the building's warmth to the sound of a tinkling bell.

The place smelled like musty wood, but before long it would smell of cranberry scones and citrus spice tea. If only she'd been able to open shop before the holiday season. She would have decorated with Grandmother's Christmas village and teddy bear collection. The owner, Virginia Pierce, had stuck with a traditional snowflake and twinkle light theme. Not very original for someone who valued vintage beauty.

"Marissa Alexander, it *is* you." An older woman dressed in a high-collared blouse with her hair piled on top of her head stepped through a door at the back of the room and wound through the maze of furniture. "I recognized your name from the Miss Ohio pageant."

Marissa would have preferred if Virginia only recognized her name. The Alexander name had been well-known since the town was founded by J.D. Alexander in 1849. It had an honorable reputation until Marissa had become known as Miss Grace*less* Springs. With the way Virginia said the name Alexander, she certainly considered it tarnished.

"Yes, that's me." Marissa extended a hand with all the graciousness of a Disney princess. Though Disney should really make a movie about the girl who didn't get the crown and aged past the point where it would be a possibility.

Because that would be a better fit for her life. "And you must be Virginia Pierce."

"I am." Virginia pinched the tips of Marissa's fingers before pulling away. "Come on back to my office, dear."

Marissa followed, taking in the overhead chandelier she would keep for the teahouse and the cracked glass display cases she would get rid of. The loft at the top of the staircase would make a great spot for tea parties. Did the antique shop sell old hats? Because those would be fun to offer her customers as costumes to wear during high tea.

Marissa entered the fancy office with its Oriental rug and the Tiffany lamp set on a writing desk. Virginia had classic taste.

"Can I get you any coffee?" the shop owner asked.

"Oh no." Coffee would never be served in this place again. "I only drink tea."

Virginia gave a knowing smile. "Of course, of course."

Marissa sank into a padded wooden chair painted off-white with gold trim. She clasped her hands over her crossed knee. "Your shop will make a lovely teahouse. I'm super excited you accepted my offer."

"Actually..." Virginia didn't sit but looked out into the larger room.

Actually? What did she mean by actually?

"I've had two offers."

Marissa's brain buzzed with the sound of static. "Two offers?" she asked as if trying to adjust an old, rabbit-ear antenna to catch a better signal.

"Yes." Virginia placed a hand over her heart. "So I thought I'd bring in the other party, and the two of you could have a bidding war right here in my office."

Oh no. No. No. No. Marissa didn't have any more money to bid. And she didn't have any way to make more money since she'd put in her two weeks' notice at the bank when Virginia invited her in to negotiate a contract. Why hadn't the shop owner been clearer? This was so sneaky.

The bell over the front door rang.

"Excuse me while I greet your competition." Virginia's voice almost purred.

Who else had put in an offer? Did they have the money to outbid Marissa? Would she have to wave the white flag and admit another life defeat?

Tandy Brandt made sure Cocoa did his business outside before bringing him in the antique store to stay warm. There wasn't much space to secure his leash with all the old furniture and knick-knacks, so she'd just keep the Pomeranian with her. When she started her coffee shop though, she'd make sure to have a corner for animals. She'd even make them homemade doggie treats.

"What is *that*?" an older woman at the back of the store asked in disdain.

Tandy glanced around and didn't see anything disdainful, but she lifted Cocoa into her arms to be safe. "What?"

"What you're holding."

"Oh." Tandy looked up from her pup to meet the woman's narrowed eyes. She was probably a cat person. "This is Cocoa. And you are?"

"I'm the owner, Virginia Pierce." The woman said it like it made her more important. She really needed to work on her sales pitch.

"Nice to meet you, Ginny. I'm Tandy."

The woman grimaced the way Tandy knew she would. "Ahem." She cleared her throat and disappeared behind a curtain into what Tandy assumed was a kitchenette area by the humming of a refrigerator. "Can I get you any coffee before we begin?"

Coffee? Tandy could use a cup of coffee. When she opened the shop, the whole place would smell like dark roast, but at the moment, the air was suspiciously absent of its inviting aroma. An empty jar of instant granules stuck out of the trash can by the curtain, confirming her suspicions. She barely refrained from gasping in horror, but her toes curled inside her fuzzy socks and biker boots. "Um…no thanks."

"Well then." Virginia reappeared with a white mug then paused to sip her imitation brew. She licked her lips and peered into her cup with a scowl. "Not the best cup I've ever made, but let's get down to business." She led the way toward an office at the back of the shop.

"Sure." Tandy studied the interior of the shop as she followed Virginia. She liked the brick wall. It would add to the retro vibe she hoped to create with reclaimed timber and chair cushions made out of burlap coffee bags. Though that ostentatious chandelier overhead would have to go in favor of something more industrial.

"Tandy Brandt, I'd like you to meet Marissa Alexander."

Tandy stepped through the doorway to find the klutzy blonde beauty she'd met earlier, sitting in the office. She was the kind of person who might not be relatable if she didn't trip over things. But she had tripped, which made Tandy like her more than she liked most people.

Cocoa barked in recognition.

Running into familiar faces probably happened more often in small towns. Tandy certainly wasn't in Cincinnati anymore. "Hi."

The blonde stared at her in revulsion. Was she afraid Tandy was going to spill the beans on her embarrassing moment?

Tandy had her own embarrassing story to keep to herself, so she wouldn't gossip. She gave an encouraging nod. They were on the same side.

Virginia motioned for Tandy to take a seat then crossed to a studded leather chair behind her desk, downing her coffee like an addict. Why else would someone drink instant coffee? That was worse than baking pastries in a microwave. As much as Tandy loved coffee, she considered herself more of a connoisseur than an addict.

Virginia finally set her mug down. "The reason I've invited you both here today is because I can't decide between your two offers."

Tandy froze mid sit. "Wait. What?" The blonde had made an offer on the shop as well? Then they were not on the same side. She shot to her full height so she could look down on the other woman.

Virginia smoothed her hair. "I believe Grace Springs could use both a teahouse and a coffee shop."

"A teahouse?" Tandy turned on Marissa. "How are you going to serve drinks in China cups when you can't even climb stairs without tripping?" Okay, that's wasn't fair, but her future was at stake here. The antique shop was the only commercial real estate available downtown, and Tandy had come to this town because it was the last place she'd made any good memories. Back when she was twelve. She was due a few more.

The blonde stiffened the same way she had on the steps outside. "I only tripped because of your silly varmint."

Oh, so Marissa was back to blaming Cocoa again, not to

mention the name-calling. Tandy would have loved to release the hound with a "sic her," but nobody was in any danger from Cocoa unless they were afraid of being licked to death. The pup hadn't even mastered the game of fetch yet.

Marissa turned toward Virginia as if Tandy and the "varmint" weren't worth her time. "Ms. Pierce, Grace Springs is so quaint and charming with Victorian homes and cobblestone streets and the historic riverboat cruises. Tourists are going to want the teahouse parties over the kind of cup of Joe they can get back home."

"Really? Who says cup of Joe anymore?" Tandy challenged. Not the best argument, but the first thought that came to mind.

"Joe does," Marissa responded just as quickly and ridiculously.

Virginia lifted her cup again and watched them over the brim.

Why was the woman still drinking that stuff? "Virginia, uh...I mean Ms. Pierce." Tandy certainly wouldn't call her Ginny anymore. Hopefully the nickname wouldn't kill her chances here. She had to make up for it. "Not everyone can brew a good cup of coffee. Let me show you how it's done. I brought you a bag of beans that I roasted myself." They had coffee in common. At least that was a start.

Virginia tilted her almost empty cup Tandy's way with a shake of her head. "I'm supposed to be cutting back, so I really shouldn't have any more."

Marissa sank deeper into her seat. Probably in relief. Though what did she have to worry about? She had hometown advantage. Even if it didn't give her priority with Virginia, it meant she had family or friends nearby who could help out.

If Virginia was setting them up to go head to head,

hoping to wring every last dollar out of them, she'd be sadly disappointed. Tandy had no more dollars to be wrung.

She dropped into a rickety old chair in resignation. "I gave you the highest offer I could, Virginia."

Marissa observed her, dark brown eyes wary. She finally faced forward again. "So did I."

"Well, girls." Virginia drained the rest of her mock coffee and set the mug on the table. "Looks like we have ourselves a conundrum."

Really? Tandy wanted to ask again. *Who says conundrum anymore?* But she kept her mouth shut. The shop owner apparently enjoyed creating conundrums.

Virginia reached across her body to rub her left shoulder. Her mouth opened as if to continue, but she only sucked at the air.

Cocoa whimpered.

"Virginia?" Marissa prompted.

Tandy leaned forward, studying the older woman's face.

The contemptuous glint in Virginia's steely eyes glazed over. She shuddered then slid off her seat onto the floor. Tandy scrambled to check her pulse as Marissa called for an ambulance. But it was too late.

The shop owner was dead.

Chapter Two

TANDY STUDIED THE POLICE DEPUTY WHO looked more like a kid in a Halloween costume. Weren't little towns supposed to have old sheriffs who loved their easy job so much they refused to retire?

This kid was making his job way harder than it had to be. He held a stylus over his phone, taking notes the modern way as EMTs released Virginia's corpse to the coroner and the Marissa chick made a panicked phone call to her mother. Tandy's mother was the last person she wanted to talk with, so she rubbed Cocoa's silky ears to comfort herself while answering the detective's questions.

"You say Ms. Pierce brought you in to have a bidding war over the shop?" The kid looked up and narrowed his eyes.

Tandy narrowed her eyes right back. Did he suspect her of foul play? Virginia had most certainly died from a heart attack. The way she'd grabbed her left arm was a clear sign. "Yes." She kept her tone even.

Perhaps her coolness made her a suspect because she wasn't freaking out like the other witness. Or perhaps it was because she was an outsider. As usual.

"Interesting." The kid acted like they were playing a game of Clue.

A turquoise vase decorated with the image of a dragon teetered from its perch on a nearby pedestal, announcing Marissa's arrival with the clinking sound of porcelain on stone. "Sorry. Sorry." She caught the vase, and though it had sounded like it might have been chipped, it appeared completely intact. Not so for Marissa, whose beanie slipped from her head. She straightened the vase then swiped her hat off the floor before standing up fast enough to whip most of her long hair behind her back. One strand remained over an eye, but she blew it to the side. "Whew, I'm super glad I didn't break that old thing. What did I miss?"

Tandy waited for the kid to resume his line of questioning, but he simply stared at the blonde with his mouth hanging slightly open. Was he in awe of her beauty or her clumsiness? Both were equally impressive. And Tandy was hard to impress.

She tilted her head toward him. "Encyclopedia Brown here thinks it's interesting that Virginia died after tricking us into a bidding war."

"What?" Marissa threw her hands wide, barely missing the vase this time. "Where is Officer Woodward?" She leaned forward to better read the nametag on the kid's uniform. "Deputy Griffin?" She stood straight. "Lucas Griffin? Little Lukey? I used to babysit you when you were eight. Are you out of high school now? When did you graduate?"

Little Lukey focused intently on his smart phone. "I graduated from college last year. Got my bachelor's in criminal justice."

"I guess I'm only six years older than you, but wow. I thought by now I'd be..." Marissa's speech trailed off into rapid blinking. "Never mind. Where is Officer Woodward?"

The kid glanced up, his expression a mix of puppy dog looking for love and kitten backed into a corner. Tandy could handle the puppy dog in him, but she knew better than to mess with a scared cat. He rubbed his clean-shaven jaw, though honestly, he probably didn't have to shave that regularly. "Woodward has been called in to investigate a heist at the Grace Springs Historical Society Heritage Museum."

The blonde nodded. "Oh, I heard about that. The six diamonds that have been found here in Ohio were on display. Super awful that anyone would take them."

Tandy hadn't heard of them, but it made sense that Marissa had. With the way she dialed her mom as soon as the shopkeeper died, she was sure to know all the latest gossip. Though a jewel heist sounded more like headline news than gossip. Definitely not what Tandy expected when moving to a small town.

"Officer Woodward knows you're here then?" Tandy asked to be sure.

The deputy's eyes snapped her direction. "Certainly. I go on routine calls all the time."

That's what Tandy had been hoping to hear. "So the officer believes this call is routine and Virginia Pierce died of natural causes?"

The deputy grunted. "We all hope it is natural causes, but Virginia was kind of a family friend. I'll make sure to do her justice by reporting any suspicious findings."

Marissa tilted her head, a lone wrinkle forming above her upturned nose and marring her smooth skin. "Such as?"

The kid read through his notes again. "Such as how Ms. Pierce drank coffee right before she died."

Tandy's heart rate shot up. "Don't blame the coffee." She would almost rather she be accused of murder than for coffee to get a bad rap. "Studies show that drinking four to five cups a day helps people live longer."

"I don't know how they can prove that." Marissa rolled her eyes toward the ugly chandelier. "However, it *has* been proven that coffee can negatively affect digestion, increase stress, and cause heartburn."

Tandy guffawed. "That can be said for overdosing on

caffeine in general—including your precious tea."

Marissa stuck a hand on her hip, ignoring the cold gust of wind and tinkling bell from the door. "Well Virginia wasn't drinking *tea* when she died."

"My mom is dead?" A woman in her early twenties with chin-length curly brown hair stood in the doorway, her skin as white as the snow outside.

Oh no. Virginia's daughter.

Marissa covered her mouth.

"Excuse me while I talk to Jenn." The deputy cleared his throat and stepped away.

Tandy pressed her lips together and nuzzled Cocoa to avoid eye contact with her new nemesis. Why did she have to have a nemesis everywhere she went? Why couldn't people get along with her the way dogs did?

"I can't believe I said that," Marissa whispered.

Maybe they weren't nemeses after all. It wasn't like they were still going to have a bidding war for the shop with Virginia gone. Who cared if Marissa drank tea? She also wore a red beanie, and Tandy wouldn't hold that against her. "You didn't know." She offered the olive branch.

Marissa lifted a finger to wipe at a tear.

Tandy shifted her weight uncomfortably and planned an escape route between an armoire and a rocking chair. Not being enemies didn't mean they were friends. And it especially didn't mean she was offering a shoulder to cry on. "I'm gonna—"

"This is like when I came home from the Miss Ohio competition to find out my grandmother had died. Nobody had told me because they didn't want to distract me from the beauty pageant, but I'd been competing for Grandmother in the first place."

Beauty pageant? Right when Tandy had started to like

Marissa...

"At least she didn't have to find out I was the first Alexander since Miss USA started in 1952 to come home without the crown. That was my last year to compete at that level, and I should have won."

Marissa had lost? Of course she'd lost. She was as graceful as a reindeer wearing ice skates.

"That would be tough," Tandy agreed. She'd stick around to protect any antiques that could get in Marissa's way. Virginia's daughter was sure to have enough to mourn without her mom's prized possessions being destroyed in the wake of the town's aspiring beauty queen.

Marissa sighed, her eyes filling up again as she looked toward the deputy discussing Virginia's death with the dead woman's daughter.

Tandy followed her line of sight and grimaced. If they were comparing Virginia's daughter's circumstances to their own lives, she'd compare Virginia's death to her own mom's decision to divorce her dad and take off with their pastor. That had kind of been like a murder.

The deputy shot a skittish glance her way. He looked how she felt—ready to run. How close had he been to the Pierce family?

"I...I can't believe she's gone." Virginia's daughter twisted her fingers, eyes on the floor. "Can I see her now?"

"I'm so sorry, Jenn." The deputy sighed and put an arm around her. "I'd like to ask you a couple questions before you go, if you don't mind. Is there anything you can tell me about your mom's health? Any new issues?"

Jenn's chin puckered. "As you know, she had atrial fibrillation." Her voice faded, and it was a moment before she could continue. "Mom was selling the shop to get rid of extra stress in her life. The doctor warned her to cut out both stress and caffeine."

Caffeine? Oh man. It *had* been the coffee that killed her.

Marissa gasped. Despite what she'd said to Tandy-the-rebel-barista, she hadn't seriously thought Virginia had been killed by drinking coffee. She'd believed the drink to be unrefined, but not deadly. This had to be rare.

Both Lukey's and Jenn's eyes focused on her.

"What are you doing here?" Jenn's voice held mistrust. Naturally, she had every right to be emotional after her mom's passing.

Marissa didn't mean to interfere. "I'm...I'm here because—"

"I know you. You were the prom queen when I was a freshman." Jenn pointed. "Though you didn't fall off stage then the way you did at the Miss Ohio Pageant."

Tandy's head cocked sideways. "You fell off a stage?"

Marissa waved her arms as if she could erase the visual. "I was tripped and—" The back of her hand smacked into something sharp, stinging like the insertion of an IV line. She knew about IVs because of the time she'd gotten dehydrated on a bike ride and passed out while riding over a bridge, fell into the river, and was rescued by the man she'd once thought she'd marry. If only this pain had been caused by something so harmless.

A vintage brass picture frame clattered sideways and slid towards the edge of the French country bookshelf. Marissa watched in horror. She'd been trying to be so careful.

In one fluid motion, Tandy lunged forward, clutching her

dog in one arm and swiping her other hand underneath the tumbling antique. Her fingers curled around the frame so quickly that by the time Marissa blinked in disbelief, the frame had been set upright and Tandy was petting Cocoa again.

Marissa exhaled in relief. She couldn't help wondering what would have happened in the beauty pageant if this woman had been standing next to her instead of Miss Cincinnati with her runway pose and pointy-toed stilettos. Maybe Tandy wasn't so bad. Even if she drank coffee.

The tick of a grandfather clock behind Marissa grew louder, and she realized that while she stared at Tandy, the rest of the people in the room stared at her.

Little Lukey rubbed his chin. "Perhaps we should all sit down."

Was he remembering the time she'd been making him macaroni for lunch then accidentally set his kitchen curtains on fire? If so, it would be best if she found a place to sit quickly so they could return their focus to the real tragedy — Jenn's mother's untimely death.

Spotting what Grandmother would have called a settee, Marissa scurried toward it and plunked down, hands tucked under her legs to keep them from waving hazardously. Mom was always trying to get her to sit on her hands to appear more ladylike. She'd never really supported this endeavor to start a teahouse, because she didn't think Marissa could handle it, but Marissa had wanted to prove her wrong. Now she might not get that chance, unless she could convince Jenn to sell to her.

Tandy followed at a slower pace, eyeing Marissa.

"I'm sitting on my hands. You're safe."

Tandy lowered onto the gold brocade cushions, giving her dog the opportunity to lean over and lick Marissa's cheek with his wet tongue. Marissa grimaced, but kept her hands under her legs.

"Sorry." Tandy caught Cocoa's muzzle between her fingers. "No licking."

Marissa pasted on a smile. It wasn't that she didn't like animals. It was simply that as often as she tripped over them, it felt like they were out to get her. Kind of like Miss Cincinnati. She turned her damp face toward the deputy she still thought of as an eight-year-old. Because seriously, his skin looked that smooth.

Lukey must have released Jenn to tend to her mother because he strode their way alone and planted himself above them with a wide-legged stance. It reminded Marissa of the way he used to play superhero with his Underoos over his pajamas and a pillow case pinned around his neck like a cape. He scrolled through his phone then paused. His gaze rose to scrutinize them. "It appears I was right to question what was in Ms. Pierce's mug."

Marissa's lips parted. Witnessing a death was hard enough, but Lukey sounded like he wanted to take it further. "Obviously, Virginia shouldn't have been drinking coffee, but there's nothing we can do about it now."

Tandy's expression remained neutral. "You know, they do make this brew called decaf."

Marissa pursed her lips in thought. "Maybe this has nothing to do with her coffee at all."

"Or maybe..." Lukey took turns at attempting to peer into their souls. "Maybe she thought she was drinking decaf, but someone made her regular coffee. *Strong* coffee."

Marissa wished she still had the power to put him in a time out. "You think somebody wanted to kill Virginia?" Her voice squeaked on the word kill. Because this was Grace Springs, Ohio. Where the worst thing that ever happened was dehydration by bike ride. Well besides the jewel robbery, but that was likely done by someone from out of town. Locals wouldn't know the first thing about planning a heist. "Who would do that?"

Lukey quirked an eyebrow. "Perhaps someone whom she was trying to take advantage of by forcing them into a bidding war for her shop?"

"What?" Marissa's hands must have escaped from underneath her legs because they appeared in front of her, fingers splayed wide as if his logic were impossible to grasp. And it really was. "Are you accusing me of murder? You know me better than that. Your mom trusted me with your life."

The expression on his baby face remained unchanged. "Until you—"

Her right hand twisted into the signal for stop. "That was an accident," she whispered, though it wasn't like she could keep Tandy from overhearing another admission.

Tandy studied her out of the corner of her eye.

Marissa bit her lip. "Nobody died."

Lukey nodded in understanding. About time. "I guess you could have accidentally made Ms. Pierce regular coffee instead of decaf."

Marissa's hands flew wide again. "I don't make coffee for anyone. I'm starting a teahouse, remember?"

Lukey's gaze sliced toward Tandy like a laser. "Did you make coffee for Ms. Pierce?"

Tandy's chartreuse eyes widened. "No way. I wouldn't even drink the sludge she was serving."

She sounded innocent, but... "You *were* with her when she came into the office with a mug. *And* you said you brought coffee beans in your backpack." Marissa pointed at Tandy's face as the realization struck. Was she sitting by a cold-blooded killer?

Tandy slapped her hand down. "Put that thing away before you hurt someone."

Marissa ignored the sting of the words. "Someone is already hurt."

Tandy shook her head. "Not by me." She faced Lukey again. "The coffee was already made when I entered the shop, and the only people in the shop before me were Virginia and Marissa."

If Tandy was being honest, then Virginia was responsible. Whether it was decaf or not, Virginia made it, Virginia drank it, and Virginia died. There was nobody to blame but herself.

Lukey slid his stylus into the side of his phone and stuffed it in his pocket. "Well, ladies. I've got both your statements. The coroner will be checking Ms. Pierce's blood, including her caffeine levels, and I'll be checking out the remaining coffee in the pot."

Marissa sank against the cushions. She was glad not to have to defend herself anymore. The evidence would do that for her.

Tandy, on the other hand, sat up straighter. Cocoa whimpered.

Lukey hooked his thumbs in his belt loops. "If you're both as innocent as you say you are, then there shouldn't be any problem."

"Great." Marissa was free to go.

"But until we know that for sure, you'll have to stay in town."

Well, not entirely free yet, but close enough. Marissa was planning to stay in town anyway. There was the tree lighting that night then the Santa fun run and the living nativity on Christmas Eve. She wasn't as excited about going to Mom and Dad's for dinner, but that never stopped her before. "Okay," she agreed. The sooner they ruled Virginia's death from natural causes, the sooner she could make Virginia's heir, Jenn, an offer for the place. This time she'd be sure to beat Tandy to the purchase.

"Okay," Tandy parroted, though by the way she shot Marissa a warning look, the competition was on.

"Good." Lukey accepted their agreement before taking off for the curtain that hid the kitchenette.

Marissa twisted to face her competitor. If she explained the fact she wanted to start the tea shop in Grandma Ettabell's honor to make up for losing what had once been the older woman's crown, Tandy might take pity on her. "I know what you're thinking."

Tandy's chest rose and fell against her pup as she took a deep breath. "No, you don't, Marissa." She sounded so calm. Like she wanted to protect Marissa rather than go into battle against her. Not to mention the haunted look in her eyes.

Dare Marissa ask? "What then?"

Tandy glanced at Lukey's retreating back then lowered her voice. "I think the police will discover Virginia was murdered, and we will be the prime suspects."

Chapter Three

HOW HAD TANDY GOTTEN HERSELF INTO this? She'd left the big city to have a fresh start and possibly reconnect with an old friend, but trouble seemed to follow her everywhere she went. No matter how much she wished she was wrong about Virginia, she knew from what she'd seen that the police were going to find extremely high levels of caffeine in Virginia's blood.

Marissa stood and whirled to face her. "What do you mean *we* are going to be the prime suspects? *I* didn't do anything."

Officer Griffin peered at them from around the curtain.

Tandy stood and motioned Marissa toward the door. If Marissa was going to cause a scene, it would be best if she did so away from view of law enforcement. "I didn't do anything either."

"Then how would you know?" Marissa planted her feet.

Tandy had only been trying to prepare her, maybe even team up with her to prove themselves innocent. But if Marissa suspected her, then the other woman would probably rather team up with the police.

Fine. Tandy would say what she had to say then let Marissa decide what to do with it. "Officer Griffin told us Virginia made a pot of coffee, but I saw an empty jar of instant granules in the garbage can so I assumed she was making instant. If someone replaced Virginia's coffee grinds with instant granules, knowing she would use it in her coffee pot, one cup of the brew would be equivalent to, say, forty cups.

Her coffee would have been strong enough to cause heart problems in one of us, let alone kill someone in her condition."

Should she be right, this was no accident. It wasn't even an act of passion. It was premeditated murder.

Marissa's hands settled over her mouth then slipped down to her heart. "Who would do that?"

Tandy glanced past her shoulder to see if Deputy Griffin was watching, but he was busy tugging latex gloves over his fingers to collect the evidence that would incriminate them. "I know who the police will suspect. The two of us. We had the means and motive of revenge."

Marissa gripped the shoulders of Tandy's leather jacket and leaned forward. Probably realizing how being a murder suspect might affect her chances of winning future beauty pageants. "We didn't do it."

At least they were in agreement there. "Right. Which means there is a murderer on the loose in Grace Springs."

Marissa's grip tightened as she craned her neck to look through the big bay window. Did she expect to find the perp peering in from the street? Only footprints in the falling snow revealed life under the old-fashioned lanterns.

Cocoa yipped and wriggled under Tandy's grip. He must have sensed they'd been headed outside and grown frustrated with the holdup.

Marissa's dark eyes returned to focus on Tandy, bringing with them an extra chill. "What do we do?"

Cocoa shifted his weight forward. Tandy lowered him so he could land lightly on the floor then double-wrapped his leash around her wrist. "Right now I have to take my dog outside."

Marissa released her hold and whirled to open the front door for them. The bell rang as she swung it wide. She jolted at the sound, letting the door swing back toward Tandy's face.

Tandy held out a palm to catch the door before Cocoa got squished. "No worries. I've got it." She shook her head. That couldn't be farther from the truth. To think when they'd entered, she'd been imagining a puppy corner for her dog. Now she had to try to figure out who would take care of Cocoa if she went to jail. It wasn't like she had friends or family nearby.

"I'm sorry." Marissa followed them out into the stinging air. A blanket of gray clouds blocked any warmth from the sun, which seemed particularly fitting for their situation. "I'm a little jumpy with the thought of a killer on the loose."

From what Tandy had learned of Marissa over the past hour, jumpiness was normal—unless Marissa wasn't always this clumsy, and she was only nervous about committing murder.

Nah. She'd fallen off a stage at a beauty pageant and also done something to cause Deputy Griffin's mom to fire her from babysitting years ago. The woman was dangerous, but not a murderer.

"It's okay." Tandy crunched through the snow as Cocoa led her toward a red fire hydrant. The town seemed so peaceful. She didn't want to think it could be hiding a killer. The problem was that the townsfolk wouldn't want to think there was a killer among them either, which was why she was going to get blamed for this. Unless she was able to point her finger at someone else.

She sighed and looked up from her pup to scan the street. In cop shows, there was always a bank nearby with cameras that would catch the criminal, but all she could see from her spot on Main Street was a restaurant, knitting shop, salon, law office, and another antiques store. Maybe someone in Mama's Kitchen had witnessed a...

Her gaze returned to the other antique store with its black

shutters and gingerbread trim. Grandma's Attic. That would have been Virginia's competitor. Of anybody in town, the owner might benefit the most from Virginia's death.

Marissa stepped into her line of site, wrapping gloved fingers around a lamppost. "Should we tell Lukey—I mean, Deputy Griffin—about the instant coffee? Or should we wait until he gets the results on Virginia's blood? Because if you're wrong, then we're going to freak everyone out for no reason."

Marissa didn't believe her? Probably didn't *want* to believe her. But if such a belief kept Marissa from talking to the deputy, Tandy was okay with that. It would give her a little more time to investigate before the murderer was alerted that they were onto him. "We should wait."

Marissa's shoulders relaxed away from her ears. "I was hoping you'd say that."

Tandy pressed her lips together. She might be better off snooping around without Marissa. It was hard to act covert when working with someone known for bumping into things.

She scooped Cocoa's shivering little body into her arms and headed toward the crosswalk. "I'll let you get back to sticking your head in the snow and avoiding the truth." Oops. She'd only meant to say goodbye.

"What?" Marissa's feet slipped. She wrapped both arms around the lamppost and hugged it to stay upright. "Where are you going?"

"Grandma's Attic." Tandy wasn't too worried about the other woman trying to follow. Not with the drop in temperature freezing what had been melting snow. Marissa would have as much luck as Bambi trying to walk across ice in her high-heeled boots.

"Why?" Marissa called after her, likely hoping Tandy was only going to Grandma's Attic to look for some vintage Nancy Drew novels to read in case she got snowed into her apartment that night.

Tandy paused at the street to stay out of the way of a giant blue pickup tossing chunks of snow as it passed. It rumbled to a stop at the curb, allowing her to answer without yelling. "'Grandma' is on my suspect list."

"Billie isn't a murderer," Marissa hissed. "Wait for me." She tentatively let go of the post with one hand and extended a leg. Finding solid footing, she pushed away.

The truck door squeaked then slammed shut. Marissa shot a quick glance over her shoulder as if afraid the truck driver was a serial killer and now after them.

Should Tandy go back and take her arm to steady her or send her home where she was safer? Cocoa shivered. She needed to get him indoors. "It's okay, Marissa. I'm only going to ask a few questions. It's not like I have the power to arrest anybody."

Marissa held her arms wide like a circus performer on a tightrope. She continued toward the street and even leaped a small snowbank. She grinned up triumphantly. "I know, but—" Both feet shot forward, sending her flying backward. At least she'd have that snowbank to land in.

The man from the truck stopped Marissa's fall with an arm behind her back and one under her knees. He squatted to catch his balance then straightened with eyes locked on hers.

Tandy rolled her own eyes. Of course. The beautiful woman *would* get caught by a strong man wearing a Sherpa lined flannel and a cute trucker hat.

Marissa glared into Connor's gorgeous gray eyes, which glinted with pride at his heroics and humor at her predicament. Even if he smelled like pine and felt like granite, she would have rather landed in the snow. He was the whole reason she'd tried to run on ice in the first place.

"What are *you* doing here?" she demanded, though if she was going to make demands, she should have demanded he put her down. Because now they were going to have this conversation with him holding her in his arms. And he might mistakenly conclude she was okay with that.

One corner of his lips curved up, revealing that he was, indeed, concluding things. "I heard Hidden Treasures was being sold, and I thought I'd offer my remodeling services to the new owner."

She grimaced. He'd apparently found out she was planning to buy the place, and as much as she wanted to rub it in his face that were she the new owner, she would never in a million years hire him for a remodel, that wasn't the biggest tragedy of the day. "Put me down, Connor."

His cheeks dimpled, emphasizing his rugged jaw. This was what a man's jaw was supposed to look like. Not that she was looking.

"Only after you thank me for catching you." He tilted his head in admonishment. "You know your grandmother would be horrified to see you not using your manners."

How dare he bring Grandmother into this? She shoved against his shoulder in an effort to force him to put her down. His hold remained firm, which irked her even more. Cocoa would have a better chance of leaping out of Tandy's arms than she would have of escaping Connor.

Tandy clicked her tongue from the curb. "I'm not sure what's going on here, but it looks like you two have some things to work out, so I'm going to go give a different grandma the third degree."

Marissa scrunched her eyes closed. She didn't want to

look at Connor. She didn't want to think about Connor. He may have rescued her from falling into a snowbank, but he couldn't help her out with any of her other problems.

"Who was that?" Connor asked, and Marissa opened her eyes to find him watching Tandy cross the street.

She huffed. Not that she cared if he was interested in Tandy, but he was still holding her while asking about another woman. "She's my competition."

Connor's gaze dropped back to hers. His eyes narrowed in confusion, and his grip loosened. "What do you mean?"

She took the opportunity to swing a leg to the ground.

Connor lowered her other leg until she was standing, but he kept one arm behind her back. He'd likely claim it was to stabilize her, but they both knew it was to throw her off balance.

She planted her hands firmly on his chest to keep from falling into it. Things hadn't worked out so well last time she'd fallen for him. "I mean she *was* my competition. She also put in an offer to buy Hidden Treasures, and Virginia Pierce, the shop owner, brought us both in for a bidding war." Marissa twisted away from Connor's warmth to catch up with Tandy. "Then Virginia died."

Connor didn't follow though he kept his arms out in case Marissa slipped again. Was he frozen with shock? Good. That would give her a chance to get away and rescue Billie from Tandy's misguided assumptions.

"Did you say the store owner died?" Connor trailed after her.

Marissa pulled her beanie down tighter so it didn't fly off as she hopped from dry patch to dry patch to cross the street. Why had she worn her boots with heels again? "Yes. Heart attack."

"Oh man. You okay?"

No, but she could pretend. That's what Alexander women did. "Fine, fine." She waved him away. "Go talk to Lukey Griffin inside the shop. He can give you more info."

She chanced a glance over her shoulder to see if Connor had taken the bait. Instead, he strode into the street after her. "Why would I want to talk to Lukey?"

Marissa stepped safely onto the sidewalk. She'd made it this far at least. "He's a deputy now."

Connor stopped in the middle of the road and scratched his head, looking back toward the bay window of Virginia's shop. "Little Lukey? He can't even beat me in the Ho-Ho-Holiday Run, so how's he gonna catch any bad guys?"

"That was *my* reaction too. But maybe that's why he returned to Grace Springs after college. There's not usually many bad guys here."

"Not usually." Connor turned to face her again, and she realized she'd stopped as well. Not good if she wanted to get away. She pivoted on her toes then angled her feet out like a penguin to waddle safely down the sidewalk.

"What are you going to do now?" He caught up in a few long strides so that they were walking side by side.

How did she get rid of him? It wasn't any of his business that she didn't have a job and might be charged with murder. Besides the fact that he'd put her in this position.

Marissa stepped under the overhang of the other antique shop that Tandy had already entered. She reached for the brass doorknob. "I'm going into Grandma's Attic."

A bell rang as Marissa tugged the door open and entered the warmth of the cinnamon apple-scented shop. This was what an antique store should look like. All festive and welcoming with a tree in the center, wreaths on the windows, the clickety-clack of a toy train circling the room, and oh crud, mistletoe overhead.

Connor stomped off snow next to her. He grinned and pointed to the mistletoe attached to the bell on the doorframe. He wouldn't seriously expect her to kiss him, would he? He had to be taunting her.

She narrowed her eyes then left him behind to head toward Tandy and Billie at the counter. Billie wore her normal contagious smile, so she must not have been accused of murder yet. That was good.

Connor's footsteps indicated he'd followed. Marissa snuck a peek to find him standing next to her with his hands in his pockets, obviously out of his element in the midst of all the throw pillows and quilts and soft things that made him appear even more masculine…if that was possible. Would a kiss have made him feel any better?

"Are you putting an offer on this place instead?" he asked.

"No." She tossed her long hair. He'd always loved her hair. "But even if I were, I would not hire you to remodel."

His eyes scanned the room, seeing it through a contractor's eyes. "It really wouldn't need that much work."

Entirely *not* the point. "Then I definitely wouldn't want to hire you because that would give you the chance to destroy it."

His eyes hardened on their way back to meet hers. "I'm not the one who destroyed our relationship."

"Yes, you are." Why did he have to look at her like that? As if he was the one who'd been hurt. He should be apologizing, not blaming her. "What did you think was going to happen when you signed the contract to tear down Grandmother's house?"

He squared off and crossed his arms. "Nothing, because I didn't realize it was your grandmother's house when I signed."

"When you realized it, you should have reneged." They'd been through all this before. Did he think she was going to suddenly give up everything she believed in to be with him? "I can't trust you if you don't put me first."

He stilled. "But if I was the type of man who reneged on my word, then *nobody* could trust me."

Sure they could. It would mean he'd seen the error of his ways and was making the changes to improve. For example, if he'd agreed to help someone steal the Rare Ohio Diamonds, he shouldn't break the law to keep his word. But it was pointless to say any of this to him because he'd heard it already. Multiple times. What he didn't know was the situation he'd put her in. So she'd tell him.

"Reneg is short for renegotiate. That's not a bad thing. If you'd renegotiated your contract, then I would have had the time to get my loan and buy Grandmother's house from the bank. I would have not only saved a piece of history but had a location for my teahouse." Her voice rose, attracting attention from Tandy and Billie. But she couldn't stop now. She was having a tough day, and Connor was making it worse. Maybe he'd leave if he knew this was all his fault. "Because of you, I had to go up against this city girl in a bidding war, which is why the police are going to suspect me for murder if they conclude Virginia died of a premeditated caffeine overdose."

Connor blinked. His expression wasn't one of blame anymore, but he still looked innocent. Which wasn't fair. Not when it was his fault she could go to jail.

She poked him in the chest, frustration tensing her fingertips. "I have *no* fiancé, *no* job, *no* chance at regaining my good name, and…" She waved her arm toward the other two women in the store, accidentally knocking a vintage ornament off the tree. "Now I'm following Tandy around to keep her from accusing people like Billie here of killing off her competition!"

Chapter Four

TANDY COULDN'T TAKE HER EYES OFF Marissa. It was like watching a figure skater miss a landing. The beauty queen wasn't only clumsy physically but also careless with words.

"I'm being accused of what?" Billie's tiny hand adjusted her red plastic glasses.

Oh boy. Tandy gave her best remorseful smile. She'd been planning to investigate, not accuse anyone of murder, especially after meeting the little Chinese shop owner. The sweet woman had short, spiky hair that had lightened with age to be the color of creamer and a laugh that overflowed like a cappuccino with one too many shots of espresso. "I think what Marissa was trying to say is that—"

"I heard what she said." Billie stumbled backwards and sank into a creaky rocking chair. "Virginia is dead. I can't believe it."

Even if Tandy had been suspicious before, she wouldn't be now. Billie was clearly in shock.

Marissa rushed over, hair flying, hand on her heart. "Billie, I'm so sorry. I didn't mean for all that to come out." She wove her way behind the counter and dropped onto her knees at the woman's side.

Tandy let her take over. This was her mess. She could clean it up. Besides, Marissa knew Billie better than Tandy did. Tandy had barely met the woman before she'd been offered a piece of homemade apple cake and told stories of growing up on an apple orchard and how apples were exchanged at Christmas time in China as a symbol of goodwill.

Billie was the kind of person Tandy moved to a small town to get to know. Could they be friends after Marissa explained what happened to Virginia, or would Billie turn her suspicions on Tandy, being that she was the outsider?

Tandy's shoulders sagged with the weight of it all. She'd wanted Billie to be creepy and villainous so the police would have a suspect besides her. Now where did she look?

The guy from the truck joined her, watching Marissa. He'd apparently been engaged to the blonde at one time and still had a thing for her, based on the fact that he'd stuck around after her tirade. Too bad he'd accidentally agreed to demolish her grandmother's house, thus ending their engagement.

"Hi." He held out a hand to shake.

Tandy shifted Cocoa to her left arm so she could grip his calloused palm. He was more rugged up close with laugh lines in his bronze skin and a golden five o'clock shadow. If he ever got his own renovation show on TV, she'd watch it.

"I'm Connor, the destroyer of dreams."

Whether Connor felt guilty about his mistake or not, Tandy found it refreshing that his introduction wasn't an attempt to impress. He might be exactly what the beauty queen needed.

"I'm Tandy, new to town and already in trouble for something I didn't do."

He nodded acceptance before glancing at her Pomeranian. "And this is?"

She liked him even more now. "Cocoa. He's tougher than he looks."

Connor let Cocoa lick his hand then stuffed it back in his pocket. "I can tell." They both turned their attention toward the women on the other side of the counter.

Billie took off her glasses and dabbed at her face with a handkerchief. "I'd been worried something like this would happen."

Tandy's heart rate tripped. Her eyes widened. Did Billie say she'd been worried someone might kill Virginia? What did she know? And what other dangers might be lurking around the street's deceptively quaint corners? "Come again?"

"I prayed for her..." Billie slid her glasses back up her nose then focused on Tandy, fingers trembling. "We'd both go to auctions and estate sales, and I'd always take the books because I love first editions. She was into genealogy, so if I found old journals, I'd sell them to her. They were all old enough that it didn't really matter, until recently. I found a diary belonging to an upstanding member of the community and didn't feel it was right to sell."

Tandy tilted her head. What was the danger in an old journal?

"She argued, and I caught her sneaking into my shop and taking pictures of the pages." Billie inhaled. "I had the feeling she was up to no good. Possibly even blackmail. That was the last time I saw her."

Tandy's lips parted though no sound came out. She'd wanted one other suspect for police to investigate, but with the possibility that Virginia was a blackmailer, every person in town became a suspect.

Marissa looked Tandy's way, as well, as if asking for help. Or maybe she was expressing gratefulness that she hadn't won Miss Ohio after all. Then she wouldn't be in the public eye as coming from this sinister little town when the news broke.

Tandy might be safer moving back to the city since there was no one here she could trust. Everyone had secrets, and they seemed to be worse than hers.

Connor stepped forward. "Do you still have the diary, Billie?"

He really was a hero, wasn't he? Fighting for Marissa despite her rejection. Tandy's heart constricted with a twinge of jealousy. She didn't want to think she needed a man in her life, but it would be nice to have someone who cared for her this much. She nuzzled her nose into Cocoa's fur.

Billie glanced from Connor to Marissa, concern turning her eyes from the shade of a macchiato to deep roast. "I do, but—"

Marissa rocked forward and grasped Billie's hand between her own. "Oh, please, Billie. We aren't going to blackmail anyone. We need to take it to the police. Then they can question the right suspects."

Billie stilled, indecision creasing her face. "I'm afraid people will be hurt when the secrets are exposed."

Tandy moved closer to the counter so as not to miss any of the conversation. Who did Billie think was going to get hurt? Taking the information to the police would reveal what the killer was trying to keep quiet. The bad guy would be the only one hurt, and it would keep him from hurting others.

Marissa shot Tandy another glance. Maybe they were going to be a team after all. Of course, Marissa would probably choose anybody to work with over her ex.

Tandy blew her bangs up. She had nothing to lose. "Billie, you know how you were telling me about plucking blossoms off young trees in your apple orchard to keep them from being infected by Fire Blight?"

Billie shifted to look at Tandy though her expression didn't change. "Yes."

"Well, this is like that." Tandy bit her lip in hopes the older woman would understand. "You sacrifice a few apples to keep the whole orchard from being destroyed."

Connor nodded encouragingly. He got the analogy.

Billie closed her eyes. They could always take this information to the deputy, and he could subpoena the diary. Tandy couldn't imagine Billie as being uncooperative though. The woman was all warmth and grace.

Billie peered at Marissa. "You sure you want to see what the diary has to say?"

Marissa widened her already wide eyes. "Yes. Please. This is very important."

Billie winced and shot a warning look toward Connor. What was that about? Did the journal contain secrets on him? Had he killed Virginia to get Marissa to run to him for help? He'd certainly been there at the right time.

Billie stood. "It's in my safe. I'll be right back."

As Billie headed toward a back room, Tandy scooted sideways so she wasn't as close to Connor and scanned the area for a weapon. A silver coffee and tea set was the closest thing she could reach. She picked up the larger pot with her free hand and pictured herself knocking Connor unconscious with it then riding to safety on the old-fashioned unicycle in the corner.

"Ooh...that's pretty," Marissa cooed, standing from her kneeling position. "Does it have a price tag?"

Tandy blinked. Were they really talking about purchasing antiques at a time like this? Of course, Marissa didn't have as much to worry about as Tandy did. Connor wouldn't kill *her*.

Connor stepped closer and reached toward Tandy.

Her stomach lurched, and she raised the teapot, ready to strike. "Back off."

Connor lifted a quizzical eyebrow then looked above her at the little white tag dangling from the handle. "It says three-hundred dollars, but I think Tandy wants it for herself."

"Figures." Marissa pursed her lips in a pout, drawing all Connor's attention.

Tandy shivered in relief. He'd only been trying to find the price for Marissa. She lowered her weapon as well as her eyelashes to act like everything was normal. "You wouldn't want this anyway, Marissa. Silver requires a lot of polishing."

Billie joined them once again, a brown leather journal covered in gold filigree clutched to her chest, and her cheeks drained of color.

Tandy set the teapot down and hugged Cocoa tighter in anticipation. Inside Billie's book were the answers they'd been looking for.

Billie stopped in front of Marissa, bowed her head then extended both arms carefully as if holding a bomb.

"That's Grandmother's diary," Marissa exploded.

She stared at the familiar journal in Billie's hands. It was a priceless treasure, but surely it didn't hold secrets that would motivate murder. It held family history. Memories from her childhood and beyond. A beautiful heritage.

Billie's eyes pooled with tears. "I'm sorry, Marissa."

"For what?" Marissa asked even while retreating.

She didn't want to know the answer. Whatever skeletons were in her grandmother's closet, they would be best left undisturbed. Especially by her. Especially if she didn't want to destroy her family name any further. Mom would flip.

While Marissa had grown up with pride at being related to the founding fathers, as a kid she hadn't realized that meant the bar was set higher for her. Normal kids got paid by their parents for getting straight A's. She got reprimanded for a B. Normal teenagers whispered together in the high school bathroom. She got whispered about. Normal summer vacations were spent on Lake Erie while her education continued in museums and on tours...besides that one summer where she was sent to fat camp even though she hadn't known she was fat.

Being crowned Miss Ohio hadn't been an option. She'd practically been born royalty.

Yet she'd somehow lost the title.

Instead she'd determined to start the teahouse in Grandmother's Victorian mansion.

Then her fiancé demolished the place.

And now that she faced the possibility of being accused for murder, the only way to save herself was to tear her family down even more?

She ran fingers into her hair and gripped their roots, barely aware of her beanie sliding down her back and landing with a whisper.

Billie didn't answer, she simply turned toward Connor.

He stepped forward, retrieving the beanie and reaching for the diary.

No. Connor couldn't know her family's secrets. That would give him the power to use them against her. Use them to soften her towards him.

She snatched the diary before he could get it, heart throbbing. "You need to leave." She made her voice as forceful as she could. Steeled her eyes. Dared him to defy her one more time.

She was defending her family from him. From his suggestion that maybe she wasn't the only one who made mistakes. From his suggestion that the Alexanders weren't any better than he was, and more importantly, they weren't any better than her. If that were true, she'd have no hope for redemption.

But her strength was an act. If Connor stayed, he'd witness her breakdown. She'd probably even cry in his arms. And then where would she be? Who would she be?

Connor held out her beanie while studying her with the kind of look that threatened to melt her witchiness like Dorothy's bucket of water. She snatched her hat and narrowed her eyes to keep the liquid from forming.

His jaw hardened, its edge working up his expression until the light died from his gaze. "All right."

He did an about face and marched toward the door, and just like that he was gone. No condolences. No second chances. No teasing or promises or begging for mercy.

It's what she'd asked for, but it left her empty. Alone. Well, not literally alone. But lonely. Like she'd been her whole life.

The clacking of the toy train interrupted her thoughts, bringing her focus back to the other women in the room. The one who'd hid her grandmother's secrets and the one who needed them to be set free.

Tandy stood in place, hanging onto her puppy like a kindergartener with a blanket. "What was that about?"

Marissa shrugged and looked away. She was going to be okay. It was no big deal. She'd wave off her issues with Connor. Because likely the stuff in the diary she wouldn't be able to wave off, and that's what mattered now. "He's an old flame."

"Not that old," Billie countered.

"Yeah, it looked like there were still a few sparks," Tandy added.

What did it matter? Connor was gone, and she had other

things to worry about. She inhaled courage then lowered the diary to the counter, running her fingers along the buttery material and inset design. The woman who'd written inside had passed before her time. Passed before Marissa could make her proud in return.

Billie and Tandy joined her at the counter. She couldn't look at them. She couldn't face the pity on Billie's face or intrigue on Tandy's. Billie knew more than Marissa did, while Tandy knew nothing.

"Shouldn't we take this to the deputy across the street?" Tandy asked in what she might consider to be a gentle tone, though from anyone else it would come across as sardonic.

Marissa looked up but only to glare. She wasn't going to hand over Grandmother's most intimate memories to a kid she used to babysit.

Tandy increased the pressure like handcuffs against a struggle. "How come the diary was sold in an estate sale anyway? Why didn't your family inherit your grandmother's belongings?"

Marissa looked down again, her guts twisting in shame. She didn't want to dishonor the dead, but she had to answer, or Tandy would keep going. "Grandmother had some debt that needed to be paid off. She was used to living in luxury, and without my grandfather around to manage his real estate holdings, she lived above her means."

Tandy nodded, her eyes wandering along the ceiling as she thought. "She must have had a reverse mortgage then too, which is why the bank owned her house and it wasn't passed down to her children."

Marissa's stomach warmed. Nobody had known about the reverse mortgage before Grandmother's death. The Alexanders had all assumed her historic house would remain in the family for generations to come. "Unfortunately," she admitted.

If Grandmother was capable of that kind of secret, what else had she been capable of? Marissa really didn't want to know, and she didn't want anyone else to know either.

Tandy turned from her to face Billie. "Did Virginia blackmail Marissa's grandmother?"

"Hm..." Billie tapped a finger to her lips. "I don't know about that, but if Ettabell Alexander was ready to come clean with her story, it could have created issues for someone else."

Wait, Tandy thought Grandmother was being blackmailed too? That would explain her finances. And if she was going to come clean with whatever it was Virginia was using for blackmail, then could she have been killed, as well? Marissa needed to know.

She flipped the diary open. "What page, Billie?"

Billie pointed to the ribbon that acted as a bookmark. "I didn't read this to pry into your personal life, Marissa. I want you to know that. I read this to see what Virginia had been taking pictures of."

Marissa swallowed down the ball of uncertainty at what she might find. Whatever it was, it wasn't Billie's fault. "I know. You were trying to protect me." Billie understood being a grandmother. Though she was more of the down-to-earth kind. She'd lost her husband a while ago, but she didn't live above her means or keep secrets from her grandchildren.

Billie met her gaze and nodded solemnly before flipping to the page she'd marked. She started to read aloud, but Marissa impatiently read ahead.

I'm going to go to the pageant board and let them know the Miss Ohio contest was rigged for me. Governor Joseph Cross counted the ballots and lied about who had the highest score in order to get Grace Springs on the map, thus promoting tourism for his riverboat cruises. Miss Sandusky should have won.

Chapter Five

MARISSA COULDN'T HAVE READ THAT RIGHT. Her eyes leaped back up to the beginning of the paragraph to reread it correctly. But the words didn't change. The meaning didn't change. Never in her life had she imagined such a scenario.

Grandmother hadn't been the true Miss Ohio.

The room spun. Her skin burned. Her chest heaved. She gripped the edge of the counter to hold herself upright.

"Sit down, Marissa." Billie's soft voice barely broke through her blizzard of thoughts, but she couldn't make her legs move to obey.

What would Marissa's life have been like if Grandmother hadn't been crowned? Would Grandmother have met Grandfather at the homecoming parade for WWII on which she reigned from a float? Would Grandfather have made so much money in real estate if Joseph Cross hadn't turned Grace Springs into a tourist town? Would Dad have had the funds to attend the prestigious Ashby College where he met Mom? Would Marissa have been born?

"My whole life is based on a lie." Had she just said that out loud?

"Uh..." Tandy shoved her little fur ball into Marissa's arms. "Here."

Marissa let go of the counter to embrace the bundle of warmth and softness. Cocoa's damp tongue scrubbed her face. This time she didn't care. Because the dog would love her even if everyone else found out she was a nobody. She needed more dogs in her life. She stroked his silky fur as a rogue tear mingled with the saliva on her cheek.

Something solid bumped the back of her knees. Billie's rocking chair. Marissa let herself sink into it, though it would take longer for reality to sink in. Her grandmother was a fraud and had apparently known she was a fraud. But for how long? And had Tandy's mother known? Had she even earned her crown, or had that been rigged as well? Would Marissa have wanted the pageant to be rigged in *her* favor?

No. It had been rigged against her, and that was also wrong.

"Does Joseph Cross live in Grace Springs?" Tandy asked, drawing Marissa back into the present.

Tandy was thinking of Virginia's murder. That's why Billie had brought out the journal in the first place. Tandy didn't care about the Alexander heritage or the legacy Marissa was going to leave behind. She only cared about clearing her own name. Which was safer for Marissa in a way.

If Marissa focused on finding Virginia's killer, it could take the sting out of this discovery. Like, *Yeah, Grandmother stole the Miss Ohio crown, but at least I'm not a murderer.*

Billie cleared her throat like it was hard for her to speak ill of anyone. She may live in a small town, but she wasn't a gossip. She probably knew more dirt than most, being that she bought people's old belongings, but she always took their problems to God first. Apparently even Virginia's. "As far as I know, Joseph Cross sold his sternwheelers and moved into the retirement community by the river—Grace Springs Manor."

Marissa leaned forward, her grip on Cocoa tightening unintentionally. The dog wiggled. "Mr. Cross sold his boats?" That had been his whole reason for rigging the pageant. Ever since she could remember, he would invite the reigning Miss Ohio to serve as hostess during his annual Christmas Cruise aboard The Ohio Queen. If he sold the boats, then the woman who'd tripped Marissa wouldn't be coming to town for the event. What a relief.

Not a relief was the idea Mr. Cross might have sold the boats in order to pay a blackmail fee.

Tandy scooped Cocoa out of her arms, so Marissa squeezed the armrests instead. Was anybody else thinking what she was thinking?

"Cross might have needed money to pay off Virginia," Tandy read her mind. "And he might have been angry enough to kill her."

Yes. Exactly. Could he also have been angry enough to kill Grandmother?

Marissa's heart thrummed in her ears as she tried to recall the medical examiner's cause of death. He'd said Grandmother had died from natural causes in her sleep, but how hard had he looked? As hard as the EMTs across the street who'd claimed Virginia died of a heart attack? If they'd known to look deeper, would they have found suspicious signs? Like the evidence Little Lukey was probably going to find in the coffee pot?

Billie tugged at the collar of her blouse. "Girls, we don't want to accuse Joseph of murder if he's innocent."

Marissa's spine snapped straighter. She wanted Mr. Cross to be guilty. She wanted him to go to jail. Not only for Virginia's murder but as punishment for the burden he'd heaped on Grandmother's shoulders. On all their shoulders. It was like Mr. Cross didn't think her family had what it took to make it on their own, and she wanted to prove him wrong.

She'd do it. She'd visit him and get a confession.

Tandy slid the diary off the counter and held it up. "We should give this to the deputy, so he has the evidence needed to find out for sure if Cross is innocent or not."

Marissa shot to her feet and reached for the diary. Cocoa growled, and she pulled back, which was silly. Being scared of the tiny dog was like being scared of a mouse. Except she'd once fainted at the sight of a mouse in a corn maze.

She wouldn't give up. She'd trade Billie's silver teapot to get the diary from Tandy if necessary. She'd trade Virginia's whole shop, should her daughter keep it on the market. That journal belonged to Grandmother. Her secrets didn't need to be revealed if Marissa could get Mr. Cross to take responsibility for Virginia's death without it.

Marissa had to speak Tandy's language if she was going to try to reason with her. "Let's go talk to Mr. Cross first, so the police don't think we're attempting to frame him."

Tandy's light eyes narrowed to slivers. "I'd rather end up in jail than get myself killed."

Maybe Tandy was being the reasonable one here. But Marissa knew Joseph Cross from attending Grandmother's dinner parties when growing up. He was like another grandfather. He'd never suspect her. "You'll be fine. We'll take Mr. Cross a piece of Billie's apple cake and ask him to tell stories about my grandparents." Did that guarantee her safety? She needed to talk both herself and Tandy into this crazy idea to prevent the diary from becoming public. "Plus, he's in a retirement center. We'll be surrounded by other people."

"Other people stuck in wheelchairs and with forgetful minds."

"Surely there will be nurses and staff around."

Billie's forehead wrinkled in consideration. "I do have some leftover apple cake." She probably cared more about tarnishing Mr. Cross's reputation if he was innocent than keeping the diary a secret.

"And..." Marissa would not be deterred. She motioned

between the two of them. "If Mr. Cross tries anything, it's two against one."

Cocoa yipped.

"Three against one." There. That would seal the deal.

Tandy smirked. "Nice try." Apparently, she hadn't bought Cocoa to be a watchdog.

Billie ducked behind her counter and returned holding a rectangle serving platter decorated with a vintage painting of Santa Claus. "Joseph Cross may not be guilty at all. Virginia could have been blackmailing people we don't even know about." She retrieved her sheet cake from the other side of the cash register to scoop large slices onto the dish. She paused and looked up. "To be safe, please promise me you won't drink any coffee he makes."

Marissa raised a finger in protest. "I don't—"

"Or tea," Billie amended.

Marissa lowered her hand. "I promise."

Tandy clicked her tongue. She studied Billie, blinked, then studied Marissa. "I'll go with you if you let me lock the journal in the glove box of my car."

Marissa's blood sprinted through her veins. She needed the diary back, but at least the glove box was safer than the police station. One step at a time. "Okay."

Tandy nodded slowly before facing Billie again. "If anything happens to us, you can tell the deputy where to look."

Marissa's pulse pounded like her heart was playing Carol of the Bells. What was she getting them into?

Tandy eyed Marissa while moving Cocoa's pet car seat to the back of her Volkswagen, then she stuffed the old journal in her glove compartment and locked it. She got the feeling the beauty queen wanted to keep the family skeletons hidden in her closet. Tandy could totally relate to such a sentiment, but not to the point of going to jail.

Marissa positioned the platter of apple cake on her lap and buckled in. "You drive a Beetle and own a Pomeranian. You really aren't that tough, are you?"

Tandy climbed into the driver's seat with a groan. Were people going to assume she was tough because she was from the city? She'd let them. Safer that way. Though it might require not letting on what a softie she really was when it came to animals. Like how she'd rescued Cocoa from an abusive owner and slept on the floor with him for a week before she could get him to snuggle in bed with her. "My apartment complex didn't allow big dogs," she said instead. Which was also true.

Marissa flipped down her visor to check her reflection in the tiny mirror and put on lip gloss that matched her beanie. "As for the slug bug, you bought it as an excuse to punch people?"

Tandy huffed then started the engine. "If I punch somebody, there's a good reason for it." She'd actually bought the little black car when her last boyfriend broke up with her to go work for an auto company in Toledo. Since he'd claimed America made the best cars, she'd bought a German design out of spite.

Marissa returned her lip gloss to her purse and looked up, wariness darkening her eyes. She didn't ask, but she was obviously questioning whether Tandy would also kill someone if she had a good reason. Maybe Tandy shouldn't try to come across as too tough after all.

She shifted, stepped lightly on the gas, then tensed in preparation of pumping the brakes if the car started to slide. Visiting a suspected murderer might not be the most dangerous part of their evening. She would have been better off buying a Jeep with four-wheel drive even if the company employed her old boyfriend.

"You shouldn't stereotype people, you know." Tandy slowed to a stop at a red light and adjusted the heat as the blast warmed her cheeks. "I mean, look at you. You're a beauty queen with a stolen crown."

Marissa sat up even straighter, which was quite a feat considering her already perfect posture. "First of all, my grandmother did not steal the crown. Someone else rigged the competition, probably without her knowledge. And in case you forgot, she was planning to come clean."

That was true. Tandy gave an understanding nod then looked both ways when the light turned green. All clear. And quiet. Who would ever have thought a killer was on the loose in this picturesque setting? Was he really an old man in a retirement center or was he a stranger watching them from behind the giant Christmas tree next to the gazebo? She shivered.

"Second, *I* did not steal any crown. I'm a contestant without a crown."

Tandy inched between the town square and an old brick church, heading toward the river.

"Third, the only reason I don't have a crown is because Miss Sassy Cincinnati tripped me." Marissa adjusted her beanie as if imagining it were a tiara. "Nothing good ever comes out of Cincin-nasty."

Whoa now. Tandy pressed her lips together and tightened her grip on the steering wheel. This was what she should have expected, wasn't it? As if worrying about finding a murderer wasn't enough, she now had an enemy right there in the car with her?

Tandy really wanted to punch the other woman. And that very woman had actually given her the excuse needed to do so. She balled her right fist and jammed it against Marissa's left arm. "Slug bug."

"Hey." Marissa rubbed at the spot with a gloved hand. Her rubbing slowed. Her eyes darted up. Awareness dawned. "You're from Cincinnati, aren't you?"

Tandy might as well admit it. If the police were to investigate her, they'd find out anyway. "I am."

Marissa froze except for a crease marring her perfect forehead. "Oh, I'm sorry, Tandy. I didn't mean anything by that." Her hands came back to life, flying up in a shrug. "It's been a super emotional day."

Tandy checked on Cocoa over her shoulder. He could always bring her comfort in the midst of chaos. And he certainly seemed comfortable, head resting on his paws, eyes closed. She'd snuggle with him later.

Marissa twisted toward her. "I'm sure Cincinnati has plenty of nice things too. We went there for Christmas one time and saw the lights at the zoo and went ice skating at Fountain Square and…and…there was that really cool parade with all the horse drawn carriages. We don't have a whole parade of them here—just one that brings up the rear of the Santa Claus fun run on the morning of Christmas Eve."

Memories tugged at Tandy's heart. She'd enjoyed those events as a child, and like Marissa, she'd also almost forgotten them. "It's okay. There's a reason I left."

Marissa leaned forward as if expecting her to continue, but Tandy wasn't going there today. She had enough problems to deal with in their current situation.

"I'd hoped Grace Springs would be warm and friendly

like I remembered it." So much for that idea.

Marissa sank back, and they watched the snow swirl around them as businesses were replaced with houses then fields. "You've been here before?"

Tandy exhaled. She'd been trying to skip over this subject as well, but Marissa read between the lines. "I visited a few times as a kid." She downshifted to a stop at a T in the road. A good distraction. "Which way?"

Marissa pointed, her eyes sliding Tandy's direction, apparently still fascinated with the idea that Tandy had been to her town before. Perhaps she thought that maybe they'd met in the past. They hadn't. Tandy would have remembered meeting Marissa. Even in elementary school. Someone that beautiful and charmingly clumsy would be hard to forget.

"Do you have relatives or friends here in town?" Marissa pressed.

Tandy eased into the turn, using the excuse of focus for time to consider a response. She'd be as honest and vague as possible. "I knew people from when my family visited, but I'm not sure if they're still in the area."

"They" being Greg's family. She wasn't going to look them up because that could seem stalkerish. And it could also set her up for more disappointment. The kid she used to catch fireflies with probably wasn't anything like how she remembered him. It was best to savor those memories and use them as motivation for returning to the simple life.

"What's their last name?" Marissa broke into her thoughts.

Huh-uh. There was no way Tandy would answer that question. It was a small town. Greg probably went to school with Marissa. Could have taken her to prom or worse—been turned down when he'd asked her out. Tandy didn't want to get that personal with a stranger. It wasn't like Marissa opened up about her former fiancé. "What's Connor's last name?" she asked in return.

Marissa's eyes widened in what might be considered alarm then she tossed her hair like she wanted to convey the message it had been a false alarm. "His last name is Thomas. You…uh…you know Connor's family?"

If Tandy had been trying to get out of the line of fire, then she'd hit the bullseye. She bit her lip to hide a smile. "There was a boy I used to play with who would now be around Connor's age, but the name Thomas doesn't ring any bells."

"Oh." Marissa shifted in her seat and looked out the passenger window.

The silence invited Tandy to ask more questions. Or perhaps it was Marissa's discomfort. "How long have *you* known Connor?"

"My whole life." Marissa shivered then reached to fidget with the knobs on the dashboard. "I'm still cold. Is it cold in here to you?"

Tandy shrugged. She was on the warmer side, but if Marissa was cold, she didn't mind her adjusting the heat.

"I think we should listen to music." Marissa flipped the radio on, and the melody to *All I Want for Christmas* floated around them.

This wasn't the Christmas Tandy had wanted. She'd begun the day with plans to start a business, and now she was only hoping to not be accused of murder. Plus, she was on her way to meet the very person who might have committed such a crime, giving him a motive to want to kill her also. Not to mention she was partnered with an overdramatic tea drinker. Whatever she'd done to deserve this, she would have preferred the standard punishment of coal in her stocking.

She slowed for another curve then stared in awe at the

view said curve revealed. Beyond the gently falling snow stood a massive brick structure with steep rooflines, multiple chimneys and balconies, black shutters, and white dormer windows. The place made retirement living look glamorous.

"Cross can't be too worried about money if he's staying here." Another dead end?

Marissa leaned forward to get a better look. "Or maybe he's worried about money *because* he's staying here."

Only one way to find out. Tandy took her eyes off the gorgeous building to find a parking place. On their way inside, Cocoa growled at the snowmen wearing Santa hats that someone's grandkids must have built. She hushed him then wiped snowflakes from his fur as the automatic front doors slid open with a whoosh.

The luxurious lobby was decorated for the season with garland around pillars, white lights up the curved staircase, and a Christmas "tree" made out of poinsettias pointing toward the center of a soaring ceiling. Marissa didn't even pause to take it in, but she was probably accustomed to such elegance. She marched across the marble floor toward a man in a gray suit behind a counter. Was he a businessman or were all employees of Riverwood Estates required to dress like Cary Grant?

"Hello. We're here to see Mr. Cross." Marissa wobbled for absolutely no reason at all, and the dish of cake landed with a clank on the granite counter before she stepped wide and caught herself.

The Cary Grant impersonator arched an eyebrow before lifting his disdainful gaze to rest on Tandy and Cocoa. "Is Mr. Cross expecting you?"

Tandy grimaced. If this had been Cincinnati, she would have asked Marissa to call first, but with Grace Springs being such a small town, she'd figured they might be more personable here. Rather, this retirement center employed bouncers.

"No, but I brought him some cake." Marissa flashed a stunning smile that said she was used to getting her way.

The man's lips pinched into an attempt at a grin as he picked up the phone. "I will tell Mr. Cross you are here, Miss…"

"Alexander."

Recognition dawned in the man's expression. Marissa might as well have said, "Miss Grace Springs." If Virginia's daughter had known her as the beauty contestant who fell off the stage, she apparently had a reputation that preceded her. Not good.

They all listened to the tinny ring of a phone that could be heard on the other end of the line. What if Mr. Cross wasn't here? What if he'd stayed in town after tampering with Virginia's coffee grinds to make sure his scheme had been successful?

Voices, footsteps, and laughter broke the silence from behind them. Tandy glanced over her shoulder to find a group dressed in ugly Christmas sweaters and reindeer antlers holding sheet music and filing into the lobby. Carolers?

The man set the receiver back in its cradle. "Mr. Cross must still be at lunch. I can tell him you stopped by and give him the cake."

Marissa frowned and pulled the plate along the counter protectively. "No, I'd like to—"

"Come on." Tandy gripped her sleeve and tugged. They weren't going to get anywhere with this guy.

"Wait, Tandy." Marissa tugged back. "I have to talk to Mr. Cross."

"I know," Tandy hissed out the side of her mouth then

raised her voice to address the man who wanted to stop them. "Thank you, sir. Please give Cross the cake for us and wish him a Merry Christmas."

"Certainly." The guy smirked.

Marissa glared then twisted to focus her rebellion on Tandy. "What are you doing?"

Tandy practically dragged her out the automatic doors into the chilly air. "The question you should ask is what are *we* doing?"

"Fine." Marissa yanked her arm away hard enough to send herself stumbling sideways, which probably wasn't that hard. She regained her balance. "What are *we* doing?"

Tandy snagged the Santa hats from the snowmen with her free hand. She tossed one to Marissa then stuffed the other one over her own head, its icy temperature sending a blizzard of goosebumps down her body.

"We're Christmas caroling." She nodded toward the last of the group headed inside. "Hurry so we can blend in."

Chapter Six

BACK IN THE WARMTH OF THE building, Marissa switched out her beanie for the stocking hat then ducked behind a big man in an elf costume to keep from being spotted by the snooty front desk attendant. "With a little more time, I could have sweet-talked our way past him."

Tandy tucked Cocoa inside her jacket. "Now you don't have to."

Not exactly a vote of confidence, but Marissa would let it go. She was on her way to find Mr. Cross, which had been their goal. What Tandy lacked in the art of small-town charm, she made up for in resourcefulness.

Should it bother Marissa that the other woman was okay with breaking the rules? It definitely bothered her that Tandy was so quick to punch if she felt someone deserved it. Things could go from bad to worse that way. Maybe Marissa's assessment of how nothing good came from Cincinnati had been accurate after all. Even the stitching on the white trim to Tandy's hat read "Naughty" as if she belonged on Santa's naughty list. Marissa's hat must appropriately declare her "Nice."

She followed the crowd down a side hallway, stopping at the first door on their left. The giant elf resembling the choir director from her church knocked, and once the door swung open, the people around her burst into a lively rendition of "Rudolph the Red-Nosed Reindeer." She and Tandy would have to join in until they reached the cafeteria.

Marissa sang along, looking from face to face. Vanessa.

Marie. Opal, the old lady who loved organ music. This *was* her church choir, and they had no idea a murder had been committed in their little town. If they'd known, they might prefer to sing Elvis's "Blue Christmas." Instead, they chorused together about how the other reindeer called Rudolph names.

"Like Bozo!" she soloed.

A familiar hand with black fingernail polish hooked her bicep and tugged. "Come on, Bozo."

Tandy was a pushy little thing, wasn't she? Marissa emerged from the group then untangled herself from the other woman's grip. "Don't call me Bozo."

"You're the one putting on a show."

Opal sent her a scowl before returning to her song book.

Marissa lowered her voice. "I'm singing along because we don't know where we're going."

Tandy pointed past her. Marissa followed the direction with her eyes. A map hung on the wall. It had a red "You are Here" circle on one side of the outline and a large rectangle on the other side printed with the word "Cafeteria."

"Oh."

Yet another scowl.

"I mean ho. Ho-ho-ho." Marissa held her belly like a bowl full of jelly.

"Come on." Tandy took off. Figured. "At least the cafeteria will be a public place for confronting Cross."

Tingles shot from Marissa's heart. Maybe she didn't want to do this after all. But what was her alternative? Letting Tandy hand over Grandmother's diary to the authorities? She dug her fingernails into her palms and jogged to catch up.

The spicy scent of fried chicken grew stronger as they followed the Berber carpeting down navy blue hallways trimmed in white molding. Wreaths decorated with shiny blue and silver balls hung on each door they passed. Finally, they arrived at the entrance to a cafeteria that doubled as a giant sunroom with a roof and walls made entirely of glass. Linen-covered tables dotted the room, giving patrons a beautiful view of the lazy river outside.

Tandy unzipped her jacket, lowered Cocoa to the floor, and hooked his leash over the pole that held a sign with the day's menu. It wouldn't be sanitary to let a dog who liked to lick things into an eating establishment. "What's Cross look like?" she asked.

Marissa scanned the residents seated at tables. "Last time I saw him, he had a full head of white hair and a trim beard."

Tandy patted Cocoa on the head and stood. "So he looks like Santa?"

Marissa pictured Mr. Cross in her mind. "Honestly, he looks really good for being in his eighties. He doesn't wear glasses, and he has leathery skin from the sun. Maybe he's a GQ Santa. But more like Sean Connery without the accent."

"Good." Tandy pulled off her "Naughty" hat. "Because it's hard to picture Santa killing someone. Sean Connery, on the other hand..."

"He had a license to kill."

Tandy tilted her head, chin puckering in thought. "I think Timothy Dalton was in that movie."

Beside the point. "Both played James Bond."

"Marissa Alexander?" The deep voice interrupting their conversation came from the table on their right. The man in question stood and circled toward them in his pressed burgundy shirt with a popped collar that somehow made him look sophisticated rather than slimy. He wrapped Marissa in a side hug. "Sorry about the Miss Ohio pageant, my dear, but you recovered well."

Marissa snorted. They hadn't proved the man a murderer

yet, but he was definitely a liar. Probably what made him so good at rigging beauty contests.

He let go to extend his hand toward Tandy. "Cross." Pause. "Joseph Cross," he introduced himself as if he was employed by British Secret Service.

Tandy shook hands with Mr. Cross but raised her eyebrows at Marissa in an expression of disbelief. Had he overheard their conversation or was he used to being compared to the agent for M16?

"I'm Tandy Brandt. I...um...came with Marissa to bring you some cake from Billie at Grandma's Attic."

Good cover.

"I love Billie's apple cake." Mr. Cross smiled, glancing at their empty hands.

Good cover except for the fact that they didn't have the cake with them anymore.

"The guy at the front desk—"

Mr. Cross held up a hand. "Say no more. I'll make sure to retrieve it from Kent. For now, you can join me for dessert." He motioned them to pass him and sit down at his table.

He sure didn't act like someone guilty of murder. Maybe he had no conscience, thus no guilt. Marissa had met a few people like that during her pageantry days.

She sat, shooting a quick glance at Tandy to read her expression. Tandy seemed as aloof as usual. At least she wasn't punching people.

Mr. Cross introduced them to the ladies at his table like visiting royalty, as if she'd really won the crown for Miss Ohio. This would have made her angrier at him if he wasn't so darn likable.

A waitress arrived then, reciting the dessert menu. The other residents at the table all rose with the excuse of a Christmas cookie exchange. They giggled when saying goodbye to Mr. Cross like teenagers with crushes in a school lunch room. Apparently, he was the retirement home equivalent of the football quarterback.

Marissa watched them leave with envy, wishing she could get out of dessert as well. Usually she was too preoccupied with counting calories to eat sugar, but she needed a reason to stick around. "Crème brûlée."

Tandy waved away the options. "I already had a slice of cake, so I'll just take a cappuccino if you serve them. I haven't had a good cup of coffee all day."

"Yes, ma'am, we do."

Ugh. Why hadn't Marissa thought of that? "And a tea. I'll take a green tea. Caffeine free please." The caffeine could make her more nervous, and she was already feeling shaky sitting next to the man who could have killed Virginia...and her grandmother.

The waitress left with their orders, and Mr. Cross gave them his full attention, propping one ankle over a knee and resting an arm on the back of Marissa's chair.

She scooted closer to Tandy so his hand didn't touch her. The hug had been more than enough.

His chestnut eyes lost their shimmer. "To what do I truly owe this honor? Why didn't Billie bring me the cake herself?"

Oh no. Where did she start? As she spoke, would he be planning her death? She pressed a palm over her pounding heart in hopes it might quiet the noise in her ears. "Do you remember my grandmother?" Dumb. Dumb. Dumb.

"Yes. I saw you at her funeral."

Tandy pinched Marissa's side. She elbowed Tandy's arm away. She was doing her best. Though maybe she should leave this job to Little Lukey after all. "Right. You've known her longer than I have. Which is why I thought you might have some stories you could tell me about her that I don't already know."

His gaze didn't move, but his chest rose and lowered.

She reached for Tandy's arm that she'd earlier elbowed away. She needed support. Tandy's warm fingers clasped hers. This city girl wasn't all bad. Though if it was true that the good died young, then Tandy was safe while Marissa was still conspicuously wearing the "Nice" Santa hat.

The hard glint in Mr. Cross's eyes faded. "Are you talking about how I rigged the Miss Ohio pageant?"

Tandy's grip tightened, and Marissa prepared herself to be yanked down another hall by the other woman. She wouldn't complain this time. Because with her body frozen in fear, it was the only way she'd be able to escape.

Tandy tensed to run. If Cross had killed Virginia for knowing his secret, was he also going to kill the two of them after this confession?

If so, she might as well see how much information she could get out of him first. "You rigged the contest to make sure Marissa's grandmother would win?"

Mr. Cross leaned back in his chair and looked out one of the many windows. He appeared more contemplative than dangerous. "Regrettably, yes. I was young and ambitious. I saw an opportunity, and I took it. I justified my actions by telling myself Ettabell would be the best queen."

Tandy shook her head. If he could justify cheating, then could he also justify murder?

He rolled his lips together like the words struggled to get out after all this time. "I kept it a secret for years, but it slipped to Ettabell at a dinner party after I'd had a few too many drinks."

Would a slip like that really ruin a career as a politician? Was the threat of discovery bad enough that he would have been willing to pay blackmail or commit murder? It was only a stupid beauty pageant.

"Ettabell slapped me as she should have. Shocked me sober. She wanted to come clean with it right away..." His voice faded like he was being drawn back in time with his memories.

Marissa had gone just as still. Numb maybe. Hopefully she'd snap back to life if they had to run. Because Tandy would also have to rescue Cocoa.

Tandy curled her fingers around the cell phone in her pocket with her free hand, ready to call the deputy if needed. "You didn't want the truth to come out, did you?"

The foot on Cross's knee dropped to the floor. His arm on Marissa's chair took its place on his thigh as he curled forward and into himself, head bowed. "I asked her to wait until I sold my riverboat company because I knew there would be bad press, and I didn't want my mistake to sink the town, so to speak. I think she agreed because she felt like it was a fitting punishment."

Tandy narrowed her eyes. If he'd been preparing for the news to break, then he wouldn't have needed to pay a blackmailer. There was only one way to find out. "Did you sell your business before Marissa's grandmother passed?"

Marissa's hand trembled in her grip as they waited for the answer.

Cross looked up, dark eyes wry in self-deprecation. "I did. Ironic, isn't it?"

Marissa slid her hand away to wave emphatically. "Ironic isn't the word I'd use."

Oh boy. Should Tandy try to restrain the princess's passion or wait and see how Cross reacted? She'd remain in her seat for a moment.

Wrinkles lined Cross's distinguished brow, his confusion ruling him innocent in Tandy's mind. "What word would you use?" he asked. He wasn't Santa Claus, or even Sean Connery. He had the appearance of being wise like a Roman emperor and in need of a laurel wreath around his head. Though it was more likely Marissa would smash a Christmas wreath in its place.

She shot to her feet, and flashed her straight, white teeth when enunciating slowly. "I'd use the word *convenient*."

Tandy rubbed at a sudden throb in her temples.

Cross tilted his head. "You mean the *opposite* of convenient, don't you? If I'd known your grandmother was going to take our secret to the grave, then I wouldn't have had to sell the business at all."

Marissa leaned forward to get in his face since he was still sitting down. "You *did* know she'd take it to the grave since you put her there."

Cross sat in silence. The Christmas music playing in the background grew louder. The waitress arrived with their orders, her friendly smile faltering.

Tandy tugged Marissa down, took her tea from the server, and slid it across the table. "Here, drink this." Tea was supposed to be soothing, right? Maybe that's why Marissa preferred it. If Marissa drank coffee, the caffeine might rile her up enough to accuse all the patrons in the cafeteria of being in on the imaginary crime against her grandmother.

Marissa shoved the cup away, causing her tea to slosh. "I'm not drinking my tea until Mr. Cross confesses to selling his company to pay Virginia's blackmail."

Cross sat back and scratched his head. "Honey, I don't

know what blackmail you're talking about. I can't be sure I heard you correctly a moment ago either. If you think I killed your grandmother to keep from having to sell my river tour company, then you can check the dates on the sale."

Marissa crossed her arms. "Then where's all your money? Why do you live here?"

Cross turned from them to study the room, and with the way his jaw twitched underneath his ear, it looked like he was using the time to calm himself. He wasn't thinking up a lie, was he?

He slowly faced them again, his stare gouging her conscience with its sharpness. "I built this place."

Marissa wilted like a poinsettia in January.

Tandy studied the man. Was he telling the truth? That would be easy enough to check out. As were his whereabouts at the time of the murder. "Have you been here all day?"

"Here? Yeah." Cross shrugged. "I played snowshoe golf this morning, but that was on the premises. You can ask our events coordinator."

Tandy heaved a heavy sigh. They'd both wanted Cross to be guilty. Then he could be locked behind bars and the two of them could go home safely and sleep soundly that night. Instead, he was simply a man who'd made a mistake in his past that shook Marissa's current world. Tandy would still be a suspect in Virginia's murder, and somewhere out there, the real killer wasn't even a blip on their radar.

"I'll double check your story, Cross." Tandy eased away from the awkwardness. "But I do apologize for making assumptions. We are only trying to help the police figure out who killed Virginia Pierce."

Cross's eyes bulged. "Virginia Pierce is dead?"

Marissa shot Tandy a skeptical look as if she still wanted to believe Cross to be the bad guy.

Tandy pointed at the tea. She needed to keep Marissa's mouth too busy to talk.

Marissa picked up the cup, though her expression remained rebellious.

"Yes, sir," Tandy answered. "She died this morning, and the police suspect foul play. We know she was taking pictures of pages in Marissa's grandmother's diary, and we thought she might have been blackmailing you."

Cross ran a hand through his hair. "That's why I saw Virginia's sister crying earlier."

Tandy slid her eyes toward Marissa to check if the other woman knew about Virginia's sister, and if their relationship had any significance. She seemed to know everybody in this tiny town, but she didn't even flinch at this knowledge. Just continued to stare Cross down.

Cross shook his head, defending himself. "Virginia wasn't blackmailing anyone. She wanted to use me to rig the downtown holiday decorating contest in her favor."

Marissa rolled her eyes. The girl couldn't hide her thoughts, though Tandy was thinking the same thing. How would Virginia have won since her place was hardly decorated?

"I told her no, of course, but..." His eyes scanned the panes of glass overhead

Tandy looked up also to see what he saw. Silver snowflakes similar to the ones dangling in Virginia's shop.

Marissa set her cup down with a clank. "But what?"

Cross's gaze lowered though the blank expression masked his thoughts. "I wouldn't be surprised if there was some foul play involved."

Marissa inhaled sharply. "Why?" The girl was as subtle as an ice scraper. Tandy should have left her in the car, as well.

Cross grimaced. Was he truly reluctant to tell them info that would keep them off his tail? "It may be nothing, but while I was at her shop, I overhead an argument on the phone. It sounded like it was over some rare piece of art or artifact she'd acquired. She wasn't willing to work out a deal."

Of all the reasons to kill someone, Virginia was killed for *stuff*? Couldn't the bad guy simply steal the item? Though if he did, she'd probably know who he was and report him to the police.

Marissa leaned forward. "Who was it?"

Cross lifted a shoulder. "Maybe check her phone records or question local art collectors?"

That didn't do them much good. Anybody could have wanted anything from Virginia. They were back at the beginning of this whole mess. At least Marissa didn't have to worry anymore about her grandmother's diary being evidence, though Tandy would have preferred that scenario.

Marissa stood to her feet. "I know who it was."

Chapter Seven

MARISSA HELD HER PALMS TO HER CHEEKS. It was shocking how much sense her realization made. "Randon Evans killed Virginia."

Tandy remained in her seat, unfazed by the bombshell. "As I'm new to town and haven't met anyone before today, you're going to have to give me a little more information than a name."

Oh. No wonder she didn't get it. Though Marissa had thought the man was known worldwide. "Randon is the famous app designer. He's become a millionaire off his apps while working at home in his pajamas."

Tandy shook her head.

"Excuse me, girls." Mr. Cross stood. "I'm going to go call Billie and see how she's doing." He took a few steps before pausing and stroking his beard. "Don't you think you'd be better off leaving the detective work to actual detectives?"

Tandy still didn't rise. Only deadpanned, "Not if they're investigating us."

"Ah. I see." He continued on past. "In that case, Merry Christmas to all, and to all a good alibi."

Tandy watched him leave. "I'll double check the date when Cross sold his company, but I really don't think he's guilty. Why do you think this Randon guy did it?"

"He's new to town."

That got Tandy's attention. Though not in a good way. She scowled. "Oh yeah. He should definitely be locked up. A real menace to society."

Marissa dropped her head back. Why did Tandy have to take every statement the wrong way? "That's not what I meant." She huffed and reached for Tandy's arm. "I mean, I don't think he cares about our residents. He only wanted a house in the woods to go with his hipster image. He also collects art since he considers himself an artist."

Tandy lifted her chin in acknowledgement. "Interesting."

"Even more interesting is the fact that he's been writing letters to the editor of the Grace Springs Gazette, complaining how locals don't appreciate all the culture and money he's brought to our community." Marissa's mind rewound through the different letters she'd read. The memories of his words sent chills down her arms. "I think there was even one where he mentioned Virginia by name."

Tandy chewed her lip. "If anybody was going to murder someone with an overdose of coffee, it would be a hipster."

"Exactly." Now they were on the same page. Well, kind of. Tandy rose, and Marissa could have simply let her walk away, but the coffee comment bugged her. "You realize that if you started a coffee shop, you'd be catering primarily to people like Randon, right?"

Tandy tossed her ponytail over her shoulder and sailed past to retrieve Cocoa. "While your teahouse would cater to Virginias."

Marissa glared at the other woman's back, not that her opinion even mattered anymore. "I guess we don't have to worry about that now unless Jenn decides to go back overseas to continue teaching English after Christmas, but my guess is she'll stay here to keep her mother's heritage alive. That's what I would do."

"I know." Tandy said it like following in your parent's footsteps was a bad thing.

Simply because Grandmother hadn't truly earned the

Miss Ohio crown, it didn't mean she wasn't an honorable person. She'd been honest enough to want to confess she was a fraud. More evidence that she was a better person than Marissa. Because Marissa was glad the secret hadn't been revealed.

With the heat of shame burning in her chest, Marissa removed the "Nice" hat from her head. Being nice was more about making people like you than actually caring about their well-being, wasn't it? She needed to work on being kind rather than nice. And she would. Once she reclaimed her place in society by opening a teahouse in Grandmother's honor.

Tandy hooked Cocoa's leash around her wrist and paraded him out of the cafeteria, checking once to make sure Marissa was following. "If this Randon fellow lives in the woods like you said, then I'm not sure we should go out to his place alone."

Marissa shook away her depressing thoughts to focus on the reason she was dealing with them in the first place. Had Randon not killed Virginia, then Marissa would most likely already be the proprietor of a new teahouse. And she wouldn't know a thing about the diary or the black mark it left on the history of her family. She needed to make sure the millennial was arrested so she could go back to enjoying her small-town Christmas.

She trotted after Tandy, the heels of her boots clicking on tile as they entered the foyer. How would she lure Randon to town? He'd only leave his home to make himself look good. Like when he had a debate with her father at the college over whether God existed or not. He preferred to be his own God. Which must take a lot of the joy out of his holidays...

Holidays! That was it. "He's coming to town tonight."

Tandy waved boldly at the man they'd snuck past earlier.

He glared, and Marissa sped up to match the other woman's stride in an effort to hide from his view. The front doors slid open with a whoosh of icy air, cooling her burning blush.

Were it up to Marissa, she would have gotten out of there as quickly as possible. But Tandy stopped and handed Marissa her dog's leash so she could return the Santa hats to Frosty and his wife. What an odd mix of indifference and ethics. Tandy didn't seem to care what others thought, but she lived up to her own standards. Such as not stealing from snowmen. Marissa could respect that. Even if they weren't friends.

Tandy picked up Cocoa and continued on toward her car. "How do you know he's coming to town?"

Marissa tugged on her gloves and extended her arms wide to balance and prevent a fall like she had that morning. Landing in the parking lot would hurt more without Connor around to catch her. Not that she wanted him around. She took small, even steps as she considered options for "accidentally" running into Randon that night. "After all his whining in the newspaper, the city council finally decided to shut him up by giving him the honor of putting the star on the Christmas tree at the tree lighting."

Tandy clicked her remote to unlock the car with a beep. "It's kind of late in the year for a tree lighting, isn't it?"

Marissa's foot slid wide, and she grabbed onto the door handle just in time. Her heart lurched then eased back into its normal rhythm. She was okay, and she had to make sure she stayed that way. "They do the tree lighting every Friday night for tourists, but on the last Friday before Christmas, it's tradition for someone special to put the star on the tree. Lucky for us, this year it's Randon."

Tandy bent to settle Cocoa into his spot in the backseat. "Yes, we're lucky he's going to be surrounded by people because it's good for our safety. But how are we going to get to him to question him?"

Marissa's stomach rumbled. Empty calories or not, she should have eaten her crème brûlée when she'd had the chance. Maybe she could see if Randon wanted to go to dinner with her before the tree lighting. No. She didn't want to spend that much time with him. "I'll be his date for the tree lighting."

Tandy gave her a quizzical look over the roof of her car before dropping into her seat. "Just like that? It's that easy for you to get asked out?"

"I haven't dated anyone besides Connor for a couple of years, but it can't be hard." Marissa joined her on the chilly car seats, mulling over her strategy. "I'll be smooth. I'll text him and tell him how impressed I was when I saw him at the college and act thrilled that he's being honored by the city." She shrugged. "You know."

"No, I don't know."

Marissa pursed her lips. She and Tandy really didn't have much in common, did they? "You don't ever massage a man's ego to get him to like you?"

"Uh...no." Tandy turned the ignition. "Though if it's that easy, why haven't you dated anyone since Connor?"

Marissa snapped her seatbelt tight. She could wave off Tandy's comment, or she could...what were her other options? She'd never been very good at letting go. "If you're so worried about Connor, why don't you date him?"

Tandy grinned before she shifted into reverse and backed out of the parking spot. "We could make tonight a double date."

Marissa's palms itched at the idea, but why *wouldn't* Tandy want to go out with Connor? He was cute. And strong. And pleasant. And...he'd probably love to put his arm around someone else with Marissa watching. "Never."

Tandy pulled forward toward the street. "You'd be safer that way."

She'd be safer if she never saw Connor again. "I'll be fine." The itch in her palms spread to her chest. Her heart. If Tandy was going to date Connor, she didn't want them around her at all. "In fact, I really don't need your help tonight. I can do this without you. I'm the one who had the idea to talk to Mr. Cross. I'm the one who figured out Randon is the killer."

Tandy snorted. "Without me, you'd still be Christmas caroling at the manor."

No, she wouldn't. Well, maybe... She did like to sing. Marissa relented, sinking deeper into her seat. "Fine. You can come tonight. But no Connor."

Tandy slowed at the parking lot exit. "Which way do I go?"

A nice change in subject. Marissa should appreciate the change. She pointed to the curve ahead. "You'll turn right once you get past the bend."

The river ran along the left side of the road and a hill on their right. It was beautiful, but also dangerous. She was glad not to be driving, though they should have taken her Jeep.

Tandy slowed for the curve. They'd barely made it around the bend when a rockslide appeared in front of them, blocking their path.

Marissa's heart leaped into her throat. She braced her hands on the dashboard and screamed.

Tandy slammed on the breaks and gripped the wheel at the sight of the rocks in the middle of the road. Adrenaline surged through her veins in an effort to speed up her reactions and slow down the coming impact. The snow-coated pavement wasn't nearly as helpful. It carried her forward with the momentum of an avalanche.

She could try to avoid the rocks, but that would either send the car into the side of a hill or down an embankment into the river below. If she headed toward the river, they wouldn't only crash but also possibly drown or die of hypothermia. She'd err on the side of running into the hill.

The rocks grew larger as the car continued to ice skate. Tandy had to act. She cranked the wheel to the right. Her little car continued forward even as the windshield pivoted to face the hill, so her side of the car slid sideways toward the very rocks she'd been trying to avoid. She braced for impact.

Metal crunched. Glass shattered. An explosion rang in her ears as the airbag hit the side of her face, sending her head bouncing toward Marissa. The front airbag slammed her forearms into her chest, leaving behind the sting of rug burns. Pain shot diagonally across her torso from the seatbelt.

Some kind of powder rained around them like snow inside the car, and the Sulphur smell of gunpowder singed her nose hairs. It took a moment to realize both were from the airbags.

Then all went calm, though not all was quiet. Marissa continued to scream, mouth open and eyes closed.

Tandy unhooked her seatbelt to relieve the pressure on her ribs and survey her passenger. No blood. No bones sticking out anywhere. Not even any damage to the other side of the car besides the deflated airbag hanging from the console. "You okay?" Tandy asked so Marissa would realize that she was, in fact, okay, and hopefully stop the noise.

Marissa's screams died. Either she'd become aware that the car had quit moving, or she'd run out of breath. She peeked one eye open, then followed with the second. Finally, she lifted her hands in front of her face before using them to feel up and down her body as if expecting to find something missing. She twisted toward Tandy. "I'm alive."

Tandy shifted to ease the ache in her gut, sending up a cloud of powder. She grunted. "Good, because I need you to call 9-1-1." She gingerly craned her neck to check on Cocoa. The dog sat upright in his little basket, tongue hanging out as if trying to figure out what new game they were playing. She'd pet him later when she could reach him without having to twist her body into the shape of a candy cane to do so. "Good boy."

Marissa leaned forward, searching through the contents of her purse scattered on the floor. "You want me to call Little Lukey?"

Tandy swept the airbag out of her way like a curtain to look out the window. A few boulders had been lodged into the side of her Bug. She wasn't likely to be able to open the door, but she could crawl through the space that had once held a sheet of glass.

"I don't care if the deputy comes or not. We just need someone who can get these rocks out of the road before another car crashes." Plus a tow truck to haul them and her poor car back to town. She tugged her legs up to kneel on the seat and lean through the window, but the movement ignited a fire down the side of her torso. Wrapping arms around her waist, she fell back against the upholstery. "And maybe an ambulance."

Marissa paused mid dial. "Are you hurt?" She looked up from her phone, peering through the grey daylight. "You look like you've been punched in the face."

Tandy lifted her fingers to gingerly test for swelling or scratches. The throbbing in her cheekbone at even a gentle touch told her more than she wanted to know. In case being a suspect in a murder investigation wasn't the worst way to introduce herself to her neighbors, she'd now have a black eye and fat lip to help destroy their first impression. Not to mention the fact that her car had been totaled and she was still unemployed. "Joy to the world."

"I'll get you help." Marissa finished dialing and held the phone to her ear.

Tandy glanced past her to watch for any cars coming their way. They should probably get to the side of the road in case more vehicles rounded the curve and couldn't stop before crashing into her Beetle. Didn't she have some flares in her emergency kit that she could use to warn other drivers?

Thankfully, there weren't many others driving around in the snow. Probably home for the holidays. If only she'd stayed in bed that morning instead of living this nightmare.

"Hi, Lukey. It's Marissa."

Tandy motioned toward the door for Marissa to climb out. She'd retrieve Cocoa and follow through the passenger side rather than climb through her own window. With the way her ribs throbbed every time she twisted, it would likely be the less painful route.

Marissa shoved her door open. "Sorry. I mean Deputy Griffin," she said into the receiver even as she shot Tandy a wide-eyed expression that told how she was still trying not to laugh at the joke of Griffin working for the police.

Tandy didn't see the humor. She simply wanted his help. She nodded toward the door. "Keep going."

Marissa stepped into the snow, giving Tandy the space she needed. "I'm with Tandy Brandt... Yes, my competition for the teahouse... Never mind that. We ran into a pile of rocks on Riverside Road. We need a tow truck and an ambulance."

With a hand supporting her ribs, Tandy turned on her flashers, hooked her backpack over her shoulders, then flipped around to face backwards. She gingerly leaned through the bucket seats and scooped Cocoa into her arms. "Hey, buddy. We're going to go for a walk."

He nuzzled against her neck, tickling her ear with his fur.

She shivered, and she wasn't sure if it was from his tickle, the icy breeze, or a delayed adrenaline rush. But if she was cold, she should keep moving. She crawled across the seats to join Marissa in the middle of the road.

"Yeah, it looks like a rockslide," Marissa spoke into the receiver.

Hopefully the deputy was carrying on this conversation while on his way to rescue them, because Tandy wanted nothing more than to head to the safety of her little apartment and let someone else take over this ridiculous investigation. Hopefully, they'd uncovered enough clues now that she couldn't be arrested for the crime. She grunted and adjusted Cocoa to her left arm so she could pop the trunk with her free hand.

Marissa watched her walk behind the car. "I'm okay, but I think Tandy is hurt."

Tandy wouldn't dwell on the pain until later. She had to prevent any more injuries by setting up a road flare as quickly as she could. She braced for the ache then tipped forward to unzip her emergency kit. It took a couple jerks of the zipper to open the pouch with only one hand, but then she realized she'd never be able to light the flare while holding Cocoa.

"Marissa," she called.

"Oh, Tandy needs me. Please hurry." Marissa shoved the phone in her pocket then wobbled to the back of the car.

"What's wrong?" She may not have been the most level-headed individual, but at least she cared.

Tandy gritted her teeth against the throbbing from her insides to keep from revealing her discomfort when lifting the stick that looked like dynamite. "I need you to hold Cocoa so I can light this."

"Sure. Of course." Marissa grabbed onto the trunk to steady herself before reaching for the dog.

Cocoa nipped at the other woman's hand and turned to burrow against Tandy's neck once again. He never nipped. "Cocoa," she admonished. She had enough to worry about without her dog acting up.

Marissa pulled her hands to her chest. "You think he knows you're hurt?"

Oh. That could be it. He wanted to protect her. She tilted her head to hug him against her shoulder. His affection touched her, but now what did she do?

"Here." Marissa grasped the flare. "I'll light this."

Tandy wanted to retort. Something about how dangerous Marissa already was on ice without holding an open flame in her hands, but she should give the other woman a chance. She was, after all, trying to help.

"All right. Take off the cap then strike the scratch pad against the igniter button."

Marissa nodded, the tip of her tongue sticking out the corner of her mouth as she concentrated. Blinding fire shot from the end of the stick and sparks flew toward her wool coat. She squealed.

Tandy would remain calm enough for both of them. "You need to take the flare around the bend and place it down gently."

Marissa eyed the road in trepidation.

Tandy should have told her to walk around the curve

before lighting the flare, but it was too late now. She needed to position the stick before it burned her. "You have fifteen seconds before the fire grows."

Marissa's eyes widened. She jerked into action, her baby steps as quick as Tandy had ever seen them. She disappeared around the curve in the road to the crunching rhythm of boots in the snow. The little crunches were followed by a big crunch then silence as if her whole body had landed on the ground. Hopefully she didn't drop the flare and brake off the tip.

"Tandy," Marissa called her name.

Tandy looked down at Cocoa and shook her head. If only her dog had let Marissa hold him so she could have taken care of the flare.

"Tandy, come look at this."

So much for wanting to be rescued. Tandy was going to have to do the rescuing. Bearing down against the ache in her ribs, she tromped along the road until Marissa appeared. Sure enough, she lay flat on her belly. But that wasn't what caught Tandy's attention.

Where Marissa's footprints stopped, another set of footprints began. Larger footprints, belonging to snow shoes. And they led up the hill to the pile of rocks from where the rockslide must have originated.

The roadblock was no accident. Someone had tried to kill them.

Chapter Eight

MARISSA STARED AT THE FAINT FOOTPRINTS directly in front of her face, barely registering the snow melting against her clothes. She didn't want to believe it. She didn't want to believe someone had deliberately caused the rockslide to block their path. She could have been killed. One murder that day was more than enough for her.

"Did the killer know we are looking for him, or was this trap set for someone else?" Tandy asked.

Marissa couldn't imagine either scenario.

Sirens sounded in the distance. She had to get up or Lukey would find her on the ground next to a burning flare, and he didn't need any more examples of her klutziness to make him suspect her. Nor reminders of the fire she'd once started in his home. She pushed to her knees. "If Randon is the killer, he wouldn't have known we were looking for him."

Tandy's eyes roamed the crime scene. "Could Cross have warned him? He heard us say Randon's name."

Marissa sat back on her heels and brushed at the flakes covering her belly. "Maybe Randon wasn't trying to kill us. Maybe he was only setting up a roadblock to give himself enough time to get out of town."

Tandy grunted. "Then he wouldn't have put it around a bend in the road so that we wouldn't have time to stop."

Marissa bit her lip. She had a point.

Tandy continued her thought. "I liked Cross, but there's the possibility he's in on it. He did leave the cafeteria before we did."

Mr. Cross and Randon? Together? If Mr. Cross had the time to warn Randon then he possibly would have had the time to cause the rockslide himself. Didn't he say he'd been snowshoe golfing? What if the activities director had dropped him off for what she'd expected to be an innocent hike and he'd caused the rockslide then disappeared into the woods? He was pretty fit for an old guy. "It could also be only Mr. Cross. He told us to check the dates for the sale of his company. What if he wanted to stop us before we could do that?"

Tandy's eyes narrowed. "You want it to be Cross, don't you?"

Marissa gave her best nonchalant shrug though she'd never done nonchalant very well. She pushed to her feet and brushed the snow from her knees. "We know he's a liar and cheater." Speaking of his lies, she needed to get Grandmother's journal out of the glove compartment before the car was hauled away. And she needed to do that before Lukey—

A door slammed. Lukey strode around the corner. His eyes took in everything from the flare to the wet spots on her clothing to the footprints in the snow. At least now he would know they weren't the murderers. Someone else was out to kill them.

"Glad nobody had to die for you to call me this time, Marissa."

She frowned. Had he attempted a joke? If so, it was in very poor taste. Plus, she and Tandy could have both died here. Then who would have called?

He crossed his arms and stared at the hill. "Those kids have gone too far this time."

Tandy glanced at Marissa, eyebrows lifting.

"What kids?" Marissa spoke for both of them.

Lukey turned toward her. "We've had a few reports lately of hooligans on this hill. They've been building snowmen in streets and throwing snowballs at cars. I'm really hoping this rockslide was an accident. Of course, they could still end up in juvenile hall for not reporting such a road hazard."

The weight of his words sunk in like an anchor in a storm. Nobody had been trying to kill her. It was an unfortunate mishap. Insurance would cover Tandy's claim under the header Act of God clause. Though maybe the fact that they were still alive was the real act of God.

More doors slammed, and men dressed in blue rounded the corner carrying EMT equipment. "Who was driving?" asked the tall Mexican with a deep voice.

Tandy raised a hand, and they surrounded her.

Lukey pulled out his phone and stylus. "What are you two doing together anyway? Aren't you competitors?"

Marissa groaned. How was it that she'd called him for help, and he was interrogating her again? Not fair. Especially while Tandy got doted on by a bunch of big hunks.

Did she tell Lukey what they were really doing together? If someone had been out to kill one of them, then she definitely would have. But since it was only a bunch of kids playing pranks, she had nothing to worry about. They had simply been in the wrong place at the wrong time.

As for Virginia's killer, if the shop owner was murdered, it may or may not have anything to do with Grandmother's secret. And if it didn't, then there was no reason for Marissa to reveal the skeletons in her closet. The townsfolk would be shocked enough over a murder. To have the pillars of their community come crashing down would cause even more chaos. She was only thinking of *them*. She wanted to protect her town.

"Tandy went with me to deliver some apple cake to Joseph Cross," she said.

Tandy caught her eye as another muscular man dabbed at her cheek with gauze. She didn't seem to approve of Marissa's secrecy, but the guy with the gauze spoke, pulling her attention back toward him.

Marissa let out a sigh of relief.

"Joseph...Cross..." Lukey pronounced the name slowly as he scribbled it on his screen. He stopped writing and looked up. "Why?"

"Uh...Billie asked us to." That was true, wasn't it? Or was she being as dishonest as Mr. Cross? Fine. She'd tell the police what was going on. Just not Lukey. He wasn't a real detective, let alone an actual officer. She used to have to help him when he played Where in the World is Carmen Sandiego. She'd wait for the sheriff to finish his investigation of the jewel heist. In fact, she'd make an appointment with him the following day if she could. *There, take that, overactive conscience.*

"Billie Wu?" Lukey made another note.

Marissa scrunched her nose, hoping Lukey wouldn't try to follow up with her and find out about the diary. "Yes."

"After Virginia died, you both headed over to Grandma's Attic where she gave you the cake." He peered up at her. "Is she selling her shop too?"

He said it like he thought one of them might kill Billie next.

She narrowed her eyes. "No."

An engine revved on the other side of the bend. There hadn't been any traffic on this side, but maybe there was a line of cars around the curve, waiting to pass through.

"Should I help with Tandy's car so you can get a crew to start removing the rocks?" she asked.

Lukey scrolled through his notes like he thought there might be something he missed. "Don't worry. I've got a tow truck already taking care of it."

She blinked. A tow truck? Right then? Taking off with Tandy's slug bug and Grandmother's diary? "I've got to get my stuff out of it."

Lukey pointed to the purse hanging bandolier style across her torso. "That stuff?"

"Uh…" Okay, yeah. "I mean Tandy's stuff."

Lukey leaned backwards to see Tandy around an EMT's large frame. "Tandy, I called a tow truck for you. Is there anything important you need to get out of your car?"

Tandy lifted her puppy. "Got him," she called. He licked her cheek, and she let out a laugh, which turned into a moan as if her laughter caused pain.

Marissa was going to hurt her a lot more for not remembering to retrieve the diary. "Are you sure?" she asked between gritted teeth.

Tandy had her eyes closed. Was she really in that much agony?

The EMT unzipped Tandy's jacket and ran his hands along her ribs. "I think you need to get x-rays. If you have any broken ribs, then you might also have a punctured lung."

The rumble of the tow truck cut off her response, but it looked like Tandy would be leaving in the ambulance. Marissa needed to act quickly. "I'll ride to town with the tow truck, and make sure your car is taken care of," she offered.

Tandy backed away from the EMT. "They don't want to take Cocoa in the ambulance with me, so I'll go with you. Hopefully the tow truck driver will drop me off at the ER."

Even better. "Okay."

"You don't have to do that." Lukey stepped forward. "I'll give you ladies both a ride to town."

Marissa cringed. How was she going to get the diary back now?

Tandy gingerly lowered herself into the molded plastic seat in the back of the cop car to avoid igniting the burning sensation along her side. The ambulance would have been more comfortable, but she couldn't leave Cocoa behind. Not after he'd freaked out when Marissa tried to hold him earlier.

Now the locals were going to see her riding around in the back of a police cruiser before they even met her. There went her last chance of being welcomed into the small town. Might as well get used to being the outcast.

She twisted sideways in her seat to keep the seatbelt from rubbing against the epicenter of pain above her waist. Cocoa stood on her lap, lifting his front paws to the windowsill to watch the commotion outside.

Marissa opened her door and brought the commotion in with her. She dropped to the seat, brooding like Scrooge. What was she upset about? She wasn't the one whose face looked like it had been used in place of a punching bag. It wasn't her car that had lost the game of Chicken to a pile of rocks.

Dare Tandy ask? "What?"

Marissa's long locks flew as she spun about, getting buckled in. Only Marissa could make putting on a seatbelt so dramatic. "Your glove compartment is locked, isn't it?"

Her glove compartment? Oh...the diary. Marissa was upset because she didn't want anybody to find out she came from a family of frauds. Tandy leaned back in her seat and tried to hide a smile. She may have problems, but at least she wasn't pretending to be someone she wasn't.

"Stop smiling and answer the question."

Shoot. Marissa had seen her smile. No reason to hide it now. "Yes."

Marissa tossed her hair over her shoulder. "Yes you'll stop smiling, or yes it's locked?"

The driver's side door snapped open.

For some reason this made Tandy smile a little bigger. Maybe because Marissa wouldn't get away with being so moody around the cop. "Yes, it's locked," she said.

Marissa pressed her lips together and faced forward in silence.

Griffin strapped himself in before starting the engine. "What's locked?" he questioned while doing a three-point-turn to head back toward town.

From Marissa's behavior, it was obvious she hadn't told Griffin about the journal. Should Tandy spill the coffee beans now or let Marissa keep her secret?

Marissa leaned forward to answer for Tandy. "She locked her seatbelt in even though it hurts her ribs."

Really? After what they'd just been through, Marissa was still trying to keep the journal a secret? This girl was willing to get her killed to save face. Did she honestly think the footprints in the snow were caused by children? Children didn't normally wear snow shoes, did they?

"I'll try to drive smoothly." Deputy Griffin studied her from the rear-view mirror as if to assess her pain for himself. He wasn't as bad as Marissa made him out to be.

"Thank you," Tandy said. He wouldn't really put her in jail, would he?

Marissa rummaged through her purse, pulling out her phone. "Let me get your phone number, Tandy. Then we can stay in touch after Lukey drops you off at the hospital."

Tandy wasn't sure she wanted to stay in touch. Marissa only wanted her phone number in case she had trouble getting into Tandy's glove box. But maybe if she did this favor for Marissa, Marissa could help her out in the future. The woman had a lot of connections, and Tandy needed a job.

She rattled off her digits then settled against her seat, longing for a mug of cappuccino and the peace of her apartment. Her phone buzzed in her pocket.

Dad? Maybe he'd be able to visit for the holidays after all.

She retrieved the device to find a text message from an unknown number. She tapped on her phone to read it.

Please don't tell Lukey about the diary.

Marissa. Tandy closed her eyes, the puffy one stinging a bit. Could she pretend to go to sleep to avoid this conversation? Her phone buzzed again. She relented and peeked at the screen.

I'm going to tell Officer Woodward everything tomorrow. He'll be able to help and understand the importance of not spreading gossip about Grandmother.

Finally. Tandy nodded in approval. Virginia's blood results would probably be in by then anyway, which meant the police would know the woman had been murdered. If Marissa didn't tell them the whole story by that time, Tandy would when they hauled her in for questioning. Wouldn't the fact that someone intentionally caused the rockslide be evidence enough of her innocence?

The phone vibrated on her lap. She'd need another pain killer to battle this headache Marissa was giving her.

I messaged Randon, and he agreed to take me to the tree lighting, so you can join us after your x-ray.

Oh, no. Marissa truly thought the rockslide was a fluke, and she was going ahead with their private investigation.

Tandy grimaced and texted back. *I don't think that's such a good idea anymore. The guy could be after us.*

Marissa read her message, shrugged, and shook her head.

"Marissa," Deputy Griffin broke into their conversation without knowing it. "Where are you parked? I'll take you to your car after we drop Tandy off."

"Uh..." Marissa tapped her phone furiously. "I'm on Main by the town square."

Tandy's phone buzzed. *Bring that cute EMT with you for protection if you want.*

Tandy scrunched her nose at Marissa before silently responding via text. *He's married. Invite Connor.*

Talking about Marissa's former fiancé had silenced her last time.

Marissa bugged her eyes then typed a message. *Get your own date.*

Tandy should have expected as much. Though by not setting her up with Connor, was Marissa setting her up with trouble?

Randon could be the killer. And Cross could have warned him they were onto him. What if he pretended to flirt at the tree lighting and Marissa fell for it? Then he could get her alone to finish what he'd attempted with the rockslide.

Tandy focused on her phone to write her response. *What's Connor's phone number? I'll invite him.*

"Bah!" Marissa couldn't keep quiet after that one.

Deputy Griffin glanced at them in his rear-view mirror. "You okay, Marissa?"

Tandy grinned at the other woman's reaction. She didn't really want to date Connor. He was Hollywood handsome, but he was obviously still smitten with his former fiancée. And though Marissa tried to pretend otherwise, she was rather territorial about him, as well. Tandy only wanted him there as a bodyguard.

Marissa cleared her throat. "Yes. I'm good. Fine. Great. No problems back here."

"Good." Deputy Griffin pulled in front of a one-story building Tandy would have normally considered too small for a hospital. At least the newer construction had a glass lobby that revealed a Christmas tree and zero patients, so there shouldn't be much of a wait for her x-rays. "I'll have to let you out, Tandy. Hold on." The deputy hopped from the vehicle to circle around and open her door.

Tandy unsnapped her seatbelt and hugged her dog close. "Since you say you're good, Marissa, I'll plan to see you and Connor at the tree lighting then."

Marissa's mouth opened to argue, but Griffin cut her off by swinging Tandy's door open.

Tandy winked before standing. It had been a while since she'd gone on a date. Even if her date was still in love with his ex, he would be fun to hang out with. But better yet, he'd figure out what was going on and never leave Randon alone with Marissa.

Tandy's phone pinged once more as Griffin chauffeured the beauty queen away.

Over my dead body.

That's what Tandy was afraid of.

Chapter Nine

MARISSA CONTINUED TO STEW AFTER LUKEY dropped her off at her Jeep. Was Tandy really attracted to Connor? Was *he* attracted to Tandy? And, if so, why did he have to fall for someone else now? She needed to be focused on finding Virginia's murderer.

That's what she was trying to do when heading to the auto body shop to retrieve Grandmother's diary. Okay, that wasn't the only reason she was retrieving the journal. But it very well could play a part in it.

She drove through the dusk to the garage with the big red letters across the front spelling out BODYSHOP. Surely Jumpsuit George would let her look in Tandy's car. He knew her, and he'd know she'd been involved in the accident.

She reapplied her lip gloss before entering, just in case she needed to use her feminine wiles.

George stood behind the counter, wearing his standard navy-blue coveralls of course. She'd never seen him in anything else. Even at church. Hence the nickname.

"Hey, Jumpsuit George." She tossed her hair and leaned against the counter.

"Hey." George glanced at her once before doing a double take. He lowered the volume on the football game he was watching and rested his hands on his protruding belly. "Glad to see you're okay, Marissa. The crash looked pretty bad. Was it only the other girl who got hurt?"

The other girl. Tandy. He didn't even know his customer's name? Tandy might have been right about being considered an outsider. "Tandy is at the hospital right now, but I think she'll be okay. I just want to retrieve a couple things she forgot to take with her."

"Oh." George frowned. "I wish I could help, but the police had me haul the car to their impound lot."

Marissa's heartrate tripped. Her stomach churned. Grandmother's diary was in police possession. Surely, Lukey wouldn't use it to smear her family's name, but if he used it in his investigation at all, the Alexander name would be smeared in the process. It could affect both her parents' careers. It could affect her success at starting a teahouse. It could affect her scores when she was moved up into the Ms. Ohio category next year for women over the age of twenty-eight.

The last thought ate at her. Is that really what she cared about? She'd worry later.

"Why is it at impound?" Tandy hadn't done anything wrong. Well, not really.

George unclasped his pudgy fingers to shrug before clasping them atop his head this time. "I guess so they can use it as evidence when they track down the kids who caused the wreck."

Marissa pressed her hands to her cheeks. It was going to be okay. The police weren't even interested in the diary. In fact, they might even let Tandy pick it up from the impound lot. Why not? It was her car.

She took a deep breath. "Okay, thanks, Jumpsuit George."

"You shouldn't knock the jumpsuit until you try it. They're really comfortable."

"One of these days." She smiled at the image. She rarely dressed for comfort. "Enjoy the rest of your game."

"Will do, Marissa."

Back into the icy air she marched, the streetlights popping on to reflect off fresh snow and brighten the dark night with an eerie golden glow. If only her day hadn't been so dark. After days like this, she used to be able to find comfort in Connor's arms. She missed his strength. Now she had to do everything on her own. Well, not completely on her own. Tandy was going to meet her at the Christmas tree lighting to confront Randon. But that wasn't the same. Especially not if Tandy was interested in Connor.

Marissa ignored the emotional itch underneath her sternum as she drove back downtown. She'd focus on the growling of her stomach instead. She parked in the elementary school parking lot with everybody else and planned to grab something to eat at Mama's Kitchen on her way to meeting Randon at the town square. Going all day without eating was not good for her metabolism.

Icy air stung her face as she stepped into the chilly night and joined the crowds flowing down the street. But she couldn't help stopping in front of Virginia's Antiques and staring in the unlit window. Everything would be different if Virginia had lived. Everything except the fact that Marissa still wasn't spending her favorite night of the year with Connor.

With a sigh, she continued down the sidewalk until she reached the wooden double doors to Mama's Kitchen. Matching potted evergreen trees wrapped in white lights flanked the entryway under the green awning. She lifted a hand to press the door open.

A solid chest belonging to a large man slid between her palm and the wood, freezing her in her tracks. The murderer? The police?

No, Connor.

She defrosted enough to drop her hand to her side. No

need for panic. She could handle him. Except she thought she'd handled him that morning. What was he doing here?

He crossed his arms, his facial features set like concrete. "I saw you getting a ride through town in the back of a police car."

Was that all? From his expression, one would think she'd committed murder. Oh... "Don't worry. I didn't get arrested."

"I know." He didn't relax. He didn't move out of the way. "I called Lukey. He said you'd been in an accident."

She fought a losing battle with her smile. Had he been scared? Did he care that much about her wellbeing? It was kind of nice. She had to wave him away before she let herself enjoy the feeling too much. "I'm fine. A couple of kids were playing pranks and accidentally caused a rockslide."

His head tilted. His eyes pierced. "That's what the deputy said, but he doesn't know you're snooping around, trying to find a murderer. If he knew that, he might think otherwise."

Uh-oh. Connor assumed the rockslide was an attempt on her life. No wonder he was acting all bodyguard-like. "You didn't say anything to Lukey, did you?"

"Not yet." His gaze softened. "I wanted to find out what was going on from you first."

Her heart squeezed in her chest. If only he'd checked with her like this before tearing down Grandmother's house. Since he hadn't, she couldn't trust him with Grandmother's other secrets. She swallowed them before they came out. "You want to know what's going on? Uh...I'm...I'm grabbing something to eat on my way to watch the tree lighting."

"May I join you?" He didn't take a step closer, but she could suddenly feel his warmth and smell his piney scent as if he had.

Her heart thrummed in her chest.

"She's already got a date, dude."

Marissa didn't have to look to know the man who strode up behind her was none other than Randon Evans. She could tell by the way Connor's jaw turned to stone and his eyes narrowed into lasers.

Of all the places for Randon to run into her. But of course, she was standing in the middle of the route from the parking lot to the tree lighting.

What did she do now? Offer Connor contrition for parading another man in front of him? Or play it up to make Randon feel special the way she'd planned? While she felt contrite, her goal *had* been to make Randon feel special.

Connor didn't move. He watched her. As if waiting for her to confirm she was really on a date with the man in rolled up skinny jeans, loafers, black glasses, and gauge earrings. Well, why not? She'd been needing to put some space between the two of them anyway.

"Randon. Glad you could make it." She tucked an arm behind her date's back and tilted into a side hug. He wasn't much taller than her height of 5'7", and his goatee scratched her cheek.

Connor's chin lifted. He wasn't buying it.

She slid out of her date's reach. "Randon, meet Connor Thomas."

Randon reached for Connor's hand. "Nice to meet you, Connor Thomas."

Connor shook without repeating the sentiment.

"I'm flattered that Marissa thinks I need no introduction, but I'll give one anyway. I'm Randon Evans. I design phone applications. Started a little company you may have heard of—App Entertainment."

Connor crossed his arms again, his chest sticking out

farther than before, if possible. "No, I haven't." He focused on Marissa. "I don't play games."

"Ouch." Randon laughed like it was funny to be rude. "Maybe I'll see you around town again sometime." A clear dismissal.

Connor's gaze remained locked on hers. It said he wasn't going to interfere while Randon was involved, but he'd want answers later. Had he guessed correctly that Randon was on her suspect list?

She gave a tight-lipped smile. If he had figured out she was suspicious of Randon, then he would know she couldn't say anything at the moment.

"Maybe I'll see you around town," Connor repeated Randon's words though he looked straight at her.

There used to be no "maybe" about it. Even after she'd ended their relationship, Connor continued to seek her out. He'd been reliable. A constant. And now it sounded like that would all end. Was it really what she wanted?

No, she'd wanted him to fill her empty spaces, but he'd left her emptier than ever. She couldn't bring herself to say goodbye.

"Connor." Tandy joined them and sent Marissa a smile of pure delight in spite of her bruised cheek, puffy eye, and the scab on her temple. "I was hoping you'd be here."

Marissa curled her acrylic nails into her palm, wishing she'd said goodbye a little faster. Because now Tandy would think Connor was joining them, turning their interrogation into that double date she'd suggested.

Connor lifted an arm in front of Tandy to hold her back after Randon and Marissa filed past down the sidewalk. "What is going on?" he whispered.

Tandy clicked her tongue. It seemed that as much as Marissa liked to play the drama queen, Connor preferred to stay out of the limelight. The two could perfectly balance each other if they'd both stop being so stubborn. "Marissa should have called to fill you in."

"Well, she didn't." He was really cute when angry. How did Marissa resist those lowered eyebrows and smoldering gray eyes?

Tandy grabbed his gloved hand and pulled him after her so they didn't lose sight of the other woman and the possible murderer. She spoke quietly over her shoulder. "When Marissa decided to meet up with Randon at the tree lighting because we suspect him of killing Virginia, I suggested you be my date because I don't feel safe around suspected killers."

"Ah..." His grip tightened, and he caught up enough to whisper into her ear. "You wanted Marissa to ask me out for you, but she wouldn't."

He seemed more interested in the part about how Marissa wouldn't ask him out for her than the part about how Tandy wanted him to. Which was to be expected. "Uh...yeah." She stopped to keep from running into a little blonde girl whose hat fell off. The girl was like a mini Marissa. Or maybe Marissa was like a child. "If she didn't invite you to join us, how did you end up here?"

Connor motioned toward the crowd around them. "How did *anybody* end up here?"

Tandy knew better than to believe Connor was attending a tree lighting by himself. She lifted an eyebrow.

He looked away, probably keeping an eye on his ex. "I heard about your car accident and tracked Marissa down to make sure she was all right."

That made more sense. He was there because he cared. There should be more men like him in the world. At least one more. For her. "Marissa isn't hurt, but I got a little beat up."

"I see that. Did you get checked out?" Connor released her hand and led the way single file between two slow families.

"Yes. Cracked ribs but no punctured lungs." Her ribs still stung underneath the rib belt the doctor had given her, and she'd prefer to be home in a hot bath, but she hadn't wanted to leave Marissa alone with Randon. Marissa, however, seemed to prefer Randon's company over Connor's.

"That's good." He glanced at her again. "Is Cocoa hurt? Where is he?"

How could anyone pass up a man this perfect? "Yeah, he's with my neighbor. She picked me up at the hospital and dropped me off here." Tandy looked from him to find the woman he adored.

Marissa stopped at a spicy scented food truck to place an order for pizza in the shape of a candy cane with pepperoni stripes. She kept peeking sideways to watch Connor.

Tandy's stomach rumbled, and not only from the nausea caused by the lovesickness around her. If Marissa was going to practically drag her here then stick her with a jealous ex, the least she could do was provide dinner. "Can you get me a piece too, Marissa?"

"I'll get it for you." Connor stepped forward to join his former fiancée in line. "Since I am your date and all."

Tandy rolled her eyes towards the silvery sky. "Merry crustmas to me."

"Pizza on Earth, goodwill toward men," called the woman in an elf hat serving food from the window above.

Tandy's laugh turned into a groan at the intense throb in

her side. Her painkillers didn't kill the pain so much as make her loopy.

Connor dug his wallet out of his pocket to pay for her dinner. He brought her back the pizza cane. "You okay?"

Okay was relative. She'd been more okay before, but today she would settle for not being murdered. "Yeah."

Connor turned to face Marissa's date. "Randon, did you hear what happened to these ladies this afternoon?"

Oh boy. Connor was going to do their interrogating for them.

Randon lifted a shoulder before flashing his superior smile. "Cat fight?"

Tandy blinked. Did the man really care that little, or had he caused their accident and was playing innocent to an extreme?

Marissa joined their circle and narrowed her eyes at Tandy. "More or less."

Tandy frowned then took a greasy bite of pizza. She needed nourishment if she was going to have to deal with this kind of tension. Was the beauty queen more upset about Tandy vying for the location she'd wanted for her teahouse or vying for Connor's attention? Either way... "If I was in a cat fight, I wouldn't look like this because I would have won," Tandy said around the food in her cheek.

A mom with a baby in her arms sent Tandy a startled look before darting the opposite direction. Awesome. One more local she'd scared away.

She consoled herself with another huge bite of gooey goodness, the yeasty crust and tangy sauce almost making up for the fact that she'd have to ask one of these crazies for a ride home after the tree lighting. At this point, she might actually choose their murder suspect just to avoid being a third wheel.

Marissa took a prim bite of her pizza, the challenge in her gaze for Tandy alone. So much for being on the same side.

Connor cleared his throat and leaned forward. "Our lovely dates were in a car accident, Randon. Marissa didn't tell you?"

Randon pulled out his phone and opened his camera app. "No, I hadn't heard that. I bought an all-wheel drive vehicle when I moved here. Subaru Outback. Nine out of ten drivers rated it as one of the best cars in snow. I also bought studded tires. You should get a set of studded tires, Marissa." He held the phone screen up and leaned toward her. "At least you're not the one with a fat lip. Here. Smile."

Tandy would like to give *him* a fat lip.

Marissa's mouth turned up in an automatic pose, though her eyes kept their matte finish.

Tandy swallowed down her bite of pizza to glare as Randon took a selfie with Marissa. She reconsidered her idea of riding home with such a jerk. Even if his car was rated best in snow. How insensitive and shallow to joke about her injuries. Especially if he'd caused them. She wanted him to be the killer now. And she wanted him to get arrested before he put the star on the town tree.

He lowered the phone to study the image he'd captured. "You're gorgeous, 'Rissa. You make me look good."

Connor's lips parted. He eyed Tandy in disbelief though she wasn't sure if he was more shocked by the arrogance or the presumptuous nickname.

Marissa shifted slightly away, her eyes wide with aversion as Randon tapped his fingers on the screen. "Hashtag Miss Grace Springs, hashtag tree lighting, hashtag hometown hero."

Connor pointed in contempt. "You? You're calling yourself a hometown hero?"

Randon stuffed his phone in the pocket of the military jacket he must have bought at a consignment shop. "Uh...yeah? I'm the one being honored tonight. Have *you* ever put the star on top of the tree?"

Connor's hand curled into a fist.

Tandy hooked her fingers in the crook of his elbow to hold him back. She wanted Randon getting arrested, not Connor for starting a fight.

Chapter Ten

MARISSA DROPPED THE REMAINS OF HER pizza in the trashcan so she could separate Connor and Randon. This was why she hadn't wanted her ex here in the first place. He wasn't the jealous sort; he was the protective sort. And any woman Randon dated needed protection from his superiority complex.

She took a step between the two men and continued her act of adoration. "Speaking of your honor, Randon, we better get you over to the gazebo. Wouldn't want you to miss—" Her foot hit a slick spot. Her body careened backwards right into Connor's chimney of a chest.

His arms locked around her waist, holding her upright but also against himself. The heat of his breath tickled her ear. She shivered though she hadn't felt this warm in a long while.

"Hashtag be careful," he whispered.

A laugh threatened to spill out. Laughter at how ridiculous it was to hear his husky voice use the term "hashtag." Laughter at the double meaning to the phrase "be careful." And laughter at how sad life had to be for her to exchange the safety of Connor's arms for hanging onto the arm of a possible killer.

She turned her head sideways and tucked her chin to respond without being overheard. "I know what I'm doing."

He lifted her upright but didn't let go immediately. "Did you plan for me to catch you just now?"

"No…" She used her most haughty tone for the one word since she couldn't think what else to say. The truth was that if she were to plan falling into his arms, she would have done so in a more private setting.

"I gotcha." Randon wrapped a weaselly arm behind her back to ease her away from the other man. "I'll support you if you want to escort me over to meet the mayor."

She did her best to keep from gritting her teeth in distaste, but Connor could read it on her face anyway. She knew by the way he crossed his arms and smirked as Randon lead her off.

Tandy wasn't any better. "Way to go, hometown hero," she called.

Those two had a little too much in common for Marissa to be content with leaving them behind. They'd eat pizza and make their jokes, and if Tandy slipped, Connor could catch her like he'd caught Marissa.

Tandy had better not slip.

"You used to date him, huh?"

Randon's question attempted to pull her into the present, though she sent one more warning look toward Tandy.

"I can tell," Randon answered for her. "I don't think he's quite over you. Makes me feel like a king to have a beauty queen by my side."

A king? Wasn't hometown hero bad enough? Marissa gave her best pageant giggle and grin. If she wanted to get this night over with, she'd better ask some questions. She'd start with an easy one. Like alibi. "So what else did you do today, Randon? Were you busy getting ready for tonight?"

He wove a path through the crowds toward the gazebo at the center of the square. "Computer coding," he said without pause, then launched into a monologue most likely designed to impress her with his intelligence.

"Fascinating." She stifled a yawn. "That must take a long time. Were you home on your computer all day?"

He led her to the gazebo stairs, where she gripped the railing. Mayor Kensington stood in the center with a microphone. On one side of them loomed a large unlit Christmas tree. On their other side, a fire engine lowered a ladder with a bucket toward the ground. She pulled away from Randon to wave at both the mayor and Troy Younger, the firefighter operating the bucket.

"Not at all. Coding is a breeze." Randon shrugged. "I still had plenty of time to pick up my grandmother from the retirement center and take her out to eat at Mama's Kitchen."

Marissa's feet froze in place and she gripped the railing tighter. Randon had been both downtown and at the retirement center? Was he arrogant enough to have committed murder and attempted murder without even trying to hide his whereabouts?

"My grandma is the reason I moved here in the first place. Nine out of ten grandchildren don't take care of their grandparents, but I'm sweet like that." He paused at the step above her. "What?" He looked the direction she'd been staring blindly and shook his head. "Did you date the firefighter too?"

One thing at a time. She'd answer then she'd move again. And maybe after that she could think of a way to get even more information out of him. What had he asked again? Oh, the fireman...

"Troy?" Had she dated him? It would have been years. He was married now. "I think we went to a high school dance once."

Randon clapped his hands together. "This is great. You should come up with us in the bucket to help put the star on the tree."

"Wh-what?" No. Not if he was a murderer. Not with her clumsiness. He could throw her over the side of the bucket and everybody would assume it had been her own fault.

"Yeah. Come up. It'll be our official introduction to the town as a couple." His teeth flashed in the darkness, giving his smile a creepy feel. "I have to confess, I've been dying to take you out."

That wasn't the confession she wanted to hear. Especially if by taking her out, he meant killing her.

She held a hand to her racing heart and twisted to look out at the crowd, but without the tree lit, it was too dim to see faces. Where was Connor? She wanted Connor.

"Don't be nervous."

Did he really think she was nervous about standing in front of a crowd, or did he know she had other things to fear?

A speaker crackled, and a spotlight lit up the mayor at the podium in the gazebo. "Merry Christmas, Grace Springs."

Wild applause. And a whistle. That would be Connor. Sounded like he was at the back of the crowd.

"I'd like to thank you all for coming. Here with me tonight is our guest of honor Randon Evans." He held his arm wide to welcome Randon to the stage.

The spotlight shifted to blind Marissa. She squinted and shaded her eyes with a hand and hoped it hid her from view. She could let Randon hog the limelight while she removed herself gracefully. She slid a foot behind her off the step and bent her front knee to descend backwards.

Mayor Kensington continued. "He may be new to Grace Springs, but he's known around the world for his game designs. And it looks like he's brought a familiar face with him."

Her face? No...

"Miss Grace Springs, are you going to assist with placing the star on the tree?"

Her attempt at a playful laugh came out sounding more

like the donkey's reaction to having baby Jesus take over his manger. She added a wave of refusal.

Randon caught her waving hand and tugged. "Of course she is."

The crowd cheered.

She stumbled up the stairs to keep from getting pulled off her feet. Though it would have been better to fall from this distance than from fifty feet in the air. She found her balance and peered up toward the tip of the tree. Her toes tingled at the height. The sensation of falling made her grab tighter to Randon's hand.

He squeezed. "I'll take care of you."

Her pulse throbbed harder against her joints. What did he mean by taking care of her? Was he trying to comfort her or talking like a mobster?

She sidestepped. "I'm just going to—"

The fireman's basket lowered to the edge of the gazebo. Troy swung the little door open, blocking her path.

Randon motioned for her to enter ahead of him. "Your sleigh awaits."

Her slay? "I don't want to..."

Troy laughed. "Yeah, you didn't want to go on a helicopter ride with me before prom either, but you loved it, remember?"

That's right. But that had been about wind from the helicopter propellers messing up her hairdo. This was about her date wanting her dead. "This is different." She pivoted to head the other direction.

Randon blocked her path. "Afraid of heights, huh?" He stepped forward.

She stepped backward. Into the basket. Oh no. She'd have to wait for him to follow then scoot around him and escape off the contraption.

Randon stepped onto the rectangle platform. He moved to one side.

Hope surged through her veins, propelling her forward. Straight into Troy.

"Watch out, Marissa."

That was good advice. Except he meant watch out as he closed the door, not watch out for homicidal hipsters.

She leaned forward toward Troy. "I think Randon is trying to kill me," she whispered so as not to be overheard by the other man, but she couldn't even hear herself over the church choir bursting into song.

They had apparently changed from their ugly sweaters into golden robes to fill the night with a chorus loud enough to be mistaken for angels in Israel.

"What?" Troy asked as he snapped the door shut.

Should she try to explain or simply swing a leg over the side and...

The bucket shifted, knocking her sideways. She grabbed the edge and watched the ground sink away. Was it too late to jump? It would be if she wanted to land safely in her heels. Was it too late to kick off her boots and jump?

"Marissa," a deep voice called from below. "What are you doing?"

Connor. He'd found his way to the front of the crowd, arms wide as if presenting the vulnerability of her situation.

She pointed to the tree and leaned forward to yell down that she was supposed to help hang the star. "Help—" was all she got out before the basket bounced.

She jerked upright and spun to find Randon hopping in place.

He chuckled at her expression. "You're too easy to scare."

He wanted to scare her, did he? Well, she was probably

right to be scared. Didn't Troy see that?

Troy grinned, but shook his head. "Knock it off, man."

Marissa glared then peeked over the side again to find Connor. If he'd thought someone had tried to kill her earlier with the rockslide, then he was definitely going to worry about her here. Even if there wasn't a suspected murderer next to her, Connor would probably still worry. Was there anything he could do to help?

Tandy stood next to Connor, her mouth hanging open like she was about to join in with the lyrics to "Oh Christmas Tree."

They both grew smaller as the bucket continued to rise. If Marissa jumped from the bucket, could Connor catch her?

Troy peered down at her ex from where he worked the controls. "I still can't believe you two broke up. I thought you might be trying to make Connor jealous by getting on stage with this guy—"

"This guy has a name," Randon interrupted.

Marissa shot This Guy a sharp look.

Troy ignored him. "But it appears that Connor is dating someone else too. And I don't think he would ask out another woman unless he was truly interested."

Marissa's spine stiffened, which was ridiculous. She knew Connor and Tandy weren't on a real date. And even if they were, Marissa had other things to worry about. She peered down at them anyway just to see what Troy saw.

Connor and Tandy faced each other, intense expressions on their faces. They were talking about her. They had to be. Why else would they be leaning in so close?

Marissa's stomach clenched. She hated that it clenched. She really shouldn't care if Connor wanted to date someone else. She should care more about Tandy. She should warn her new friend away from the man who would destroy other people's dreams to build his own.

Nobody else seemed to see this about him. Not even Troy who'd assumed Marissa was more likely to date for selfish gain.

The pair separated below, and she sighed in relief. Connor wove through the crowd to follow underneath the bucket as it swung toward the tree while Tandy jogged the direction of the fire truck.

At this height, an icy breeze lifted Marissa's hair off her shoulders and made the bucket rock, bringing her back to the present danger. She should focus on staying as close to Troy and as far away from Randon as possible.

She turned to scoot toward the real hometown hero.

Randon stood in her way. His eyes narrowed.

Her throat clamped shut. She gripped the side of the bucket behind her. Internal warning sirens almost blocked out his next words.

"Did you only want to come with me to make your ex jealous?" Randon challenged.

No. No. Absolutely not. She didn't have enough spit to form the words, so she shook her head violently.

His eyes stayed squinty as he took another step forward. He reached out a hand.

Marissa whimpered and jerked toward the corner.

The bucket stopped. But she didn't. She'd lurched hard enough to tip forward over the side.

A scream escaped her lips, and her gloved fingers slid along the fiberglass, feeling for something to grab to hoist herself up.

The crowd below gasped. The choir stopped singing like a scratched record.

Something hard snagged her fingers. The door handle. She gripped it, her shoulder lit on fire, and her feet toppled past her face to swing freely above fifty feet of nothing.

Tandy charged towards the fire truck, looking over her shoulder when the crowd around her gasped. Marissa's form hung from the outside of the bucket, and Tandy's heartbeat sputtered like *she* was the one about to plummet to her death. Randon must have pushed Marissa in the way Tandy had feared. At least Marissa had caught onto something. And the fireman in the basket was reaching toward her to pull her back to safety.

But how could they be sure Randon wouldn't push him over as well? And how would the firefighter lower them all back down if he was holding onto Marissa.

Tandy continued her race. If Marissa fell, would Connor get there in time to catch her? At that height, they'd still both likely be severely injured.

Two men in bulky yellow jackets leaned lazily against the fire truck, apparently joking with each other and unaware of the peril overhead.

"Lower the bucket," Tandy yelled.

Their faces swiveled her way. One cupped a hand behind his ear to signal he couldn't hear her though the other's jaw tilted up then dropped open. He jerked to attention, pointing to the problem.

"Lower the bucket," she repeated breathlessly, hoping she wasn't too late.

The men scrambled for the controls, so she spun around, her heart in her throat.

Marissa shrieked, her free arm waving overhead,

reaching for the firefighter. He clasped her firmly around the wrist.

A collective sigh puffed up from the crowd, and as if the sound was the release of air from an inflatable lawn decoration, Tandy's shoulders sagged. It was going to be okay.

The bucket began its descent, thanks to the firefighters in the truck.

Tandy narrowed her eyes at Randon. He wouldn't try anything else up there would he?

The man stood frozen, and not only from the arctic temperatures. With the kind of horror that chiseled his expression taut, he appeared to be neither hometown hero nor a murderer. Was he nothing but talk?

She shook her head at the absurdity of the idea. Could Marissa have tipped herself out of the bucket in clumsiness and fear? If so, Tandy didn't know whether to be relieved or disappointed. Now what?

She took a deep breath, braced a hand against her left ribs where the deep breath stung, and made her way to meet Marissa when she landed. Once firefighters got her to solid ground, would they take Randon back up to put the star on the tree, or would she be able to confront him then? Whether he was a killer or not, he had some explaining to do.

The firefighter in the bucket hung over the side, reaching for Marissa's other hand as the firemen in the truck used their controls to continue to lower them past the midpoint of the tree. Marissa let go of the handle she'd been holding and swung her arm to grab onto the firefighter with both hands. She missed the connection, causing her body to spin around like an ornament.

The firefighter growled and made a jerking grab to catch her free hand but came up empty.

Marissa continued to swing by one arm again. She slipped lower. And lower. Until gravity completely tugged her out of the glove gripped by the man above.

She screamed and disappeared into the bushy tree branches.

Tandy ran.

Chapter Eleven

MARISSA'S BODY CAREENED TOWARD THE GROUND. She squeezed her eyes shut as pine branches scraped her jacket. Good thing she had on extra padding. Maybe she should always wear heavy clothing to keep her safe when she fell. Though she wasn't safe yet. Below the tree limbs and strands of lights that juggled her body, waited a landing pad of cement and ice.

Blindly, she groped for some kind of hold amongst the branches racing by. It had miraculously worked when she'd tipped over the side of the bucket. This time her hands fisted around nothing, and she tumbled out of the tree. Where was her guardian angel now?

The open air soothed like when driving her Jeep with the sunroof open, but it also stepped on the gas of her descent. She braced for impact against the unforgiving ground.

Something as strong as tree limbs caught her again. Then, "Oof." She landed on what felt like a pile of leaves. Had the firefighters brought out a safety net? Because shouldn't her body be hurting more?

She pried an eye open to find herself face to face with Connor. He *was* the pile of leaves. Catching her must have knocked him to the ground since they lay there in front of the whole community. Of course, she couldn't really be embarrassed about her current position after what she probably looked like when pinballing her way down the Christmas tree. Her dive off the stage at the Miss Ohio pageant had only been a warm up act. Though it was much nicer to be caught than pushed.

Warmth released through her body as if she were eating lunch in the Soup Cellar, and a laugh bubbled out.

"Are you okay, Marissa?" Connor practically grunted the words. "It sounds like your fall knocked a screw loose."

She'd be worried about how he was feeling if he weren't making jokes. He was the same old Connor. There to catch her when she fell. If only he'd caught her when she'd fallen for him.

"Yes." She planted her gloved and ungloved hands against the cold, rough ground on each side of his face to push herself up. She was okay only because her situation could have been a lot worse. She met his gaze. Her breath hitched. "Thank you for stopping my fall."

He didn't move. Only returned her gaze. It said he also left words unspoken. Did her expression hold the same longing as his? If so...

Hands lifted Marissa from behind. Then she was surrounded by emergency workers and separated from Connor. A couple of paramedics tried to keep him on the ground to check him out, but he shook them off and pushed to his feet.

"Where's it hurt?" a deep voice tugged at her attention.

Where did she hurt? Besides her heart? She blinked then looked down at herself in case there was a bone sticking out of her body or something. She knew from experience you couldn't always feel pain right away if your body was in shock.

Her shoulder burned, but she rolled it out and reached for her face. Blood smeared her one glove and wet the fingertips on her other hand. What must she look like? Randon wouldn't want to date her anymore, though that probably had more to do with the way she'd ruined his shining moment than with her damaged appearance. Since he hadn't pushed her, he might not be worthy of investigation after all.

Though was she really worthy of being an investigator? Police investigated things all the time without getting in car accidents and falling out of fire truck buckets. She wanted to clear her family name, but what good would that do if it got her killed?

Tandy wanted her to go to the police. Might as well. After she got her diary back of course.

"I think I only suffered a few scratches," she said.

A medic dabbed her face with damp gauze. "You're really lucky."

"Nah." Tandy joined them. "She's just a pro at falling. She has a lot of experience."

Marissa shook her head at Tandy's silly perspective. "Maybe next time I'm in a beauty pageant, I'll save my fall for the talent competition."

The EMT pulled the gauze away to get a better look at her face. "You're *that* Marissa?"

She smiled her beauty queen smile.

A man in a bright yellow jacket joined them, motioning toward Tandy. "This woman saved your life. She got me to lower the basket when Troy was busy hanging onto you."

Marissa's heart dropped the way she should have. While she'd been annoyed by Tandy's offer on Virginia's shop and jealous of her instant kinship with Connor, the other woman had saved her life more than once now.

Tandy shrugged and looked away, but Marissa wouldn't let her shrug off such a huge act. She reached out to offer a hug. The real kind.

"You." Connor's voice boomed above the surrounding chatter, stopping her in her tracks.

Marissa looked up to find him storming toward the fireman's bucket now at ground level.

Randon stood frozen with one foot in the bucket and one foot on the ground, wide eyes focused on the man confronting him. Though Connor had been the one to land on his back, Randon looked to be the one who'd had the breath knocked out of him. And with the way Connor was glowering, that might not be all that got knocked out of him.

Marissa broke away from the medic to separate the men the way she'd done before. Only this time because she believed Randon to be innocent.

Connor pointed. "You pushed her."

The crowd gasped.

Randon retreated into the bucket and closed the door to separate them. "N-no," he stammered.

"Police. Arrest this man."

Marissa continued her pursuit in hopes of reaching Connor before Lukey did. The deputy might very well arrest Connor for disturbing the peace if he didn't calm down. "Randon didn't push me." She grabbed Connor's arm.

"Of course he did. You yelled to me for help." Connor shook her off, shooting her a warning glance. "I'm going to stop this before you get hurt, Marissa."

"No." She scampered to stand in front of the bucket door. "I said 'help' so you would know I was helping him put the star on the tree."

Connor tilted his head in disbelief.

"Okay, I was afraid at first, but that's why I accidentally..." She scrunched her face at how her next words would sound. "...backed up over the edge."

Connor crossed his arms, the intensity in his stare making her heart burn. "You..." He apparently had as much trouble with the idea as she. "...Knocked yourself out of the bucket?"

Marissa bit her lip. Not ever a conversation one wanted to have with an ex. It was better for old boyfriends to think that they were missing out, not dodging bullets. "Uh...yeah."

Connor glanced above her head to make eye contact with Randon. "Well, if you were that afraid, then you must have had reason to be afraid."

He'd let her off the hook, but he was still fishing. And he could be right. She'd certainly been afraid.

That's what she would tell the police. But she wouldn't accuse Randon of pushing her.

Tandy jogged over and grabbed Connor's hand. "He didn't push her, Connor."

Connor lowered his gaze and his defenses. "What do you mean?" He didn't shake off Tandy's hold the way he had Marissa's.

"I mean, while you were down here focusing on Marissa, I was watching Randon. He was in shock." She motioned toward the man with her head. "Kind of like he is right now."

They all turned to stare at Randon.

"Of course I'm in shock." He backed up even more. "Why would I possibly want Marissa to steal the spotlight from me by toppling to her death?"

Connor released Tandy's hold to step forward. "I'll put the spotlight back on you if you like."

Marissa held a hand to her heart. She was glad he'd let go of Tandy, but not so glad he was threatening Randon.

"Stop." Lukey pushed into their circle. "Why did you think Randon might want to hurt you, Marissa?"

Marissa blew out a white puff of air. She was ready to tell all. Even to this kid she used to babysit. She wiped her numb fingertips down the side of her face and opened her mouth.

"Marissa?" A sing-song voice interrupted her thoughts.

A voice she recognized. A voice she hated. "I have something you might want."

Her guts churned, but she forced herself to look into the over animated face of Lavella Moon. Big eyes. Big lips. Big hair. She was practically the big, bad wolf. What could she possibly have that Marissa wanted? Besides the crown? And title? And oh yeah, the grace of a ballerina?

Marissa secretly gritted her teeth before forcing a pained smile. Had Lavella seen her fall? Had she noticed that Connor was not her fiancé anymore? Was she currently giddy over the scratches on Marissa's face that could potentially turn into hideous scars? "Miss Cincinnati, what a nice surprise."

Lavella tossed her hair. It slid perfectly into place. "It's Miss Ohio now."

Marissa wouldn't acknowledge the win. She tossed her own hair. A twig fell out. "Did you bring me a Christmas present?"

Lavella shook her head slowly as if filled with great regret. "I would have if I'd known you were going to be here, but I can give you this." She lifted up a red leather glove with a cashmere lining.

Marissa took the traitorous glove then pressed her lips together to keep from losing her cool. Of all the people to find it for her, Lavella just happened to be in town and...

What was Lavella doing in town anyway? She'd sabotaged Marissa's goals once before. Was she here to do it again? Had she killed Virginia as an attempt to frame Marissa?

"Great." Lukey waved the other woman away. "Now that you've got your glove back, Marissa, you can tell me—"

"Lavella," Marissa called out, heart pounding. She wouldn't let the other woman get away with it. Not this time.

Lavella glanced over her shoulder, penciled eyebrow

arching villainously. "What's that, sweetie?"

With that counterfeit endearment, Marissa took longer than she should have to mold her face into an innocent expression. "Will I see you again?" Yes. Yes, she would. But where? "What brought you to town?"

"Joseph Cross invited me for the Christmas Cruise."

What the jingle bells? How did Mr. Cross still have a cruise if he didn't own any boats? Marissa didn't even try to control her reaction this time.

Tandy adjusted her ponytail and wished for earmuffs. How long did they all have to stand around waiting for Marissa to catch up with her pageant pals before they could get back to business? She had a cracked rib, for Santa's sake.

"Can I put the star on the tree now?" Randon whined.

"I'd love to help you see stars," Connor offered.

Tandy rolled her eyes. As much as she liked Connor, he was overdoing the protective detail. Of course, if he'd caught *her* the way he'd caught Marissa…

"Somebody better tell me what's going on before I throw you all in jail," Deputy Griffin threatened.

Fine. Tandy stepped forward. As far as she knew, she was the only one who couldn't go to jail because she had a pet at home to take care of. Though Connor very well could have a dog waiting for him too. A big dog. Maybe a black lab. She'd ask later. "Marissa suspected Randon of killing Virginia because she wouldn't sell him the art he wanted."

Randon raised his hands as if under arrest. "Are you kidding me?"

Connor lifted his chin. "Do you see anybody laughing?"

Marissa pealed with laughter. Fake laughter. The kind that scraped like a snow shovel against cement.

They all turned to look at her. She faced the exquisite Miss Ohio. Had Marissa been crowned queen, her little stunt tonight would have landed her on national news. And she could still trend on Twitter if anybody in the community recorded the botched tree lighting ceremony.

No wonder the woman was losing it. She probably would have rather been in a coma then have her fall posted on social media.

Deputy Griffin raised his bullhorn. "All right, people. The ceremony is cancelled for this evening."

Murmurs of confusion rose around them. Marissa wiped at her eyes even as she laughed with her frenemy. If she'd wanted people to remember something other than the Miss Ohio pageant when they thought of her, she'd succeeded.

Griffin lifted the bullhorn once again. "Don't worry, Miss Alexander is fine. We ask you to head home for the evening. Mayor Kensington will announce changes to the annual festivities once new arrangements have been made."

Marissa remained focused on the conversation with Miss Ohio while fanning her face. Was she warm from blushing? Did she need oxygen? Was she trying to fly away? "You thought I'd be offended if you told me you were coming to town?" she over enunciated. "That's hilarious."

Connor scratched his head, his gaze connecting with Tandy's. They both knew there was nothing that could offend Marissa more than Miss Ohio coming to town.

"Miss Graceless Springs," the Deputy interrupted.

Except maybe that. Marissa's eyes glowed amber when she turned to face the deputy.

"We need to talk. Would you like to do it now, or should

I take you down to the station?"

Miss Ohio made a mock cringing face. "Oops. I don't want to get you in trouble."

"Don't be absurd," Marissa returned to her playful self, though her words spoke what Tandy knew she believed to be the absolute truth. "I'll see you tomorrow."

Miss Ohio wiggled her fingers and disappeared into the crowd.

"'Bye, Miss Ohio," Marissa called cheerfully before slipping beside Tandy and lowering her voice to murmur, "It was her. She did it."

Goodness and mercy. Was Marissa claiming the reigning Miss Ohio had replaced Virginia's coffee grinds with instant coffee? For what possible reason? Tandy dropped her hands to her sides in helplessness.

"Was that Miss Ohio?" Randon's voice lowered. "Had I known she was in town, I would have invited her to put the star on the tree with me. Since, you know, she doesn't think I'm a murderer."

Marissa shook her head. "Oh, I don't anymore."

Griffin's eyebrows shot toward his prematurely receding hairline. "Did someone else tell you Randon was the killer? Did someone else try to scare you?"

Marissa tugged off her remaining glove and tossed them both in the trash. Had they been ripped? Because those were some high-quality gloves. "*You* scared me, Lukey. You're the one who suggested Virginia may have been killed. If that's the case, how can I trust anyone?"

Tandy huffed. They were supposed to be interrogating Randon here. "Randon, when was the last time you were in Virginia's shop?"

Griffin gave her a once over before turning toward Randon to wait for an answer.

Randon pulled out his phone and flipped to a calendar app. "I went to her shop when I first moved here. I was decorating my bachelor pad. Nine out of ten bachelors wouldn't go to an antique store to decorate, but I'm a little classier than most." He tapped on his screen and turned the phone to face them. "October eighteenth. Ha-ha!"

Like that proved anything. Even if he was an app engineer, he wouldn't schedule a murder on his phone.

"Was there a painting she wouldn't—"

"Miss Brandt." Lukey scolded. He pulled out his own phone to take notes. The pair faced off over their devices. "Now, Mr. Evans. Was there a painting that Ms. Pierce wouldn't sell you?"

Randon made a face. The kind of face a person makes when pretending not to know what someone is talking about. "No."

Could Griffin not read through it? He suspected *her* easily enough, and Randon was almost as much of an outsider.

Tandy dug deeper. "But you said in the newspaper—"

"Miss Brandt."

Marissa stood by quietly, though with the way her eyes rolled about, she clearly had a lot of thoughts in her head. Was she purposely letting Tandy take the heat here? Marissa was the one who'd suspected Randon. She was the one who claimed he'd written a letter to the editor.

Randon's eyes twinkled in their know-it-all way. "I said there was a piece of art she wouldn't sell me. But it wasn't a painting. It was a vase."

Connor cringed. "Why would a man want a vase?"

Tandy snapped and pointed at him. Exactly.

Randon adjusted his glasses. A clear indicator he was about to bore them with his brilliance. "Connor, Connor,

Connor. I wanted the vase because not only am I a man, I'm an art history major. I recognized the vase as being similar to one seized from Chinese royalty during the Second Opium War. I'm sure it's worth more money than you've made in your entire life."

Connor glowered. The glower said he didn't have a comeback, and he didn't care.

"I, personally, don't need the money. I want to give the piece the care it deserves. Virginia had wheat it in at the time. Wheat."

"So you killed her in hopes of getting your hands on it by buying it from her daughter?" Connor asked for Tandy. She appreciated that they were on the same wavelength.

Griffin however did not. "I ask the questions here," the deputy growled before motioning for Randon to continue.

Randon's arrogance returned with enough force to ridicule them with a blank stare for questioning him. "If you knew anything about art collecting, you'd know that Virginia recently changed her will to donate everything in her store to the Historical Society."

Tandy's lips parted. Her pulse thrummed in her ears, made particularly loud by the fact that everybody else had gone silent. Could this be a coincidence? Or was the recent jewel heist at the museum somehow related to Virginia's death?

Chapter Twelve

MARISSA BARELY CAUGHT RANDON'S LAST STATEMENT. All Virginia's antiques were to be donated to the Historical Society? If that had anything to do with the murder, then Lavella would have to be involved in it. What if Lavella's plans were bigger than simply taking Marissa down? What if she wanted to take down the whole Alexander family to keep anybody from ever believing that she'd tripped Marissa on stage? If she had the diary, she could do that.

As far as Marissa knew, the only people aware of the staged results of Grandmother's win, besides Tandy, Cross, and Grandmother, were Virginia and Billie. Though if Virginia knew, she could have sold that information to anyone. And Lavella would have been top bidder.

Hmm... Did Lavella somehow think Virginia had the diary in her possession? Had she gone looking for it, and Virginia lied, saying she'd donated it to the Historical Society? Then Lavella broke into the museum, stealing the jewels as a decoy? Marissa pictured her dressed in all black pulling off a ski mask with a triumphant cackle.

The theory couldn't be more farfetched than any other theory that included both robbery and murder. She already knew Lavella was a thief as she'd stolen Marissa's crown by tripping Marissa. Unfortunately, it wasn't likely that anybody else would believe that story. Even Tandy gave her a skeptical look. She'd have to keep investigating for herself.

Lavella had probably only given Marissa a ticket to the Christmas Cruise to rub it in her face that she was the new

Miss Ohio. The second ticket was to rub in the fact that Marissa was single and had nobody to share it with. But she'd consider both tickets an opportunity to spy on the queen of lies.

All she had to do was convince Tandy to get Grandmother's diary out of her glove box at police impound then talk Connor into being her date for the cruise. With the way he'd wanted to kiss her under the mistletoe earlier that really shouldn't be too hard.

Her toes curled in her boots.

"Marissa." The man in question planted himself directly in front of her.

She smiled up at his smoldering gray eyes and clenched jaw. It would be fun to be his fake date. At least then he couldn't go on any more fake dates with Tandy. Marissa was really a better partner for him anyway. They could sleuth together. Like Nancy Drew and Ned Nickerson.

"No more sleuthing."

She frowned. Just because she'd been in a car accident and fallen out of a fireman's bucket on the same day didn't mean she should let Miss Ohio get away with stealing her crown—ahem—murder. "Connor…"

He turned his back and strode away.

She shook her head to clear her mind then looked around. Everybody was disbursing. Tandy jogged after Connor, probably going to ask for the ride he was sure to give. Lukey scanned their surroundings as he called someone on his phone—probably Officer Woodward. And Randon stopped a passerby to ask which way Miss Ohio had gone.

Marissa's ego twinged. Even Randon was abandoning her for someone else.

She was going to stop Lavella. But first she had to stop Tandy. Because if Connor wasn't going to help her, she needed Tandy's help. And also, she had to protect the other woman from Connor's destructive ways.

She jogged through the snow to catch up.

"What's his name?" Tandy's voice floated back as though she was completely oblivious to Marissa's crunching and huffing behind them.

"Ranger," Connor responded.

Ah. Connor's dog. At least they were sharing small talk and not discussing anything important.

Connor glanced over his shoulder at her. He stopped though he didn't turn her way. "I think Marissa wants to offer you a ride home, Tandy."

How did he know? Did he think she was jealous?

She narrowed her eyes. He probably couldn't tell she was scowling in the dim light, but the scowl made her feel better. "I can...sure...if you need a ride, Tandy." There. Take that. "But what I really want are my personal items out of your glove compartment. Do you think you could pick them up from police impound tomorrow?"

"Them?" Tandy shifted her weight to the other leg and clutched the side of her torso.

"Yes." Marissa would give Tandy the benefit of being testy because she was in pain. When she felt better, she'd realize Marissa didn't want to talk about Grandmother's diary in front of Connor after his no sleuthing decree. He wasn't the boss of her, which is why she was simply going to avoid him altogether. "My feminine items," she said as insurance he would tune out and never speak of this conversation again. It wasn't really a lie. Diaries were kind of feminine.

Tandy's lips twitched. "I think the pharmacy carries feminine items if you need more."

Connor waved to Troy as the fire engine rumbled to life,

and Marissa took the opportunity to bug her eyes at Tandy. "I've had a really hard day, you know."

"Oh, I know." Tandy looked her up and down. "Did you realize it hasn't been much fun for me either? Not only did I total my car, but I got the puffy face and cracked rib to prove it. And also, the deputy, who suspected me first of murder, now thinks even less of me because you didn't back me up with your suspicions of Randon."

What? That didn't even matter anymore. Lavella was in town. They needed to investigate her. And they couldn't do it with Connor right there. "This isn't about you, Tandy."

Okay, Connor could step in here if he wanted to. Defend Marissa. Protect Marissa. He always had before.

Tandy stuffed her hands in her pockets. "If you're not worried about me, I'll get a ride home with Connor, though thanks for the offer."

Connor pressed his lips together as if to signify he wasn't coming to Marissa's rescue this time. Then both he and Tandy turned and walked away.

Connor pulled into Tandy's modern apartment complex.

She pointed to the building across the parking lot above the empty stall where her Bug should have been parked. He could probably figure out her unit was the one with the giant lit-up Snoopy on the balcony.

"That was kind of harsh," Connor said as he rolled to a stop and shifted into park, and she knew he wasn't talking about the Snoopy balcony decoration. He was talking about her treatment of Marissa.

Tandy sighed. "I know." She was tired and achy, and while she'd come to town with a plan for her life, she now had nothing. Except her dog. At least the only game Cocoa ever played was fetch. Well, she was trying to get him to fetch anyway. "Marissa's harsh to you all the time. Doesn't it ever bother you?"

"It wasn't always like this," Connor defended, as if that made Marissa's behavior better. "She has a tendency to throw the baby out with the bathwater."

The way she'd thrown away her perfectly good gloves earlier? And the way she'd taken her fiancé to the dump when their relationship could have been salvaged?

"Like if she spills a drop of coffee, she just pours the whole thing out."

Tandy sat up straighter. "She drinks coffee?"

Connor laughed and leaned back in his seat. "Sorry. *I* drink coffee. She drinks tea. I meant to say, she dumps her tea out."

Tandy sank back into her seat. Why did opposites have to attract? Wouldn't life be easier if coffee drinkers dated coffee drinkers?

"I think it's because her parents had really high expectations of her," Connor continued. "She could never meet them."

Tandy grunted acknowledgment. She didn't relate. Her parents had never had any expectations of her. They were too busy fighting their own battles. Who would have thought parents with high expectations could also mess up their kid?

"I think her problems stem from the fact that she drinks tea," Tandy countered. "I mean, if she tried coffee, she'd learn to treasure every drop."

Connor smiled a sweet smile. He was the Caramel Macchiato of men. "Perhaps."

"She's not a cat person too, is she?"

"She's more of a fish person."

Tandy smiled back. While she really liked this Connor guy, what she liked most about him was how devoted he was to one woman. "She'll come around."

"To dogs?"

"To you."

The frost on his smile melted away. He leaned forward conspiratorially. "I'm not the kind of guy to try to make a girl jealous, but I liked the way she didn't want me pretending to be on a date with you tonight. It gives me hope."

A laugh rumbled up, and Tandy gripped at the pain in her ribs to help push it back down. "If not for the way you left me to roll around in the snow with her, it would have been the best fake date ever."

He grimaced. "You really think that was an accident? And you think the rocks in the road were a juvenile prank? Or do you think someone is after you?"

Tandy stared out into the dark night. Thinking that someone wanted to kill her made going into an empty apartment a scary thought. She already had enough scary thoughts to deal with. Like how she had no income.

"I don't know. If Virginia was killed, and I do believe she was, then it's likely related to the robbery from the Historical Society. The change in her will is too much of a coincidence for the crimes not to be connected."

"Yeah. And the police are handling the robbery." Connor eyed her. "You two will stay out of it now, right? For your own safety."

Tandy wouldn't make any promises for Marissa, but it wasn't like they had more leads or suspects. "I don't see why anybody would be after us. I mean, I'm new to town. Nobody knows me. And while Marissa knows everyone, she's her own worst enemy."

Connor gave his thinking-of-Marissa half smirk. "Poor Marissa."

He had it bad if he even adored her greatest weakness of clumsiness. "Can you believe she fell out of the bucket tonight?" she asked.

"Yes." He laughed, and she joined in until the stabbing pain in her ribs reminded her that laughter was a bad idea.

Why was she not in bed yet? She grabbed the door handle and yanked it open, letting a light snow drift in. "Thanks for the ride."

"You're welcome."

She slid to the ground and stepped out of the way to swing the squeaky door shut.

"Hey, Tandy."

She stopped. Leaned back in toward his warmth. Imagined he'd decided to take her on a real date.

"I hope you'll come around too. Marissa needs a friend."

She gave him her get-real face. "I can see why she doesn't have any with the way she treats you."

Connor tilted his head in acknowledgment. "I'm just thinking, she messed up tonight. Maybe if you accepted her anyway, she'd realize that she doesn't have to be perfect to have healthy relationships. And then maybe she'll get to the point where she'll stop expecting everyone else to be perfect too."

It was an interesting idea. How exhausting that Marissa seemed to think love had to be earned. Of course, that's why Connor wanted Tandy to play nice. He wanted her to help his ex see the value in the love she already had. "I'll think about it, Connor."

"Thanks."

She actually couldn't stop thinking about it. His words

followed her up the stairs. They stayed with her when Cocoa met her at her neighbor's door. They wove themselves around her as she trudged into bed. They escorted her memory back through the events of the day spent primarily with Marissa.

It had been a long time since she'd spent so much time with one person. Perhaps Tandy also needed to learn how to have friends, too, though it wouldn't be because she tried too hard. More like the opposite.

Hmm. She'd rather consider the facts of their mystery than try to solve her relationship issues.

Her thoughts snagged on the memory of Joseph Cross. She'd written him off her suspect list, but that was with the proviso he'd truly sold his riverboats. She'd planned to look that up tomorrow then forgotten about him with all the drama that had happened afterward. But of anybody who could have set up the roadblock for her to crash, he was the only one she knew who had both means and motive.

She really didn't think he was a bad guy. Though Marissa had.

Tandy stared at the texture on the ceiling. She'd follow up on checking out Joseph Cross's claim in the morning. Not because she wanted a friendship with Marissa. Well, not entirely. Mostly because she didn't want to get blamed again for something she hadn't done.

Marissa jolted in bed, away from the sensation of falling that had been tugging at her all night long. Whew. She was safe in her room.

Oh wait. She really had fallen. That hadn't been a nightmare.

She'd fallen out of a fireman's bucket in front of the whole town. And Lavella Moon.

Marissa cupped her hands over her face, feeling the threads of scratches against her cheeks. Yep. Her nightmare was real. Which meant she needed to put on some serious makeup. It also meant she was going to get a call from her mom.

She checked her phone. Twelve voicemails. Did she have to call back, or could she wait to get criticized on Christmas Eve? She had enough enemies at the moment without having to worry about her parents too. However, if she proved Lavella guilty, she might get to step into the Miss USA pageant as first runner up, which meant she'd be returning home with the crown.

Marissa clicked to her texting app. She'd send a quick message to let her parents know she was getting ready for the Christmas Cruise that night. They'd be proud she was still attending, right? Maybe if she acted like her fall from the fireman's bucket the night before had never happened, they would forget about it in the light of this event.

She hit send and climbed out of bed, pondering the ways Lavella was out to destroy her. How far would she go? Should Marissa ask Connor if she could borrow Ranger as a watchdog?

She grimaced at herself in the mirror. He'd probably already lent Ranger to Tandy. And Tandy didn't want anything to do with her anymore. Was there anyone on Marissa's side?

Billie. She was on everyone's side. Even Joseph Cross's side when they'd thought the man had possibly murdered Virginia.

Oh no. Marissa blindly sat herself down on the lid of the toilet. If she was right about Virginia being killed for the diary, then wouldn't Billie be at risk too? Because Billie was the one who'd owned it. She had read it. If Lavella thought she still had it, and she didn't hand it over, could she be hurt? Or worse?

Marissa leapt into action, pulling on fuzzy leggings and a tunic sweater. She'd soaked in her jet tub for almost an hour the night before, so she could skip the shower, though she couldn't skip her tea. She used her instant hot water dispenser to brew what Connor used to call her "Morning Thunder" blend in a travel mug. A girl couldn't save the world without being properly caffeinated. Then she shifted her Jeep into four-wheel-drive and powered over the fresh layer of snow from the night before.

"Billie!" She burst through the door of Grandma's Attic to find the city council members roaming the place with clipboards in their hands.

Oops. The Christmas decoration contest. Joseph Cross tossed her an irritated yet sophisticated glance.

She pivoted to avoid eye contact and ran directly into Connor's mom, Abigail. Had the woman recently been elected to the board? That's right. She had.

Marissa's gaze darted around in search of an escape. "Ooh, a vintage nativity set." She stepped past.

Footsteps followed to where she stood facing the crèche on a credenza. "It reminds me of when you and Connor played Mary and Joseph in the live nativity last Christmas Eve," Abigail said from behind her.

That was a memory Marissa preferred to forget. Which Abigail had to know. "Yes. It was...cold." Kind of like how she felt now. What was she doing here again? Oh yeah. Billie.

She spotted the older woman serving apple cider from

the beautiful silver tea set she'd been admiring the day before. Unless the cider was made from a poison apple, the shop owner was safe. And that was the important thing.

Now Marissa would change the subject to avoid discussing how she'd once been engaged to Connor the way Mary had been engaged to Joseph. "Uh... What's the prize for the decorating contest?" Yes. That would veer them away from talking about Connor.

"Connor donated renovation work to the winner."

Oh? Marissa turned sideways and peeked up to find Abigail watching her for a response. Connor's mom had never wanted to understand why she'd broken off their engagement. "That's nice." She swallowed, wishing she'd picked Chamomile tea for breakfast to battle her sudden acid reflux. "Does, uh, Grandma's Attic have a shot at winning?"

Abigail flipped through the pages on her clipboard. "I can't say anything specific, though Billie is always tough to beat. I'd heard Virginia Pierce had some grand plan up her sleeve, but now we'll never know."

Marissa's spine stiffened, and she shot Mr. Cross a wary look. "I'd heard that too." Did he feel as much shame as she did over his past deception? Had he really turned Virginia down when she'd asked him to rig the contest?

But why would Virginia want to win Connor's services anyway? She was selling the shop. "I wonder..."

Her voice faded away when the bell over the front door rang and Connor stepped inside, wearing the khaki Carhartt jacket she'd given him for his birthday. "What do you wonder?" he challenged, likely assuming it had to do with the investigation he had no right to tell her to give up.

Abigail sipped from a China cup. "Now I'm curious what you are wondering too."

Marissa blinked and realized that practically everyone

was watching her stare at Connor. She had to say something. Though what could she say in front of Mr. Cross? She shrugged. "I'm wondering what you're doing here, Connor."

His eyes told her he didn't buy it. Probably because she usually feigned indifference around him, and her deep contemplation had been the exact opposite. "Mom couldn't get out of our driveway in her Porsche this morning. I'm her chauffeur for the day."

A legitimate excuse. Abigail's husband had surprised her with the convertible Porsche when she turned fifty. Not practical in the winter, but she usually stayed home to work on their farm anyway.

"You've been giving lots of rides lately," Marissa quipped before she could stop herself. Tandy was none of her business.

One corner of his lips curved up. "A few," he said, possibly inferring that there were more than the two she knew about.

She pressed her lips together to keep from giving him anything more than a tight smile.

"Well, it's good to see you, hon." Abigail patted her arm.

Marissa turned her face toward Abigail though it took a little longer for her gaze to follow. She had trouble interacting with the woman who would have been her mother-in-law, but she had even more trouble with Connor watching. She couldn't avoid eye contact now.

Marissa gave a toothpaste commercial smile. "You too."

Abigail blinked at the unexpected volume then squeezed where she'd been patting. "I still pray for you every night."

Marissa couldn't say "you too" to that one. Plus, it kind of irked her that Connor's family thought she needed prayer. "Thank you."

"Come on, Mom," Connor prompted, holding the door

open to the sound of jingling overhead.

Marissa relaxed when Abigail and the rest of the councilmembers preceded Connor out, though she'd watch from the corner of her eyes to make sure Joseph Cross was completely out of sight before she focused on Billie. Through the window she saw Connor motion for Abigail to step ahead of him, and he started to follow, but as Tandy breezed past him toward the entrance, he pivoted and trailed the younger woman instead.

Grr... Marissa didn't want to see either of them, and she especially didn't want to see them together.

The bell rang to mark Tandy's arrival. "Oh, good, I was hoping you'd be here, Marissa."

Marissa's eyebrows leaped like ballerinas in The Nutcracker. Tandy came to Grandma's Attic looking for her? "Hi."

"Why was Joseph Cross here?"

"He's a decorating contest judge."

"Among other things..."

Whatever that meant.

The bell rang again as Connor reentered. If they kept this up, the two of them could take over for her church's hand bell choir.

He planted himself like a soldier. What? Was he *Tandy's* bodyguard now?

Tandy held Cocoa in one arm and dug through her little backpack with the other. She wore the same black boots and coat from the day before, though she'd exchanged the high ponytail for a messy bun on top of her head and added a gray scarf around her neck. Not much for color or variety, but she did have a grungy kind of beauty. If that was a thing.

"Look." She pulled out a sheaf of papers. "I checked public records, and Cross did indeed sell his riverboat company, but he sold it to the same company that owns the retirement center. He basically sold it to himself."

That's what Tandy had meant. She thought the guy responsible for Virginia's death was out judging decorating contests. If he wasn't guilty, then why would he have lied to them about selling his steamboats?

Could he have had something to do with Lavella's crown? Tandy had originally thought Lavella was out to prove he'd rigged Marissa's grandmother's win, but maybe they were in this together somehow. There was already the connection of the Christmas Cruise.

"So *that's* why Mr. Cross still runs the Christmas Cruise. Luckily, Lavella gave me tickets for tonight." She gave a sly grin before remembering she was being watched by a guy who'd forbidden her to "sleuth."

Connor took her grin as an invitation to stride forward. "What do you mean? If you're suspicious of Cross, you shouldn't go on his cruise alone."

"I'm not. I'm going with Tandy." Tandy would let her sleuth.

Tandy blinked. "This cruise isn't a dress up thing, is it? I don't dress up."

Marissa waved her hand to shush any arguments. Once she worked her makeover magic on Tandy, she'd be singing a different carol.

Tandy lifted her chin. "I'm serious, Marissa."

Connor motioned toward Tandy. "It sounds like you better take me."

Marissa held up her finger then pinned it against his chest when he didn't relent. She pushed, but he didn't move. "You could have been my Ned Nickerson, but it's too late now, buddy."

"Ned who?"

Tandy squinted. "Is that a Nancy Drew reference? Because I picture Connor as more of a Hardy Boy. Probably Frank. He had a thing for Nancy."

Connor brushed her finger from his chest. "Marissa, you are not Nancy Drew."

"Really?" She raised her other hand to poke him. "Because it looks like I was right all along about Mr. Cross."

Billie joined the group, petting Cocoa. "Are you talking about Joseph Cross again? He told me Virginia hadn't been blackmailing him after all."

Connor answered for her. "I don't know about Joseph Cross, but I know these girls were in a car accident on their way home from the retirement community."

Billie gasped. "A car accident? On top of the Christmas tree lighting incident? That's scary, Marissa."

Marissa placed both her hands on Connor's chest to shove him toward the door. At least this time he stepped backwards a few steps with her pressure. Not far enough. She leaned at an angle to push harder, but he remained planted.

"Yes, this is her second recent brush with death," Tandy confirmed.

"Are you okay?" Billie asked from behind.

Marissa nodded then grimaced. Nancy Drew probably never ruined a tree lighting by mistake, but that was not the point here. The point was that Marissa knew who the bad guy was. She just had to figure out how to prove it without destroying her family's reputation. Nancy wouldn't have had that problem either.

Nor would Nancy have had Marissa's biggest problem—getting rid of an interfering ex.

Chapter Thirteen

TANDY SENT CONNOR AN APOLOGETIC SMILE. He hadn't wanted Marissa investigating anymore, and here Tandy was, running in with clues. Though she wasn't going on any fancy cruise. Marissa had purposely avoided the question of attire for the event.

"Take it to the deputy," Connor suggested to the woman trying to shove him out the door.

Tandy nuzzled Cocoa, considering their options. Connor didn't know Marissa's secret. He didn't know her legacy was a fraud. Would it make a difference if he did? Nah. He'd likely be more concerned about Marissa's safety than her reputation.

Tandy hadn't cared yesterday, but that was before she'd seen Marissa's fall from grace with her very own eyes. Before she'd heard about how Marissa's parents set such high expectations she could never live up to them. Before she'd woken up that morning feeling a connection to another woman who struggled with friendships.

"I'll go to the police station right now." Tandy's offer shocked the other two into silence. Marissa stood upright, releasing Connor. She would be even more shocked to learn that the reason Tandy was offering was so she could get the diary out of her glove compartment. She'd let Marissa decide whether to give it to authorities or not. Tandy just wanted to see if there was anything else in it about Joseph Cross. Because the diary was what had sent them his way in the first place.

The couple both stared at Tandy. Marissa with the fear Tandy really would go find Lukey, and Connor with the fear she wouldn't.

Connor was right to be afraid. Thus, Tandy had to get rid of him.

"Hey, Connor." She pointed to the mistletoe above his head in the doorframe.

"That's cruel," Billie murmured. Obviously the older woman could read her intent and knew she was setting Connor up for rejection. But how else would Tandy get rid of him so she could talk to Marissa?

Connor and Marissa glanced up. Marissa jumped back and crossed her arms. Connor's face lowered slower, a mischievous smile sliding across it.

"Not a chance," Marissa bit out.

He stuck his hands in his pockets and shrugged. "Honey, if I'd wanted to kiss you under the mistletoe, I could have done so yesterday.

Could he really, though? It sounded like he might have tried.

"This isn't for me." Connor continued, aiming a thumb Tandy's direction. "It's for them. Billie hung the stuff, and Tandy caught us standing under it. How would it be fair to them if we didn't kiss?"

Marissa sent Tandy a glare fiery enough to roast chestnuts.

Tandy's grin spread. She really did believe that one day Marissa would realize what a fool she was to turn down such an opportunity, but until then, her little attitude ensured Connor would soon be making a swift exit.

"Just a goodbye kiss?" Tandy prompted.

Marissa didn't even pause to consider. She turned her back on Connor and strode away. "I already kissed him goodbye."

Connor's smile slipped. He locked gazes with Tandy as if to tell her she was wrong about Marissa coming around. Then he pushed out the door, more resigned than angry.

Tandy watched him go, her success tasting about as sweet as dark roast coffee beans, ground too fine and brewed too long.

Marissa's purposeful steps faltered as she stumbled over nothing and caught herself on the counter. She wasn't even wearing heels today. At least she didn't knock anything to the ground this time.

She pushed herself upright and tossed her hair as if it had never happened. "Did he see that?" she asked.

Tandy checked again on the man trudging away, head down. "No." Though if he had seen Marissa trip, he would have only adored her more for it.

"Good." She took a deep breath before widening her eyes at Tandy. "Did you come over here specifically to ruin my day? Is going to the police with my sordid family history not enough? You have to practically shove me into the arms of the man I'm trying to avoid?"

Forget beauty queen. Marissa was a drama queen.

Billie sipped her cider. "It was a simple kiss, Marissa. What are you afraid of?"

"Afraid?" Marissa spun on her. "I'm actually afraid for your life, Billie. That's why I'm here. I think if Lavella *is* after the diary, she might find out you had it and come after you."

Billie set down her China cup with a clink. "I'm in danger?"

"By Lavella?" Tandy made a face. Marissa had mentioned the other woman last night, but that was before Tandy discovered how Cross lied to them.

"Yes." Marissa glanced furtively about then leaned

forward. "She stole my crown when she tripped me, and now she's trying to discredit me by revealing the way Cross rigged my Grandmother's win. Or maybe they are working together, I don't know. Since Cross lied about his boats, he has to be involved somehow. It's the only thing that makes sense."

"How does that possibly make sense?" Tandy held out her hands. Like usual, Marissa was making this all about herself. "What connection is there?"

"She's a special guest on his Christmas Cruise tonight."

Oh. Tandy's lips parted as she considered the implications. She'd wanted to get her hands on the diary to find more info on Cross, but if he and Lavella were in cahoots, there was definitely a chance Billie could get hurt. Like Tandy had gotten hurt in the car accident.

Cross or Lavella might have caused the rockslide in the road to try to get the diary, but their plan had been thwarted when she and Marissa had survived and called the cops.

Time to call the cops again. Yeah, Officer Woodward was off investigating the jewel heist, but now that Griffin suspected said heist to be connected to a possible murder, Woodward should make it a higher priority.

"Marissa, I know you don't want your grandma's name dragged through the dirt, but we have to tell Griffin what's going on." Tandy wrapped her arm behind Billie who had gone eerily silent. "For this grandma right here."

The harsh lines in Marissa's face softened. "I want to protect Billie too, but I doubt Griffin will believe me. Especially after my suspicion of Randon last night."

A good point. Whether they needed the police's help or not, there was no guarantee the police would actually help. "I'll give him the diary."

Marissa clutched her heart. That had to be the last thing she wanted to happen, but she didn't argue. Maybe she wasn't completely selfish after all. Maybe she was learning to value what she had in front of her over what she wished she had.

Billie placed a hand on Marissa's arm. "I believe Cross when he said he wasn't involved, but in case it's anyone else after me or the journal, I can go stay with my daughter in Cincinnati. That way I'll be safe until Virginia's killer gets caught, and you wouldn't have to turn over the diary."

"Yeah, do that." Marissa nodded emphatically.

Okay then. Marissa had only been looking for a way to get what she wanted without coming across as a spoiled Grinch.

Tandy clicked her tongue. "You want Billie to go to Cincinnati? Where Lavella lives?"

Marissa spread her palms wide. "It's a big city."

Tandy swung her backpack over her shoulders and scooped Cocoa into her arms. "Stay here to make sure Billie is safe, and I'll go get the diary from impound to take to Griffin." She turned to go, but Marissa followed her out into the arctic air on the street, the overhead bell announcing that somewhere an angel was getting his wings. Somewhere other than Grace Springs, where the citizens could all use a little more heavenly guidance.

Marissa scrambled to get in front of her then gripped Tandy's forearms to either stop her or keep from slipping. "What if Billie is actually the killer, and you're leaving me here to die?"

Nice stall tactic. Marissa was the one who'd argued for Billie's innocence in the beginning. "Billie wouldn't even hurt the mouse from *The Night Before Christmas*."

Marissa refused to release her. "I didn't think she would, but remember how Virginia wanted Cross to help her rig the holiday decorations contest? Had that happened, Billie would have lost. Connor's mom told me today Billie is tough to beat."

Tandy rolled her eyes. That was the stupidest reason she'd ever heard for killing someone. Besides... "Virginia's decorations were pathetic."

"Billie killed her before she could finish."

"Go back inside, Marissa." Tandy pulled her arms free. "You can't just accuse people of murder to get your way. You can't claim Lavella is after Billie one minute then Billie is after you the next. You're here to protect her, and that's the same reason I'm going to hand over your grandmother's diary."

Marissa looked in through the window of Grandma's Attic as if afraid for her own life. "Billie knew we went to the retirement center and could have caused the rockslide to stop us from returning. Maybe she gave us the diary so she could do just that."

Tandy followed her gaze to watch the elderly shop owner wrap up the apple pie she'd set out on the refreshments table for the decorations judges. Yeah, there was the image of a cold-blooded killer. "If you're so worried that Billie killed Virginia with coffee, then don't drink any of her cider, okay?"

"I won't." Marissa pouted.

Cocoa leaped from Tandy's arms as if impatient to get on with their trip, but once his paws hit the frigid cement, he shivered. "Also, can I take your Jeep?"

It was a good thing the Sheriff's department was only a few blocks away since Marissa wouldn't let Tandy drive. She almost walked past the quaint, two-story brick building that looked more like it belonged to a cobbler in 1800s Boston than law enforcement. It was the sight of her beat up Bug behind a chain link fence that informed her she'd reached the right location. She entered the inset white door below the inset white windows. The place smelled like old wood and warm coffee. Both musty and inviting at the same time. Kind of like Virginia's shop would have smelled had Tandy been able to turn it into a coffee house.

The interior of Grace Springs PD was not as appealing with metal desks, filing cabinets, and bulletin boards. A receptionist about Tandy's age sat at the front desk, and behind her, Griffin spoke with a curly haired woman who looked familiar. Tandy's heart dropped upon recognition of Virginia's daughter.

Was Tandy going to have to talk to Griffin in front of Jenn Pierce? Definitely not. She didn't want to make the woman's mourning process any more difficult.

The receptionist, dressed in a hot pink Santa hat, set down her phone. "May I help you?" she asked in a friendly way. She must not have known Griffin questioned Tandy about the circumstances of Virginia's death.

"Yeah. Hi." Tandy's voice drew Griffin's attention, but she ignored his glance. She needed him to finish up doing whatever he was doing with Jenn before she spoke to him. What was the victim's daughter doing here anyway? Was there a morgue upstairs or something? "I was in a car accident, and my car has been impounded, but I forgot to get something out of it."

The woman grabbed a lone folder on the side of her desk and flipped it open. Besides Virginia's death and the museum robbery, Grace Springs must truly be a sleepy little town being that her car accident was the only file on the receptionist's desk.

"Tandy Brandt?" The woman set the folder down to shake hands. "I'm Kristin Shipley. Nice to meet you. I'd ask for your I.D., but your swollen lip is ID enough."

Swell.

"Here are your keys. You can go right through that back door there. And check with me on your way out. I need to make a note of your visit and anything you take with you."

Tandy nodded then shot one more look at Jenn Pierce whose shoulder slump made Tandy glad the other woman never looked up. If Griffin had discovered Virginia's caffeine levels and traced it back to the instant coffee in her pot, he could be telling Virginia her mother's death had been a homicide.

With her head down, Tandy rushed Cocoa through the back door. The snow hadn't been plowed, and her pup practically disappeared into a drift. She scooped him up and high stepped her way in a fresh set of tracks to her passenger door. After opening the only door still operable, she let Cocoa loose to run around the interior.

Her stomach clenched as she angled a smaller key into the slot on the glove box. Had someone really killed for the book that lay inside? Did a stupid beauty pageant matter that much? Marissa sure seemed to think so.

Tandy turned the key until she heard a click then cupped her fingers underneath the handle. Her pulse picked up speed. Why was she so nervous? She paused and looked around as if expecting Joseph Cross to be lurking with a sniper rifle. Ridiculous. If he was going to shoot her, he could have done it already. The only murder committed in Grace Springs had been done through coffee granules. By now Tandy had probably developed immunity to caffeine overdose, much like the Dread Pirate Roberts did to iocane powder in *The Princess Bride*.

With a breath deep enough to make her ribs sting, she snapped the console open and stared at her insurance card, registration, and owner's manual. Where was the diary? She grabbed the materials and lifted to be sure. Nothing. Nada. Zip. Coal in her stocking.

It had been there. It had been locked in there. It couldn't simply disappear like a melted snowman.

She dropped the papers and sat back, mind whirring. Had Marissa taken it? No, because she'd chased Tandy down the night before, asking about it. Had Joseph Cross scaled the fence like a ninja? Her eyes went on alert, scanning the barbed wire along the perimeter. Unbroken. He would have had to drop in on a helicopter ladder, but even then he would have needed her car keys.

Tandy opened her fist to stare at the keyring in her palm. Who would have had the key?

She slammed the box shut and ran a gloved finger over the lock. If someone had jimmied it, wouldn't there be some scratches or markings? The steel slot remained shiny.

Her Pomeranian's little body leaped into her lap, and she jolted in surprise. He walked his front paws up her torso and licked her cheek before she could exhale her gasp. "What's going on, Cocoa?" she asked.

What were the options? Someone had obviously used her keys from the police station to steal Marissa's grandmother's diary. Either a civilian had come through unsuspectingly or a lawman was in on the crime.

The fresh tracks. Those had to be from the thief. And she'd ruined them by stepping on top of them.

Tandy suspected Cross.

Marissa wanted to believe it was Lavella.

Neither she nor Marissa would have ever suspected Luke

Griffin. Though he certainly had suspected *them*. Had he known how the toxicology report would come back, and he'd wanted to make sure there were suspects other than himself?

Tandy's eyes focused on the harmless looking brick building, ready to duck should Griffin aim a gun through the window. He *would* have one.

But why would he be involved? Could he have robbed the museum then murdered Virginia to try to pull Officer Woodward away from the case? That was a bit extreme.

Was he in cahoots with Cross? Perhaps he was also a shareholder of the new company that owned the sternwheelers, and a scandal involving Cross would affect his investment too.

Or if Marissa was right about Lavella, could he be in love with the beauty queen? He hadn't seemed interested at all the night before, but that could have been a show.

The options were endless, though at least now Tandy knew the diary truly was involved, and that theory wasn't all Marissa's melodrama. What Tandy needed to do was go back in and find out from the receptionist who all had come by the department since the Bug had been dropped off. Then she'd have a more accurate suspect list.

She hoped the receptionist wasn't taking an early lunch. What if Griffin had sent her home so he could get Tandy alone and finish what he'd started with the rockslide? He'd certainly made it to rescue them awfully fast that day...

Clutching Cocoa, Tandy robotically stood and shut the door. "This is when I wish I had a big dog to protect me."

Cocoa yipped as if in offense.

"No, I don't mean that. Just kidding, Cocoa. You're all the dog I need." He could be her last dog if she didn't survive.

She took a hesitant step forward then a second with more

determination. She was going to be okay. Everything was going to be okay. She was only making herself panic the way Marissa had the night before in the fireman's bucket. Tandy wasn't like that. She was as cool as the North Pole.

She made it to the door in a blur. Peering through the glass, she didn't see either Griffin or Jenn. Maybe he'd walked her out to her car. Maybe she'd left, and he was in the bathroom. Either way, this was her chance.

Tugging the door open, Tandy darted to the front desk.

Kristin looked up, eager to please. Could she have stolen the diary? *Gah*. That was as bad as suspecting Billie.

"I'm just curious..." Tandy glanced out the front window, wondering how much time she had. Still no sign of Griffin. "With the robbery at the Historical Society and Griffin investigating Virginia's death, has it been pretty busy in here? You know, lots of people in and out?"

The receptionist shrugged a shoulder. "Not at all. Darrel—Officer Woodward—has been at the museum, and Luke has been out monitoring holiday events. He's got the Ho-Ho-Holiday Run coming up on Christmas Eve where he dresses like Santa. Well, everyone does. That's one of my favorite traditions." She grinned.

"Sounds...merry and bright." Tandy pasted on a smile the way she'd learned from Marissa. She wasn't ready to go back to the beauty queen empty-handed, and news about a festive 5K wasn't what she would be waiting to hear. "You're all alone to hold down the fort, huh?"

"I wouldn't say all alone." A wrinkle formed between the receptionist's straight eyebrows. "The other office manager took her kids to Disney World for Christmas vacation, but she'll be back on Tuesday. And Officer Woodward checks in occasionally. Griffin is right outside. He used to date Jenn Pierce, so he's really worried about her."

So Griffin had access and... Wait. Did Kristin say Griffin used to date Jenn?

A Christmas light bulb lit up over Tandy's head. She'd earlier suspected Connor of killing Virginia to get Marissa back. Could she have had the motive correct but not the couple? Murder was extreme, but maybe Griffin hadn't been trying to kill Virginia—just wanted to send her into cardiac arrest so he could comfort Jenn at the hospital. That part fit. Though why in the world would he steal the diary, unless he was trying to frame someone else? Someone like Tandy?

She had to get out of there. "I gotta go. Thanks."

Kristin's eyebrows drew together. "Wait. What did you get out of your vehicle?"

Tandy's heart hammered. "Nothing. Nothing. I must have been wrong about leaving something in the glove box." Was this going to make her look bad? Make her look like she'd taken something in secret? That could have been Griffin's goal for taking the diary.

Kristin held up a hand with fingernails that matched her hat. "Well, Griffin said he wanted to discuss something with you before you left, so if you wouldn't mind..."

She did mind. She minded that Griffin accused her of murder the moment he met her. She minded that even if he wasn't guilty of that murder, he probably wouldn't believe her claims against Joseph Cross without proof to back it up. And she especially minded that he was the only one she could think of with access to the journal and a possible motive for stealing it.

Did he want her to wait so he could either arrest her for a murder she didn't commit or kill her to cover up the murder he *did* commit? Marissa would run, but Tandy wanted to face him. Challenge him. Watch his reaction.

The front door squeaked open. Deputy Griffin entered,

mouth a grim line, gaze focused on her.

A growl rumbled in Cocoa's belly. Did he know something she didn't? She rubbed his head to calm him.

Griffin planted himself in her way and crossed his arms. "I walked Ms. Pierce's daughter, Jenn, out to her vehicle."

Of course he did. Tandy narrowed her eyes. "That's nice she has you to comfort her."

"I'm trying. Going to take her on the Christmas Cruise tonight to try to get her mind off of it."

Reeeeally?

He focused his gaze. "She's shocked from the forensics report that says her mother's death was, indeed, homicide."

Tandy's belly flipped. She'd known this was coming, but to hear her suspicions solidified didn't sit well. Especially if the deputy was involved and going to make accusations against her. "Indeed," she repeated his word. Her heart clenched at the thought of Jenn's pain.

Though Tandy wasn't close with her own mother, should the woman die, she'd lose all hope that they could someday be reunited. Along the lines of heritage, should she tell Griffin about Marissa's grandmother's missing diary to watch his response? Or should she wait for him to reveal that he knew too much? She'd try waiting first. Ask another question. "How is *my* case coming? Did you catch the culprits who caused the rockslide?"

He hooked his thumbs in his belt. Buying time to formulate an answer? Or offended by her lack of concern for the deceased? "With Virginia's death, I haven't had time to track down those kids yet. I let Officer Woodward know about the homicide, and he's returning from the museum to launch a full investigation, so I might be able to get to the rockslide next week. But that's hardly our biggest concern."

Tandy tilted her head at his disdain. Griffin looked so

smug. Like she was already holding mugshot numbers. She'd have to get him to trip up somehow.

"I pray the killer won't get away with it," she said — words that should scare him, were he responsible.

He looked her up and down. Did he honestly suspect her, or could he tell she suspected him? If he knew she was onto him, would that put her in more danger? "Until the killer is caught, you need to stay in town, Miss Brandt. You aren't planning to go anywhere are you?"

Did he want to know her whereabouts so he could set another trap like the rockslide? "I'm not leaving town," she said. Though she would see him that night on the cruise.

Chapter Fourteen

MARISSA KICKED BACK IN A DAINTY toile lounge chair, waiting for Tandy's return to Grandma's Attic. Maybe she should have let Tandy drive her Jeep. Then at least she'd know by now how Lukey had taken the news that the Alexander legacy included fraud.

She blew her cheeks out. Though she couldn't prepare herself for what else the diary might say, she could mentally prepare for the cruise that night. Did she have time to go shopping? If so, she'd get a red dress like the one she would have worn for the crowning ceremony of the Miss Ohio pageant, had she not been in an ambulance on the way to the hospital for x-rays of her wrist.

She clicked on the phone icon for her internet app to get a better idea of what she'd like to wear for the evening. The bell over the door rang, waking Marissa from her dream like reindeer hoofs on the roof.

A pink-cheeked Tandy stood in the entrance, her skin pale against dark clothing. She should wear a green dress that night. It would be a big improvement over black and gray.

Marissa slid her feet to the floor and stood. "Did you read more of the diary? Is there anything else about Mr. Cross in it?"

Tandy didn't answer. She set Cocoa down, leaving her hands empty. Had she put the diary in her backpack? "It's gone."

Marissa's eyes flew to the black straps camouflaged against Tandy's black jacket. The backpack was still there.

Was she talking about the diary? Did she think she put it in her backpack but actually set it down somewhere instead? "You lost it?"

Tandy shook her head. "No. Someone took it."

Marissa's mouth fell open. "You got mugged?" She'd been right about protecting Billie. And now she knew for certain that Billie wasn't the culprit, because the store owner had been there the whole time, meaning she couldn't have mugged anyone. Though where had she gone? The back room?

Tandy stilled. "No. Someone took it out of my glove compartment."

Marissa clutched her hands to her heart, to the burning ache at losing a piece of her history. Maybe even a piece of her future, if it was used against her. She didn't want to believe it. At least this meant Billie was safe because nobody needed to come after her for the diary anymore. "I thought you locked the glovebox."

Tandy swallowed. "I did."

If she locked it... "Did someone steal your keys?"

Tandy's chest rose and fell. "The police had them."

"Then how? Who?" Marissa's arms spread wide, unable to catch all the thoughts floating by like snowflakes. "Could someone have made a copy of the keys? I think Randon actually designed an app where you can take a picture of keys and then have a key designed from the photo."

"Of course he did." If only their mystery were as simple as a 1950s Nancy Drew novel and didn't involve technology. A recent video from a social media warning played in her memory. Marissa hadn't thought it was something she'd ever have to worry about in Grace Springs because if someone stole someone else's car, everybody would see them driving it, but... "There's also technology out now with a two-part device where the first thief holds one part by the building where the keys are while the other thief holds the second part by the car. It somehow accesses the transmitter that starts the vehicle."

Tandy twisted her lips at the idea. "Well, they weren't starting the car—they were breaking into my glove compartment. And also, there was only one set of footprints."

Marissa's eyes widened. "There were footprints? We can examine them and get shoe size and brand name."

Tandy scrunched her nose. "There *were* footprints. I stepped in them to get to my car, so now they would only show my shoe size and brand."

Marissa huffed in frustration, though she probably would have done the same thing to keep from getting her pants wet. She needed a little help here. "So what do you think?"

Tandy's chin puckered before she opened her mouth. "You're not going to like it."

"Well, that's to be expected."

Tandy narrowed her eyes before answering. "I can't help thinking Deputy Griffin has to be involved."

Tandy was right. She didn't like it. "Lukey? Is he trying to get back at me for setting his family's curtains on fire?"

Tandy's eyes bulged. "You did what?"

Nah. Marissa waved her hand. "Never mind. That can't be it. Though why else would he want to hurt me?"

Tandy glanced toward heaven before looking down to stomp the snow off her boots. "I don't think he wanted to hurt anyone, not even Virginia. He's just trying to get his ex-girlfriend back. Did you know he dated Jenn Pierce?"

Marissa jolted. She had no idea, but the discovery almost fit. Though he could simply be milking the situation and not be the real murderer. Lavella still might have killed Jenn's mom. "If he dated Jenn, that could be why he went through your car looking for a clue as to who is after us and who killed the woman who could have been his mother-in-law. Did you ask him if he has the diary?"

Tandy moved to sail past, deeper into the warm store. "No way. He's trying to pin this on me, remember? I waited for him to give himself away."

Marissa ran a hand over her face. The jumble of suspects was getting to be too much. She didn't want Little Lukey to be the accidental murderer, but she was ready to take a confession from any of them. "And did he give himself away?"

"No." Tandy sank onto the lounge Marissa had recently abandoned. "But I did learn he's taking Jenn on the Christmas Cruise tonight."

That was even better than a confession. It was the lure needed to get Tandy to attend the Christmas Cruise with Marissa. While Tandy spied on the town's sweet little deputy, she'd be cracking the case by eavesdropping on Mr. Cross and Lavella. Plus, Lukey would be there to back her up when it was time for their arrest. "I have a dress you can borrow, but you're not going to like it."

"That's to be expected."

Tandy hadn't been this scared since moving to Grace Springs. She stared fearfully into a closet so spacious that it must have once been a bedroom in Marissa's delightful little bungalow. The last time she'd worn a dress, Nora Andresen had pretended to trip and dumped a whole cup of punch down her front just because she'd been asked to the Jingle Ball by Nora's ex-boyfriend. And while Marissa wouldn't purposely dump punch on Tandy, it could still happen.

She looked down at the rows of stilettos. "How do you, of all people, walk in those?"

Marissa glanced over her shoulder from where she filed through hangers covered in fluff and lace. "In the past, I hung onto Connor's arm."

Hence the real reason Marissa needed Tandy to go with her. Stability. "I'm sure Connor wore pants. Why can't I?"

Marissa smiled sweetly then spun to lift a gown in front of Tandy's torso. "You're prettier than Connor."

Tandy rolled her eyes then glanced down to survey the damage. It was nice to be considered pretty, but not if it required twirling about and showing skin. The crushed velvet dress didn't look like it would show too much skin with long sleeves and a high collar, so it could be worse. "I guess—"

"You'll look fabulous." Marissa pulled the dress away to reveal something not so fabulous.

"Wait. Where's the back?"

Marissa beamed. "That's the best part. The gown is backless."

How could the woman act so happy when they were only going on the cruise to solve a heinous crime? The outfit was also a heinous crime. "I'm not taking off my bra to wear a dress."

Marissa shook her head. "Don't worry about it. I have these pasties that—"

Tandy held up her hand and breezed past. If she let Marissa dress her, she was going to get turned into Holiday Barbie. So much glitter. "You have to have a little black dress in here somewhere."

"I only wear black for funerals, and it's not like anybody

died."

Tandy stopped her with a look.

Marissa lifted her fingers to her lips. "I didn't mean..."

"Too late. Hand it over." Tandy held out her palm.

Marissa stayed rooted to the spot, her gaze on the carpet, probably so as not to give away the location of the desired dress with a look. "Would you consider jade green? It would highlight your eyes."

What did it matter? "As long as I can keep my bra on, fine."

Marissa looked up eagerly now. "It's just that I'm wearing red. Green and red would complement each other."

So? Was Marissa planning on having their picture printed in the paper after they captured the killer? If that were the case, Tandy would also wear a ski mask to hide her puffy lip. "I said fine."

"Wheee!"

Marissa spent the rest of the day polishing and primping while Tandy used her computer to look up Griffin's past in a failed attempt to find dirt on him. She also googled Cross then Lavella but was blinded by all the photos with gleaming white teeth in fake smiles. Why was Marissa jealous of such fakeness?

In one last ditch effort, Tandy pulled up the Grace Springs Gazette and ran a search for the recent jewel heist.

December 23—Police continue to investigate the heist of the Rare Ohio Diamonds on their last day to be displayed at the Grace Springs Historical Society. It is believed that a single thief disabled the alarm and snatched the jewels worth an estimated twenty-one grand while the guards changed shifts. Video footage shows a masked figure who appears to be a woman...

"Let's go, Tandy."

Tandy frowned at the blurry black and white image.

Griffin would probably arrest her for just thinking she wished she had a mask like that, and the figure wasn't much bigger than she was either. On first glance, she assumed the robber to be a woman as well, though were Randon still on their suspect list, his stature would fit. Of course, he might have robbed the place simply because Virginia was going to will her antiques to them.

Should Tandy look into that idea or let it go? All she really needed to worry about was not getting arrested for Virginia's murder.

As far as murder suspects went, Cross was too tall and Griffin too thick to fit the description of the robber. If the person caught on tape was linked at all to Virginia's murder, the only female suspect it could be was Lavella. Which Tandy wouldn't admit yet.

Marissa peered over her shoulder. "It's Lavella."

Tandy slid her chair back. "Stealing your crown doesn't automatically make her a jewel thief."

Marissa dug through a tiny gold purse, heading toward the door. "It should."

"Has anybody ever told you that you throw out the baby with the bathwater?"

Marissa retrieved a cranberry tube of lipstick and shot her a withering glance before pausing to tilt forward for a better view of her reflection in an entryway mirror. "I heard it once from a former fiancé who wanted to make our breakup sound like my fault."

Tandy reached for the mouse and scrolled further down the story. "You were the one to break up with him, so that pretty much makes it your fault."

Marissa straightened. "Has anybody ever told *you* that you can't arrive fashionably late for a cruise, because the ship will leave you behind?"

As that was the case, Tandy desired for the first time in her life to be fashionable. Besides not wanting to wear a slim sleeveless dress to a social event, there was the problem of finding enough room in the Jeep for Tandy to fit beside Marissa's full skirt.

She stood anyway and grabbed her coat and backpack. "Let's get this over with."

Marissa didn't move. "Um...you're wearing a backpack?"

"Um...yeah." She slid her arms in her coat then hooked on the tiny leather accessory. It wasn't like it was a JanSport or anything. Though hanging out with a drama-obsessed, cranberry lipstick-wearing, Jeep-driving blonde had a way of making her feel like they were back in high school.

Marissa fluttered her eyelashes. "At least your hair looks super good."

Tandy snorted at the backhanded compliment, but what did it matter? It wasn't like she was trying to impress anyone. She never was. Which made her feel especially out of her element once they reached the river and strolled up the gangplank from the dock onto a three-story steamboat outlined in white lights and named The Ohio Queen.

The sun had set on their drive over, preparing her for her first view of the paddle wheeler the way one might turn off the lights after ornamenting the tree. The analogy certainly fit with the way all the guests had decorated themselves like festive packages tied with ribbon. Why couldn't her suspects have simply planned to attend a Santa Paws fundraiser where Cocoa could have come with her and the only person dressed up was a big man in a red suit? That would be more her speed.

"I see Lavella," Marissa whispered fiercely over her shoulder as she led them up the ramp.

The beauty queen wasn't hard to spot. She welcomed guests at the front of the boat, wearing a white lace gown, matching long gloves, and a sparkly tiara nestled in her shiny, golden ringlets. Not to mention a white fur wrap.

Tandy grimaced at the fur. "She looks like an ice queen."

"That's a good description." Marissa nodded, twisting around to get in one more jibe before it was their turn to face her royal highness. "I'm pretty sure she has the power to turn things into ice too." With that, she forced a smile, swiveled back around, and slipped off the end of the gangplank onto the deck.

Tandy huffed, lunged forward, and caught Marissa around the waist to hold her upright. "Did she turn your shoes to ice?" she muttered before spinning them both in Lavella's direction.

Lavella lowered her hands from her mouth in an expression of mock concern. "Marissa, dear. Are you okay? At least you didn't fall off the platform this time."

Tandy tilted her head to add some contempt to her tight smile. "Don't you usually benefit from her falling, Lavella?" Sure, Tandy had made fun of Marissa's clumsiness too, but she didn't do it under the guise of being a friend.

Well, look at that. Tandy considered Marissa a friend now. If this woman was going to attack her friend, then Tandy was going to defend her.

Lavella inhaled, her plastic smile slipping for a fraction of a second. "I don't believe we've met." She extended a hand to shake. "I'm Miss Ohio. And I take it you're here with Marissa?"

Tandy shook, careful to avoid the other woman's claws. "Yes. I have a feeling it's going to be an exciting evening."

"I know it will be." Lavella retrieved her hand and motioned for a man to join them.

The man turned, his gaze piercing her first, then Marissa, and it took Tandy a moment to recognize the contractor in a suit. Connor was still rugged, but now in a classy way.

Marissa gasped.

Tandy closed her eyes. In Connor's attempt to protect Marissa, she was going to be destroyed.

"Ladies, I think you've already met my date."

Chapter Fifteen

THE ONLY THING THAT KEPT MARISSA smiling was the vision of removing her stilettos to hurl like throwing stars straight at Connor's heart. He was supposed to be here with *her*. But instead he'd demanded she give up her sleuthing and...

Oh. He was here to keep her from sleuthing. She'd tell herself that anyway. It was either that or he wanted to make her jealous. Which she wasn't. Unjealous people often imagined themselves throwing shoes at their exes when they started dating again, right?

"Connor." She stopped there. Anything else she had to say would be best done out of Lavella's hearing range. Things like, *Careful your date doesn't poison your drink.*

"Marissa." He nodded cordially. How dare he act cordial? "Tandy."

"Connor." Tandy joined in, and as fun as their little reunion was, Marissa couldn't help wishing she'd brought an actual date rather than another woman with a possible crush on her ex.

Lavella wrapped her fingers in the crook of Connor's elbow. "Now that we're all caught up, I need to welcome the rest of our guests. If you girls wouldn't mind moving along..."

Girls? Sure. She'd be Nancy Drew and Tandy could be George. This was just like the time Ned Nickerson proposed to someone else to find out what she was up to. Connor could still be Ned.

"No problem." Tandy pulled on Marissa's arm. "Thank

you for the tickets. It's an honor to see the genuine Ohio Queen. Oh, and you too, Lavella."

Marissa guffawed at the greatness of Tandy's sass. Okay, even if she could have found an actual date to get back at Connor, this was better.

Connor coughed into his fist.

Lavella's eyes narrowed.

Marissa pivoted to walk side by side with Tandy toward the cabin. "That was fantastic. Though she might try to kill you for it."

Tandy clicked her tongue as they entered a warm dining area buzzing with conversation. "That's not who I'm worried about."

Marissa would have to keep her eye on the beauty queen to protect them both. Plus Connor. Glancing over her shoulder, she found Connor watching her through one of the arched windows that circled the dining area. She shook her head in admonishment.

He lifted a shoulder in a shrug.

"There he is." Tandy pointed down the open walkway. The linen covered tables were situated on either side in a way that gave each passenger a personal view of the homes decorated with lights along the shore.

"Who?" Marissa asked. Who were they looking for? Who else did they suspect again besides Lavella? Little Lukey? Randon? Mr. Cross?

Rather than answer, Tandy headed straight for a long table of hors d'oeuvres by the bar where Joseph Cross presided over a good-natured group. For some reason Billie stood next to him dressed in a traditional Chinese gown—red with gold embroidered flowers and gold trim on the keyhole neckline.

Once they reached Billie, Marissa couldn't help but slide

her fingers over the material of the Asian's short, satin sleeves. "Billie, you look stunning."

Billie gave one of her sweet and humble chuckles. "Thank you. This dress was my mother's."

Tandy frowned. "Are you here with Cross?"

Billie looked down. "Yes, he invited me when he was at the shop this morning. I figured since he'd been ruled out for blackmail, it was safe."

Marissa arched her eyebrows. Had the pair once had a relationship? They were both widowed now, so they were free to date. It would be like if she and Connor found each other again in their 80s, and he finally admitted he'd been wrong to tear down Grandmother's home. She scanned the room to see if he'd entered yet.

"Billie," Tandy's voice lowered. "Cross lied to us. He may not be innocent after all."

Billie waved her napkin. "I think it must have been a simple misunderstanding."

Marissa's pulse picked up speed. Had Cross asked Billie out because he thought she still might have the diary? Maybe Lukey had confiscated it, and the person after it didn't even know. "We'll stick with you," she whispered then gave one of her pageant laughs to get Billie's date's attention. "Mr. Cross, even though I'm not your guest beauty queen this year, I still couldn't miss your cruise. I even brought Tandy since she's never been on a sternwheeler. Would you like to give her the grand tour?"

Mr. Cross glanced Marissa's way for the first time and a cloud of wariness shadowed his eyes before they lit up with their regular brilliance. "I gave tours earlier, but I suppose I could give one more. Let's start out on the deck for the boat launch."

A horn blared to signal they were set for departure, and

the crowd funneled through the exits. Tandy fell in step beside Marissa. "Good thinking. Now we can get Cross alone to ask him questions." She nodded her head toward the Asian woman ahead of them and lowered her voice. "You're not still suspicious of Billie are you?"

Marissa pursed her lips to convey deep thought.

Tandy narrowed her eyes. "You never really were suspicious, were you? You were simply trying to keep me from the police station, huh?"

Marissa admitted her attempt at manipulation with a sheepish grin.

Tandy rolled her eyes then reached for the door to hold it open so they could step back into the icy air.

Marissa reached to hang onto Tandy's arm in case the deck was as slippery as before. Yeah, it was completely the deck's fault she'd almost fallen on her face when getting on the boat in front of Lavella. Though the beauty queen had sure gotten a good laugh at her expense.

She peeked toward the bow to see if Connor was still with her. Nope. Lavella was surrounded by other men, none of which had Connor's broad shoulders and sandy hair. So where was...

Wait. Her eyes zipped back to the circle of men. The littlest guy in pinstripes looked familiar. She couldn't make out his face, but he had big dark circles in his earlobes. "Randon's here."

Tandy's bicep flexed under her grip. "Where?"

"Schmoozing Lavella, where else?"

Tandy steadied Marissa until she could grip the damp railing. "Don't look now, but Deputy Griffin and Jenn Pierce are on the balcony above us."

Marissa didn't have to fight the urge to look. She really didn't want to see the kid she once babysat using murder as an excuse to get back together with his ex. Some people would use any situation to try to work their way back into someone else's life.

Speaking of which, Connor appeared by her side. "I need to talk to you."

Her heart squeezed at the idea he "needed" to be with her and not her replacement, even if this wasn't the best time to talk.

The horn blared again. The gangplank lifted, still attached to the boat so that it was a walkway from the bow to nowhere. The ship shifted under Tandy's feet and the crowd cheered.

Marissa didn't bump into her at the movement, which was an improvement. Was she also craning her neck to watch Joseph Cross woo Billie? "Do you think his attention is genuine or is he after something?"

No response. Tandy turned to repeat her question, but Marissa was gone.

"Marissa?" Her heartbeat tripped, and she leaned forward to look into the inky water below for signs of a splash. Not a ripple except for the surging wave in her blood pressure. She whipped around, ready to yell for Griffin above even though she didn't completely trust him.

Wait. Something red flashed in the crowd towards the gangplank. Marissa's skirt. And Connor was with her. Tandy wanted to be upset that her partner was off being romanced while she was left to interrogate Cross, but at least the other woman was safe. Connor would take better care of her than the deputy.

The mass thinned out as passengers made their way back inside the protection of the dining room.

Joseph Cross appeared in front of her. "Did you want a tour, my dear?"

She would have preferred to have Marissa beside her, but with Billie there, she wasn't alone. And she'd have a chance to ask her questions. "Sure."

He led her first to the back of the boat where a huge round paddle churned against the water. She'd planned to ask her questions right away, but the white noise of water lapping, and the peacefulness of the stars above practically put her in a trance. Maybe if Cross relaxed along with her, she'd be able to get more information out of him.

"We have a paddle like this on display in Cincinnati," she said. "But I've never seen one at work this closely before."

"You're talking about the monument to steamboats. That paddle actually came off the American Queen." He nodded, offering Billie his jacket. "Come on. Let's go inside the steam room. It's warmer there."

The tour continued with stories about the worst maritime disaster in the United States history when the Sultana exploded in the 1800s, killing almost twelve hundred people. There were other explosions as well that eventually led to steamboat races being outlawed. In order to win, captains had started tying their safety valves closed to get the steam to heat hotter and propel the boats faster.

Lives had been lost so one person could receive glory. Kind of like how Virginia's life had been lost.

Mr. Cross pointed out the safety valves on his ship. "Here's one of those vents on The Ohio Queen. Most paddle wheelers are run on electricity now, but I like to do things the good old-fashioned way."

As in killing, like how Cain killed Abel? "Sounds

dangerous."

He narrowed his eyes. "We have to pass modern codes now, of course, so even if the valve gets stuck, it'll only cause a small explosion. Nothing to worry about." He led them toward the helm where the captain piloted them down the river. "Would you like to try steering?" he asked.

"I would," Billie chirped.

Mr. Cross motioned her forward. The captain stood by her side, giving instructions.

Tandy stayed behind with Mr. Cross. This was why she'd come. "I found the record for the sale of your boats."

Cross faced forward, rather than look her in the eye. "I told you I sold them."

He hadn't told the whole story. "Yeah, to yourself."

Cross turned toward her, his eyes clear. "I do own the majority share of stock in the corporation that bought me out, but I didn't during the sale. I purchased it later after Ettabell Alexander passed away. Even if Virginia had blackmailed me, it wouldn't have been a threat to this company because, like I told you, I sold it."

Tandy studied him. He was either innocent or a good actor. They'd already played this game before. But now she had more theories and questions. "Who else owns stock in the corporation? Anyone I know?"

Cross's brow wrinkled. "Quite a few people on this boat right now are stockholders, but I'm not at liberty to name names. Why does it matter?"

The boat shifted under their feet. Tandy lifted a hand to steady herself on a wall.

"Oops. Sorry," Billie called back to them. Could she overhear their conversation? Was she trying to interrupt, or was that an accident? A nervous twitch perhaps? Man, Tandy was getting as paranoid as Marissa.

Cross chuckled. "You're doing good, Billie." He sighed and glanced at his watch before looking at Tandy again. "I've got other guests to entertain. Do you have any more questions for me?"

Yes. A ton. But she'd probably need a warrant to find the answers. She'd settle for the one that was bugging her the most. Thanks to Marissa. "Does Lavella know about the diary, and would she use it to try to destroy Marissa's reputation? Or yours?"

Cross's gray eyes hardened to granite. "Why do you think Lavella knows about it?"

Apparently Marissa wasn't the only person afraid of the beauty queen. How much should Tandy reveal to Cross? If this was going to be her last chance to speak with him, she might as well go for the gold. "Someone knows about it because it was stolen from my glove compartment when in the police impound. Besides you, Lavella is the only other person we can think of who might want that documentation."

Cross lifted his chin, his eyes darting toward the main deck below, though it was hard to see in the dark. "If she got her hands on it, I'm sure I'll know soon. Though rather than destroy me, she's more likely to try to get me to rig the Miss USA pageant for her. Even if I had the power to do that again, I never would." He lifted an arm to motion to everyone on the boat. "I mean look at the mess that's come from doing it once forty years ago."

Tandy's eyebrows arched. That was a motive she hadn't considered yet. Could Lavella have heard about the journal from Virginia and come looking for it, not in an attempt to destroy Marissa, but to persuade Cross to help her win a national title? Could she have killed Virginia to keep her quiet?

Tandy didn't know, but at least she knew Cross hadn't

made any deals with her yet. Or so he claimed.

Billie padded over in her flats, having either grown tired of steering or intrigued by their conversation. "I almost wish I hadn't said anything about the silly diary at all."

Cross's eyes widened, and he turned toward her in slow motion. "You are the one who told them about the diary?"

Billie set a hand on his forearm. "That's why I kept turning you down when you asked me out."

His chin jutted forward. "*That's* why."

"Yes. Once I learned that you were sorry for your mistake, I felt like I could trust you." She nodded toward Tandy. "And it was good to hear you explain yourself tonight. Good to know you wouldn't repeat your mistake again by helping Lavella."

Tandy rubbed a hand down her face. She didn't know anything of the sort. She only had Cross's word for it. Though apparently that's what Billie wanted to believe. Why she'd probably given them the diary to begin with.

Cross covered Billie's hand with his own. "Why didn't you ever say anything?"

"I was afraid you might not have changed."

Tandy couldn't get away from romance. Not even when she was surrounded by people old enough to be her grandparents. Not even when one of them was a possible murderer.

She needed to regroup. She also needed to make sure Billie wasn't thrown overboard as soon as Cross got her alone. "Are you two going back to the party?"

"Shall we?" Cross held out his hand with a bow.

Billie smiled softly in acceptance.

Cross tucked her hand in the crook of his elbow and led the way.

Tandy slid her fingers against her scalp and squeezed the

roots of her hair with frustration. So much for finding another lead. So much for her "super" good hair.

She followed after the couple but paused at the stairs. They were obviously heading down into the melee. She might as well duck into the bathroom for a moment of peace on Earth. It's not like anyone would miss her anyway.

Marissa crossed her arms to face off with the guy who somehow thought dating her archrival to keep an eye on her made him a hero. "I'm supposed to thank you for being seen in public with the woman who tripped me off stage at the Miss Ohio pageant?"

He hung his hands on his waist and looked away in disbelief. "Nobody saw her trip you."

What? He was calling her a liar now? He'd been all compassion when she returned home from the competition. Had he voiced his doubts earlier, they wouldn't have even made it to the point in their relationship where he demolished Grandmother's house. "Well nobody saw her overdose Virginia either, but Virginia certainly died."

"All right." He turned back to face her and dipped his head. Was he lowering his voice to keep from being overheard, or was it an excuse to step closer to her? If that was his plan, she'd shove him away exactly like she had at Grandma's Attic. "Virginia's dead, and you're helping Tandy because she's afraid if you don't find the real killer then one of you will be accused of murder. But what if Tandy did it?"

Marissa's hands dropped to her sides and even more goosebumps popped up on her skin...if that was possible.

Despite the chills, she suddenly felt a little warm. She'd started to like Tandy. Trusted her more than anyone else in the town even though she'd known her the shortest amount of time. Even if the woman was gruff, she was also real. "Tandy doesn't pretend to be something she's not. Unlike other women you fake date."

Connor looked over his shoulder then moved even closer. "I honestly don't think it's Tandy. I just want you to be careful until we know for sure."

Okay. Was he saying that only to get back at her for questioning the person *he'd* arrived with? "You didn't seem reserved with her last night."

Connor blew out his cheeks. "I know. We had a good talk, but this afternoon after she tried to get rid of me—"

"Get rid of you?" Marissa spread her hands wide. When did Tandy try to get rid of him? What did that even mean? "She tried to kill you?"

Connor held a finger to his lips to hush her then glanced around as if worried someone was listening.

Marissa scanned the area too. Deputy Griffin did appear to be watching them from above. Could he hear her from there?

"No, she didn't try to kill me," Connor hissed, wrapping his fingers around her wrist and tugging her away from the few passengers continuing to linger on the deck. "She pointed out the mistletoe at Grandma's Attic. That was an obvious attempt to get you to reject me so I would leave."

"Oh my." Marissa pulled her arm away from him. "She wasn't trying to get rid of you. She admires you. If anything, she was trying to get me to reject you so she could step in and be your comforter."

Connor tilted his head, his gaze lifting as if to find Tandy and gauge for himself.

That wasn't the result Marissa was going for. "Not that you need comforting. You're dating Miss Ohio now." Where was his date anyway? It wasn't likely she'd pick Randon over Connor.

"Hardly." Connor grunted. "My mom ran into Lavella at Mama's Kitchen today, and the two planned this date for me. Lavella wanted me here to make you look bad while my mom wanted me here to look after you."

Marissa wasn't sure whether to be flattered or offended. But that wasn't the issue. She needed to finish warning Connor. "Your mom wouldn't have set you up if she'd known Lavella is a murderer."

Connor looked around again then tilted his head toward the swinging stage, also known as the gang plank. Steamboats used them so they could pretty much let passengers off anywhere rather than have to find a dock. "Come out here away from people if we're going to talk about this."

Marissa eyed the walkway with trepidation, grasping the railing and shaking to make sure it was sturdy. She had, after all, fallen out of a fireman's bucket the night before.

"I won't let you fall."

Like he didn't let her fall on the ice? He was going to use the excuse of a dangerous situation to hold her close. Well, okay. But only because Lavella would be watching. She was probably inside the dining room waiting for Connor to join her. Probably pulling out a vial of cyanide that very moment. Because Connor would be harder to kill than Virginia.

Marissa was more worried about Connor's safety than her own. She gripped the rail and made her way steadily toward the end of the plank before turning to face him. It really wasn't any different than standing on a pier, and she did that all the time. They both leaned against opposite sides, only a few feet apart.

Looking at him in the golden glow of twinkle lights and the breeze rustling his hair reminded her of the last time they'd been on this Christmas Cruise. When he'd proposed. When other people had cried at the beauty of it all, but she'd been too happy to cry. When she'd wished he didn't have so many romantic things to say because she couldn't wait to answer yes. It seemed like ages ago. It seemed like yesterday.

"I looked her up online."

Marissa's memories faded slower than the blink of an eye. She had to blink a few times to get rid of them. "Who?"

"Tandy Brandt."

"Okay." Marissa waited for the meaning to sink in. It didn't.

"She was fired from her newspaper for ripping on coffee shops that sold beans that aren't shade-grown. Apparently, she's a bit of a nut about her coffee, and without a job, she could be desperate. Desperate enough to kill."

"Okay," Marissa said again. Should she be afraid? No fear came. Only loneliness at the realization that while she'd been remembering the moment Connor proposed, he'd been thinking about the woman he'd gone on a fake date with.

Was he really here for her because he was worried about Tandy being a killer, or was he making up excuses to keep from starting a new relationship? Afraid of getting rejected again?

He shouldn't be. He'd been the one to hurt *her*. Or had they both hurt each other?

She didn't want to consider the possibility that she'd made a mistake in letting him go. If she had, then she didn't deserve him. Just like she hadn't deserved the crown. She had yet to live up to her family's expectations.

"I'm not afraid of Tandy," she said quietly. Evenly.

Connor studied her for a moment. "I'm not afraid of Lavella."

Here they were trying to protect each other from someone else, when they couldn't protect each other from themselves. "Who should we be afraid of?"

Maybe there was no one to be afraid of. Maybe Virginia's death had been her own fault. Maybe the car accident had been caused by kids. Maybe Tandy had simply looked in the wrong place for Grandmother's diary. Maybe Joseph Cross really did sell his boats then buy them again. Could it be that the robbery at the museum had them all paranoid?

Taking a deep breath, Marissa released the railing and stood tall to return to the deck. But before she could take a step, an explosion ripped metal, a wall of heat slammed through the air, and the gangplank jolted Marissa like a shot of matcha green tea.

Then there was no ground beneath her. Though she heard her name called and felt fingers scratch her coat, nothing stopped gravity from sucking her overboard into the icy water below.

Chapter Sixteen

MARISSA CLAWED AT THE FRIGID ABYSS. The ache that usually came with an ice cream headache raked over her entire body. She couldn't breathe in the silent, black, underwater world, but she was pretty sure her lungs had turned to ice anyway.

This was worse than falling into a Christmas tree. Worse than falling off a stage. Worse than slipping in front of Lavella.

She'd joked that Lavella had the power to freeze things, but she hadn't realized she'd be the one frozen. Had anybody else landed in the water? Did the boat break in half like the Titanic? Were there rescue boats? Would they rescue *her*?

Her limbs slowed, feeling heavy. Or maybe they were only tangled in her skirt. It threatened to pull her deeper. She forced her legs to kick, to resist. Though if she didn't dive deep, could she get sucked into the boat's paddle wheel?

Her head broke the surface. She knew from the sound of splashing and shouting and stomping of feet. She knew from the pressure leaving her ears, the hair plastered to her face, and the gentle breeze that greeted her like a snowstorm. And, finally, she knew from the burning of oxygen as it tornadoed its way into her chest.

She listened to herself gasp air. Her shiver turned into a shake. Her eyes devoured the dark night, looking for the lights that would signal the direction she needed to swim.

Lights reflected off the water. Other lights called to her from land. How did she get so disoriented? She had to figure out where she was.

If the boat had already passed, she'd head for shore. If it was right on top of her, she'd plunge back under. If it was close enough to rescue her, she'd call for help.

Something brushed her arm. She yanked away while trying to spin. She gulped the glacial air, preparing to dive out of danger.

"Marissa." Connor's voice warmed her. In her position, it was the only thing that could. "She's here. She's right here."

She spotted a glint of light off his hair then the whites of his eyes. She reached, teeth chattering. He was in an inflatable boat. With Lukey Griffin.

"Thank you, Lord," Connor said. Evidence his mom wasn't the only one to pray for her? She'd be grateful rather than offended. She'd take all the help she could get.

Both men grabbed one of her arms and drug her over the side. Her skirt scooped water in with her. They'd gotten to her quickly, but she needed them to go faster. Before the cold suffocated her completely.

Connor ripped off his suit jacket and wrapped it over her shoulders then wiped a strand of hair from her eyes as Lukey motored them toward the sternwheeler. "Are you okay?"

She did her best to nod. He'd told her he'd catch her, and here he was. She needed to thank his mom for sending him to look after her. But would she have fallen in the water if he hadn't ushered her up the gangplank in the first place? He should have known she'd lose her balance. Though this had been something more than her normal slip, hadn't it? "Wh-what happened?"

Lukey grunted as he steered them adjacent to the deck. "There was a small explosion similar to what Joseph talked about on his tour."

A steamboat explosion? Like from the 1800s? "Did anyone get hurt?"

"Only you." Lukey grabbed onto the railing to hold the rescue boat in place. "Marissa, I don't think it was an accident the explosion happened when you were standing on the swing stage. I'm starting to suspect someone is out to get you."

Tandy raced from the bathroom, still feeling off balance from the way the floor had shuddered underneath her feet. She didn't know what she'd find when she opened the door. From the sound of a nearby blast and the scent of smoke, she couldn't help thinking Joseph Cross was in one of those old-fashioned boat races that caused boilers to explode.

She scanned her surroundings while running to the railing. People poured out of the floor below to crowd the deck, but the boat looked intact. No holes in the ship. No flames. The paddle in the back continued its rotation like nothing had happened.

Next question: Where was Marissa?

Tandy's eyes picked out the red dresses from the crowd. None accentuated with her tiny waist and golden waves.

She'd look for Connor. He'd know where Marissa was.

Tandy grabbed the handrail to charge down the stairs, but movement beyond the edge of the boat's railing caught her attention. In fact, everyone in the crowd seemed to be focused there. What were they looking at?

Her heart dropped. Because if there was one person most likely to fall overboard, it was Marissa.

"Connor?" Miss Ohio pushed her way through the crowd, giving Tandy a better view of a raft floating toward the side of the ship.

A gate in the railing swung open, and Connor stepped aboard to assist the woman in red behind him. Marissa's hair wasn't bouncy and shiny anymore. It clung to her neck and shoulders. And Tandy had thought the other woman would be upset about Tandy's hair getting messed up.

Tandy didn't know what had happened, but relief flooded her at the realization it could have been a lot worse. "Marissa," she called to let her know she cared.

Marissa didn't look up, but Deputy Griffin did. His eyes narrowed, sending chills down Tandy's spine. Was the man really there to help, or had he caused Marissa to fall overboard? He could be using his power to control the situation, both making himself look good and awaiting his next chance to get rid of them.

She'd worry about it later. What mattered now was that Marissa was safe.

Cascading down the spiral staircase, she called to Marissa again. Cross and Billie joined her on the lower level.

"What happened?" She shot her question toward Cross and pushed a path through the crowd.

Cross grimaced. "It looks like someone closed the safety valve I showed you."

Tandy's exhale whooshed out. The explosion had been caused on purpose. But why? Did someone know it would knock Marissa overboard? Or were they after something else? Something like sabotaging Cross?

Marissa stepped onto the deck, her dress raining down a puddle of water. Tandy reached for a hug anyway. Marissa trembled in her arms, and it was no wonder with the way her skin felt like ice. "We have to get you out of these clothes." She twisted to look over her shoulder. "Cross, do you have blankets onboard?"

Cross scowled. "Yes, but I'm not letting you take off with her alone. How do I know you aren't the one who caused the explosion by closing the emergency valve?"

"What?" Tandy stepped away from Marissa to hold her arms wide. "You suspect me because you gave me a tour? How do I know you didn't give me the tour and wait for me to go to the bathroom so you could blame me?"

Deputy Griffin climbed onto the deck. "You were in the bathroom?" he repeated.

Tandy gritted her teeth. If only she hadn't drank so much coffee. "Yes."

Marissa took barefoot baby steps as if ready to leave them behind to argue while she warmed up elsewhere. "Tandy didn't do it," she offered weakly.

Tandy turned to follow. "Thank you."

"Marissa." Connor jogged to catch up, eying Tandy. "Remember what I told you."

Tandy frowned at the man. She'd thought they were on the same side. They certainly seemed to be the night before when she'd encouraged him in his relationship with Marissa. "What did you tell her?"

He glanced at her then looked down as he spoke. "I found out you got fired from your last position. I was simply warning Marissa that it could make you desperate."

Did he really? She pressed fingers to her temple where it pounded like the Little Drummer Boy. "You think I'm desperate enough to blow up a boat? How would this help me at all?"

"You want me to take the fall for Virginia's death," Cross called, and when she looked toward the railing, she found him standing there with his finger pointed at her.

Jenn Pierce gasped. The rest of the community stared. Tandy was going to get shunned like the Grinch from

Whoville.

She had to defend herself. She wasn't the bad guy here. She was simply in the wrong place at the wrong time. Once again. "Marissa is the only one who has taken any falls today, and I'm going to make sure someone owns up to it."

Marissa continued toward the warmth of the dining room. "Thanks, Tandy," she whispered before letting Connor hold the door open for her to enter.

Tandy turned back to glare at Cross. "You said you gave tours of the boat earlier today. Surely I'm not the only one to know about the safety valve."

Billie shook her head. "You're not. Even I knew about that."

Tandy nodded her appreciation. Though could she be sure Billie wasn't the one to cause the explosion? Someone here was guilty.

White fur caught her attention. She pointed at Lavella. "Marissa thinks Miss Ohio is after her."

Lavella froze. Spun. Widened her eyes in the art of innocence. "Me?"

"Well, you did trip her off the stage at the pageant."

All faces turned toward the beauty queen.

"I would never—"

"How about Randon?" Tandy motioned to the scrawny guy who had certainly dressed like a killer from a 20s gangster movie. "He might be getting Marissa back for ruining his moment last night."

The crowd backed away from the millionaire millennial.

Randon jerked upright from where he'd been leaning casually against a column. "Hey, you already accused me once, and I was found not guilty. Nine out of ten jurors--"

Tandy lifted a shoulder. "Nine out of ten jurors would find it easier to believe you're 'not guilty' if you weren't at the scene of another crime."

Randon opened his mouth to argue then turned toward Griffin as if not to waste any breath on Tandy. "Deputy, you don't suspect me, do you?"

Tandy crossed her arms and dared Griffin to answer honestly. "If he suspects you, Randon, he might actually be framing you. Because there's also the possibility Deputy Griffin killed Virginia himself for a chance to comfort Jenn Pierce, his ex, in her time of need."

Jenn's hands gripped her heart. Her face crumpled as her gaze rose to meet Griffin's.

He reached for her, shaking his head.

She stepped backward.

Griffin turned on Tandy. "In the dining room. Now. The rest of you too. Moon, Evans, Cross. We are getting this figured out tonight because I will not have my town, let alone my old girlfriend who is mourning her mother's death, suspecting me of being a dirty cop."

Marissa couldn't stop trembling despite shedding her dress in favor of Billie's full-length wool coat and hugging a mug of oolong tea. She wanted her bathtub. And her fireplace. And her down comforter.

Thankfully the captain was turning the boat around, though she was probably the only one thankful for that. Everyone else had their night out cut short, and by the smells coming from the kitchen, there would be a lot of prime rib wasted.

Right as she was starting to warm up, the door swung

open again. Tandy led a parade of suspects through it. Was one of them seriously trying to hurt her? Couldn't it be likely that whoever caused the blast simply wanted to make the boat go faster, and her little swim was an accident? Connor had her wanting to believe that before the eruption in the engine room.

Lukey motioned to the table next to hers. "Sit."

She eyed the other guests. "What's going on?"

Lavella eyed her back, and a cynical eyebrow found her lacking. "Tandy said you think I'm after you."

Thanks, Tandy. Exactly what she needed when on the brink of hypothermia. "I wouldn't put it past you."

Lavella tossed her hair and picked a chair facing away from Marissa's so she could turn her back on their conversation. But not before one last parting shot. "That would be a waste of time. I already beat you, remember?"

"By cheating," Marissa blurted before remembering Cross's fraud. *Please don't know about Grandmother,* she prayed, even while wanting Lavella to be the criminal. But what would she have killed Virginia over if not the diary?

Lavella's chin lifted like she was so bored she had to stare off into space. "You should thank me since you were bound to fall eventually. Aren't you glad you were able to do it here in Ohio rather than on national television?"

The boiling of Marissa's blood warmed her body faster than the heater or even Billie's coat. This woman practically admitted to tripping her. Marissa sat up straight and looked around to share the shock with others in the room.

Connor shook his head as if to say, *This isn't the time.*

Of course it was. If Lavella could trip her off stage to get what she wanted, then she was just as capable of making her fall overboard.

"Tandy?" If Tandy had openly accused Lavella in public,

then they must be on the same wavelength.

Tandy had set her jaw, but her glittering emerald gaze rested on Lukey rather than Lavella.

Connor leaned closer to explain. "Tandy didn't only accuse Lavella out there. She basically accused everyone in this room."

Marissa's chin jutted in shock. "What?" What had gotten into Tandy? Marissa was supposed to be the dramatic one.

Lukey strode to the center of the room. "I have Officer Woodward meeting us at the dock to question passengers, but I'm going to start with you all. Every one of you is going to tell me where you were when the engine exploded."

"Gangplank," Connor deadpanned.

"Not your smartest move," Lukey admonished unnecessarily. Unless he thought Connor was in on sending Marissa for a swim.

But Connor had rescued her. She may not trust him after tearing down Grandmother's house, but that was partly a result of his unyielding moral compass.

Connor leaned back in his chair. His grim expression told the cop he'd be punishing himself for the mistake far greater than the law ever could. "Agreed."

Lavella fluffed her hair. "I was looking for my date, though apparently, I was looking on the wrong side of the boat." She twisted to glare at Connor.

He shielded his eyes with a hand to avoid eye contact. Marissa totally understood his desire. However, she couldn't keep from shooting Lavella a smug smile. The other woman certainly hadn't won everything.

Lukey blew out his cheeks. "I'll confirm with passengers by the paddlewheel."

Lavella nodded, not looking guilty enough.

"I was stargazing on the top balcony," offered Billie.

"With Cross?" Lukey glanced up from where he made notes on his phone.

"Well..." Billie motioned toward Cross.

Cross cleared his throat. "I had to run back to the helm to verify our speed and course."

So neither of them had alibis either.

Lukey's gaze flicked between them. "I'll double check your story with the captain."

Randon sighed. "I had a minor issue on one of my apps that I had to fix, so I was sitting right over there." He nodded toward a spot near the bow of the boat that would have given him a great view of the gangplank. "I'm not sure who saw me because I was busy on my phone."

"Easy enough to follow up on." Lukey's gaze settled on Tandy. "And you were in the bathroom?" His tone indicated he found her story the most unbelievable.

Tandy bit her lip. "I was. Where were you, deputy?"

Lukey stared. "I was taking care of Jenn."

Randon rubbed his patchy attempt at a beard. "You weren't with Jenn when you walked by my table."

Lukey jolted. Was he lying? Had he thought Randon too preoccupied to notice? "She got teary eyed and escaped into the restroom down here for a few moments to gather her composure, which thanks to your outburst outside, Ms. Brandt, I'm sure she's having to do again."

Tandy's chest rose and lowered. "So you *don't* have an alibi?"

"I'm an officer of the law. I went to get my ex-girlfriend a pain killer for her headache, but I didn't rig any explosions, and I certainly didn't kill her mother. Why would you even think that?"

Cross wrapped an arm behind Billie's chair. "Probably because Marissa's grandmother's diary was missing from her car when she went to pick it up at the police station. She tried to blame me, but you would have the most access."

Marissa sucked in a breath. Her whole goal for helping investigate was to keep the diary out of public knowledge. If Lavella truly wasn't aware of it, and she found out about it now...

Lukey blinked. "Why would I steal a diary?"

Marissa stood, her aching bones momentarily forgotten in her panic. "I don't think you would, Lukey. That's ridiculous. Tandy probably looked in the wrong place or..."

Lukey's eyes cleared. "Or perhaps *she* stole it?"

No. That didn't make sense. Marissa closed her eyes to focus despite the confusion. Her brain seemed to be in slow motion. Perhaps from her rogue float trip. Could they just go home and continue the discussion tomorrow when she could think fast enough to keep the diary out of their discussion.

Tandy stood from her seat, eyes on the deputy. "You stole the diary to frame Cross and hide your crime. If you don't stop now, you're going to make this worse for yourself." She moved toward Lukey, her voice softening. "I don't think you *meant* to kill Virginia though. I think you only replaced her coffee grounds with instant granules to send her to the hospital. Then you could have stepped in and been the hero you wanted Jenn to think you are."

Marissa bit her lip. Was Tandy right? Had this all started with an accident, and everything since had been about Lukey cleaning up his mess?

The deputy watched Tandy move toward him, his eyes hard with fear. In one quick motion, he swiped something from his holster and pointed it her direction. "Stop."

Lavella screamed and ducked. Mr. Cross wrapped Billie in his arms. Randon froze, mid phone tap. Connor's arm and torso leaned in front of Marissa as a shield. And Tandy stood there, a regal sitting duck in her slim dress and high heels. Is that the outfit she would be buried in?

Except Lukey wasn't holding a gun. He was holding handcuffs.

"Tandy Brandt, you are under arrest for the murder of Virginia Pierce. Nobody but the killer would know why Virginia had so much caffeine in her system."

Chapter Seventeen

COLD, METAL HANDCUFFS SNAPPED AROUND Tandy's wrists before she could even comprehend the fact she was being arrested. This is what she'd been afraid of, and ironically, the whole reason she hadn't gone to Griffin in the first place. Though it was worse than she'd imagined, because not only was she being falsely accused, but it was likely the real killer was right in that room and had possibly set her up. The murderer was going to go free—was going to continue on as part of the little town that ignorantly considered itself safe.

"No." Marissa wobbled toward her. A symptom of hypothermia or her normal clumsiness? "Tandy knew about the instant coffee granules the day we met with Virginia. She saw the package in the garbage. She expected you to figure it out eventually, and she was afraid you'd suspect one of us since we were there."

Deputy Griffin yanked Tandy upright. "Well, she was right about that."

Tandy's heart sank. As great as it was that one person believed in her, it obviously wasn't going to help. Especially if the man who'd cuffed her was the man who'd caused Virginia's death.

Marissa steadied herself with fingertips on a table and motioned for Connor to back her up.

Tandy eyed Connor. He hadn't been much help earlier. Besides Tandy having the means to kill Virginia by being physically at her death and knowledgeable about the weapon, she would now also be considered to have more of a motive.

The revelation that she'd been fired from her last job surely made her seem desperate to start her own coffee shop. And as they saw it, desperate enough to kill.

Connor didn't meet her gaze. "Marissa, as I've been saying all along, the best thing you can do is let the police investigate."

He'd been saying that because he cared about Marissa. And obviously he *only* cared about Marissa.

It was a good thing Tandy hadn't spent her savings on buying Hidden Treasures before Virginia died because she was going to need every penny for a lawyer. Of course, if a lawyer couldn't prove her innocent, then she wouldn't have to worry about money anymore. The state would take care of her in prison. But not Cocoa.

She yelped. "Cocoa."

Marissa placed a chilly hand on her arm. "If you give me your keys, I'll pick him up and take care of him."

Tandy's heart quivered. Was it with concern for her pet or gratefulness for the devotion of her only friend?

"I thought you weren't a dog person." She glanced at Connor to remind him of the night before when they'd encouraged each other in friendship with Marissa. Would he take what he could get and leave her behind?

Connor shifted his jaw like she'd landed a punch under his chin.

Marissa squeezed. "If you can wear a dress for me, then I can take care of Cocoa for you."

Tandy's heart quivered again. For the friend who could have been badly hurt that night. And also with fear because if the police only suspected Tandy, the killer was still out there free to hurt Marissa for whatever reason they hadn't figured out yet. "I'll pray Cocoa takes care of you too. Be safe."

Marissa's right cheek dimpled. "You're not going to be in

jail for long. I'll figure this out."

Exactly what Connor told her not to do. Tandy narrowed her eyes at Connor, daring him to try to stop Marissa. Not that she wanted Marissa to get hurt. She wanted the opposite. She wanted Marissa safe from whoever it was that had caused their pain these past couple of days.

Maybe going to jail would give Tandy the extra time needed to figure this mess out.

Marissa cranked the heat up even higher in her Jeep. After Officer Woodward arrived at the dock and played another round of twenty questions, she'd endured a full physical with that cute EMT who'd checked Tandy out the day before. Then Connor had insisted on following her to Tandy's apartment to pick up Cocoa.

She squinted at the numbers on the buildings before noticing a balcony lit up by a Snoopy lawn decoration. That had to be Tandy's unit. And Marissa had thought her tough when they'd met.

Tandy might have to learn to be tough if she was going to prison. Though Marissa wouldn't let that happen. She wouldn't even let Tandy spend Christmas Eve in jail. She *had* to figure something out.

Connor parked beside her under a carport and met her at the bottom of a staircase. On the second floor she recognized Tandy's apartment by the doormat. She pointed it out to Connor.

Never mind the dog, beware of the owner.

Connor frowned.

Marissa slapped him. "She's all bark, and no bite."

An actual bark came from inside the building, interrupting any response from Connor.

"It's me, Cocoa," Marissa called, sliding the key in the lock.

She swung the door open to the pungent smell of coffee beans and a site that caused her heart to jolt. Though she couldn't make out the mess inside without the light on, it looked like the place had been ransacked. If all the murder suspects were on the boat, who had broken into the apartment?

Connor motioned Marissa back with an arm and flipped on the light switch.

She blinked at the brilliance, hoping the intruder had been blinded as well if he was still there. But then the large shapes all over the floor took form, and she realized Tandy's house wasn't a mess. She'd simply been storing decorations for her coffee shop.

Bags of coffee beans. Tables made of reclaimed wood. An espresso maker.

"Looks like she really was desperate," Connor mused.

Marissa ran her hand over the nubby texture of the bags. She didn't appreciate coffee, but she appreciated Tandy's passion for it. "She's a dreamer. And if we don't help, her dream will never come true."

"Even if she doesn't go to jail, hon, how can her dream come true? Are you going to give up your dream of starting a teahouse to let her buy Virginia's old shop?"

Marissa looked away. She wasn't ready to deal with either the question or the endearment Connor used. She should scold him, but she was too tired to fight. And if she wanted his help, she probably shouldn't keep pushing him away. He'd failed her, but he'd also rescued her. Twice.

Cocoa peered from around the corner, and Marissa realized the tiny rumbling sound she heard had been coming from him this whole time. Not exactly a guard dog.

Connor squatted down and grabbed a squeaky green rubber bone with a red rubber bow. He tapped it on the ground a couple times then tossed it towards Cocoa.

Cocoa bounced to claim it.

Connor patted the carpet. "Come here. Here, boy."

Cocoa stood with the squeaky toy in his mouth, eyes watchful.

"You know what? I'm used to people playing hard to get." He grinned up at her.

Marissa looked away in mock disdain but had to look back when she heard plastic crinkle. The man actually carried dog treats in his pocket.

"Come on, Cocoa. I've got something for you."

Cocoa bounded over, his allegiance apparently lying with whoever held the treats.

Connor pulled the rubber bone away, rewarded the dog, then repeated the game of fetch.

Marissa bent down next to Connor. It looked like if they were ever going to get out of there, she'd have to pick up Tandy's pet. "Hey, Cocoa. You get to come home with me, boy."

Connor handed her a treat so Cocoa would acknowledge her presence. Had it only been yesterday when she'd tripped over him and called him a varmint? She still wasn't a fan of the licking, or even the meaty scent of dog treats, but Tandy was, and Marissa was doing this for her.

Connor watched her wipe another wet spot from her cheek. "How about I take Cocoa to my house, and you keep Ranger at your place? It would make me feel better."

She studied him, not appearing quite as stiff in his suit

now that he'd lost the tie and loosened the collar. It had always been a good look on him, though it was his concern for her wellbeing that made her want to pretend they'd never been at war.

Wait. Why was he concerned if he thought Tandy was guilty? She straightened in victory. "You don't really think Tandy did it, do you?"

Connor stood a little slower. "I didn't say that."

"Well then I'm going to keep Cocoa with me the way I promised." She turned in a circle in an attempt to look past Tandy's mess to find Cocoa's food and other pet supplies. What did dogs need? A brush? A bone? A black leash hung on the wall above the counter. "You think she'd mind if I got Cocoa a red leash? Black is so boring."

"I'm sure she would." Connor strolled after her. "But don't let that stop you. In fact, get him a Santa suit to match. Then he can run with me in the Ho-Ho-Holiday run tomorrow morning."

Marissa considered. Did they make Santa Claus costumes for dogs? "With those little legs, he'd probably slow you down."

Connor lifted a shoulder. "I'm used to running with you, so it wouldn't be much different."

Marissa kept her back turned. She didn't want Connor to see her sad smile. Last year she'd made him stop at Grandma's Attic in the middle of the run to use the bathroom because she was afraid of using the Porta Potty at the finish line. Who would have thought so much would change in a year?

She took her time scanning the counter for other items that might belong to Cocoa as an excuse not to look at her ex. An old photo album sat open, displaying fading snapshots. Marissa recognized the setting of the old covered bridge in

Grace Springs before she recognized a young version of Tandy. Young Tandy also wore a standard ponytail and had a dog by her side. But there was a boy with her too.

Marissa squinted. Tandy had mentioned hanging out with a kid her age when she used to come to town. Was this a kid Marissa knew?

"Hey, that's Greg." Connor pointed.

Greg? As in Greg St. James? Attorney Greg St. James?

A kind of strangled cry erupted from within as Marissa spun. Yeah, her hand landed on Connor's chest, but only to get his attention. "We have to call Greg. He can get Tandy out of jail. He'd do it for an old friend, right?"

Connor didn't move away. "Normally I'd say you need a Christmas miracle to get a lawyer to work for free, but..." He glanced down at the hand on his chest. "It's miraculous what a guy will put up with for an old friend."

Tandy woke early on the lumpy cot, still wearing a long, slim dress. The events leading up to her arrest replayed through her mind like The Nightmare Before Christmas, as this really was Christmas Eve. She stared blindly at the cement walls that would be her home for the holidays.

At least she was safe from physical harm, while Marissa continued to play dangerous reindeer games. What if the beauty queen got herself killed in the process? Either by the murderer or by tripping over her own feet when giving chase. Connor would look after her, right?

It's not like Tandy could be there for Marissa. She couldn't even be there for herself. Deputy Griffin thought she'd killed Virginia, so he wasn't going to follow up on any of the other suspects. Especially since she suspected him.

Someone was getting away with murder, and there was nobody who could possibly help release her from behind these bars.

A door clanged, and footsteps echoed down the hallway before a man appeared in a Santa suit. It took a moment to recognize Griffin's smooth skin hidden by a full white beard.

He grunted. "I'm on my way to beat pretty boy Connor Thomas in the Ho-Ho-Holiday Run, but it looks like I'm delivering you an early gift first."

Her pulse raced like she was the one about to cross the finish line of his fun run.

He unlocked the bolt on her bars.

Should she be hopeful or cynical?

"Marissa used her resources to get you a top-notch attorney rather than let you wait for a public defender." Griffin swung the bars wide. "Which is good because you're going to need the best."

Tandy let her cynical side show in a fake smile, though hope welled from within. Her collarbones even tingled with it. This was what it was like to have somebody on her side. Even if the lawyer was paid to be here for her, he was still here. And Marissa had made it happen.

Griffin checked his watch. "Did you want to speak with him or not?"

She rose to her feet. "Sorry. I'm not used to having someone in this place actually wanting to listen to me."

Griffin narrowed his eyes, the glare almost comical coming from a character who was supposed to be known for jolliness. If the real Santa was there, she'd sit on his lap and ask for a cup of coffee. Because seriously, how could she be anything but cynical without her morning pick-me-up?

Griffin led her towards the front of the old station, stopping at a door with a glass rectangle above the doorknob. "Like I said, I've got places to go, but I'll give you fifteen minutes."

She lifted a finger. "Could I get a cup of—?"

Griffin yanked the door open. "Against my better judgment, there's already coffee waiting."

The aroma greeted her before she entered the room. And it couldn't simply be the scent of leftover sludge from the pot out front. No. This was fresh. Plus, there was a tinge of peppermint and chocolate in the air. It would be her only taste of heaven this Christmas season.

She inhaled as she entered. Sure enough. Steam seeped through the lids of two, gorgeous, red paper cups. She continued forward, hardly noticing the scrape of a chair as the man behind the table stood.

Who had done this for her? Marissa who'd claimed to hate all things coffee? It certainly wasn't Griffin.

She reached. Wrapped her fingers around the warmth. Lifted the cup first to her nose and closed her eyes. This was what hope smelled like. And it tasted even better. Like a candy cane and chocolate Kisses whirled together with the nuttiness of her favorite beverage. Smooth. Creamy. It melted all the edginess inside. "Where did you get this? I didn't think there was a coffee shop in town." Whoever made this cup of liquid bliss could put her out of business should she ever start her own place.

"I brewed it."

With this kind of magic, her lawyer might possibly be able to prove her innocent in a court of law. She looked up in wonder to find a clean-cut guy in a gray suit. He would have been your normal, everyday clean-cut guy in a gray suit except for the striking way his blue eyes stood out from his black hair. And the dimple in his chin.

She tilted her head to study that dimple. Where had she seen it before?

"Apparently you still like coffee."

Still? As in, he'd known her to like coffee in the past? How would he know, unless...

"I remembered you sneaking a thermos of coffee out of your house because your mom was afraid coffee would stunt your growth. And it looks like she was right. Weren't you this same height in middle school?"

Her heart sputtered. "Greg?" He'd certainly grown. Because though they'd been the same height, he now stood half-a-foot taller.

Could it be? After fifteen years, she was reunited with her very first crush, and he was her lawyer in a murder trial? While he was handsome and successful, how did she look?

He'd see her as a criminal. If only he'd seen her last night when she had good hair. Now she was wrinkled. Dirty. Unemployed. With a puffy face. Of all the jails in all the towns in all the world, he'd walked into hers.

Greg lifted his cup as if to toast. "I figured that with the trouble you went through to get arrested so you could see me again, the least I could do was bring you a cup of coffee."

Her heart sighed in relief. This was her old friend. Who cared if she looked like a prom date gone wrong? Though it was surprising he'd been able to recognize her at all in a dress. She'd lived in jeans and jean cutoffs for as long as she could remember. "I should have just looked you up on Facebook, huh?"

His eyes lost their shine. "Yeah, why didn't you?"

Besides the fact that she didn't want to find out he was already married with children? Though if he was more upset that she didn't let him know she was back in town than the fact she'd been arrested for murder, then maybe he was still single. She sneaked a peek at his bare ring finger then motioned to their surroundings. The perfect display of why it shouldn't matter if he was available or not. Because she wasn't. "Been a little busy."

"Apparently." He studied her with the sternness of a judge before his expression softened to the buddy she'd known as a child.

She wasn't sure which look scared her more.

He nodded for her to take a seat across from him. "I'm going to pull a few strings and see if we can get you bail today. Marissa filled me in a little, but I'd like to hear your side."

Tandy let go of her mug with one hand to pull her chair out. What would she have to say that Marissa didn't know?

Wait. Greg had spoken with Marissa. Marissa retained Greg. Was the town that small, or had Marissa somehow known he'd been her childhood friend?

"Do you know Marissa?" She sat slowly and cuddled her cup for comfort.

Greg looked up from a manila folder that had to be a file on her. How unfair. She should get a file on him.

"Yeah, I did some pro-bono work for the local children's home when Marissa was raising money for them as charity for her beauty pageant. I think she was behind me a couple years in school, so I know Connor better." He straightened his paperwork, clearly ready to get down to business.

But Tandy had more questions. Had Marissa sought Greg out because of Tandy's interest in him or her own? He didn't seem interested in Marissa, but it sounded like he assumed she was still taken. "They're not together anymore."

Greg chewed on the top of his pen. "Who? Marissa and Connor?"

"Yeah. She ended their engagement." Why was she talking about this? What did it matter who Greg was interested in dating when she wasn't even available? Though her nervous jitters weren't all from the possibility of making bail. Or the caffeine.

"Well..." Greg cocked his head, as if trying to read her. "They were together last night. They went to your house to get your dog and saw an old photo album with a picture of the two of us. Once they realized our connection, they thought I might want to help."

Her pulse sputtered. Greg was truly here for her. "You believe I'm innocent?" she asked in a rush.

Greg folded his hands over the papers that gave all the facts. Did they affect his feelings? "It's been a while, Tandy, but from what I know of you, you're a bad liar. You couldn't even sneak coffee from your mom without turning yourself in."

That was true. She'd been grounded from going to King's Island Amusement Park with Greg because of it. Back when Mom had cared enough to punish her.

"I'm curious about this article you wrote that got you fired." He arched his eyebrows. "My guess is you were fighting for justice."

"Yes." He understood her. It was so good to be known. Without realizing it, she'd reached across the table to grasp his hand. It felt warm and strong under hers, but even if he wanted to, he couldn't flip it over to clasp fingers like they used to. He was her lawyer. She pulled back. "Um...I wrote a piece about the negative effects many coffee bean plantations have on the environment as well as animals, and I encouraged readers to buy shade-grown coffee." It was a good article. Both important and true. But... "Unfortunately, I didn't think about how our biggest advertising accounts sell coffee that is not shade-grown."

He sat still, only his eyes moving as he connected the dots. He had really good posture. It made her want to sit straighter. She rolled her shoulders back and felt a small ripple of adjustment down her spine. It wasn't as comfortable as slouching, but it's not like she was comfortable to begin with.

"How did you leave things with your boss?"

She blinked. Why should her old boss come into this at all? "Uh, I disagreed with his decision."

"How so?" His pen poised to write down her answer.

"Vehemently." It was the nicest word she could think of that would describe her reaction to being fired.

Greg frowned and scribbled.

"Is that bad?"

He looked up and sighed. "Not as good as if you'd voiced your opinion respectfully and apologized."

Tandy held her hands wide. "Apologized? I didn't write anything that wasn't true."

"But you did cause your employer harm." Greg tilted his head. "The same way you did to Deputy Griffin last night."

Tandy slumped. "What if I think he killed Virginia?"

Greg pressed his lips together and shook his head. "Then you offer him the same grace you wish he would have offered you."

Tandy guffawed. Probably neither attractive nor good for her case. "I didn't do anything wrong. I don't need grace."

"We all need grace. Even if it's for harm caused accidentally."

She cringed, remembering the lawsuit against a company for serving coffee that was too hot. The company hadn't wanted to hurt anyone, but they'd ended up having to pay three million dollars. She remembered thinking how ridiculous such a lawsuit was. She'd wished the customer would have extended grace even though she'd been hurt.

Greg's mouth curved up and his eyes softened in the kind of smile that offered what she wanted. The kind that said he thought she could have avoided getting arrested, but he cared about her anyway. Which somehow made it sweeter. "Let me call Judge McMinn real quickly to see if you can post bail. And so you know, I'm not charging you a retainer fee."

Tandy's throat clogged. This was tangible grace. Not to mention ironic. Since the last time she'd spoken to Greg, they'd both needed retainers. For their teeth.

Greg made the call and worked out the details, scribbling on his notepad. One scribble caught her eye. It was a date at the beginning of the New Year. Her belly churned.

She pointed to the date as soon as he hung up. "What's that?"

Greg underlined it. "Your court date."

Not the kind of date she'd been hoping for. She'd only been released to spend the holidays broke and alone, while the possibility of prison still hung overhead like mistletoe, threatening to make her kiss her life goodbye.

Chapter Eighteen

TANDY HEARD COCOA BARKING BEFORE SHE even knocked on Marissa's red door with the big green wreath. If the beauty queen hadn't helped her out with the dog, then Tandy never would have gotten help from Greg. She'd still be behind bars. She couldn't thank Marissa enough. But she'd think of something to say. Something grateful and sincere and...

The door swung open and Cocoa ran out to paw his front legs up hers. Only he didn't look like Cocoa. He looked like a dog in a Santa costume. Marissa appeared behind him, somehow making a reindeer sweater look cute, arms wide for a hug.

"Are you crazy?" The words burst out before Tandy could stop them.

Marissa dropped her arms and pouted. "I know you're not much of a hugger, but I figured getting out of jail might be an exception to the rule."

"Not if you dress my dog up like a human. I like dogs because they are *not* human." Tandy squatted down to rub Cocoa's head and let him know she wasn't mad at him. It's not like he wanted to wear human clothes.

Marissa laughed, not seeming the least bit offended about Tandy's preference for pups over people. "Connor wanted to take him on the Ho-Ho-Holiday Run."

Tandy tugged at the strap that held a tiny Santa hat on Cocoa's head. "Connor has his own dog."

Marissa stepped back to open the door wider. "We didn't want Cocoa to feel left out, and we didn't know if Greg would be able to get you out of jail today or not. Obviously, he did."

Tandy scrunched her nose at Cocoa before standing. He cared about her whether or not she was a criminal. Kind of like Greg. Maybe it was her dog's grace that she appreciated about him so much. Maybe she should admit she needed it more often.

Like now. With Marissa. She'd smooth things out. Thank Marissa the way she'd been planning to. Work on her people skills.

She faced Marissa and entered the warm, sugar-scented home with the wooden floors and built in bookshelves. "Thank you, Marissa. Even if you overstepped your bounds in dressing up my dog, I am thankful you called Greg."

Marissa beamed then pointed down at Cocoa, still wearing a red jacket. "You don't think he looks cute in—"

Tandy glowered.

"Never mind then." Marissa turned to lead Tandy back into her cozy kitchen with the bird egg blue cabinets and white marble countertops. An island offered cranberry scones and some type of citrusy tea.

Tandy took a warm scone, thankful Greg had brought her coffee earlier. "Did Connor remodel your house?" she asked. If so, he did good work. A handy skill to have in a boyfriend.

Too bad Tandy had more use for an attorney than a contractor. Not that she was dating Greg. Or complaining about Greg. For all she knew, he was good at building things too. They'd made that tree house together once.

"Yes, Connor remodeled the place. You should have seen it when I bought it. Super old and run down." Marissa poured a weak brown liquid into a fancy cup. "Tea?"

"No comment."

"Wise choice." Marissa sipped, pinkie up.

Tandy sat on the cushioned barstool and reached down to scoop her dog into her lap. Her whole body ached from lack of sleep, and her skin felt covered in grime from the restless night on a mattress that was not her own. "I need to go home and take a shower, but I wanted to pick up Cocoa first."

Marissa sank down next to her. "Then what are you going to do? We've been running ourselves ragged, trying to figure out who killed Virginia, yet it's like we're no closer than when we began. Actually, we're farther away. Because you've been accused of the crime."

"No kidding." Tandy ran a hand over her face. Even the people who'd once believed in her had turned on her. "Does Connor really think I'm guilty?"

Marissa lifted a shoulder but looked away. "He's not convinced you did it, but he's suspicious of the way you got fired from your old job."

Would things have turned out any differently if Tandy had apologized and offered to try to fix her mistake? If so, then Connor wouldn't be suspicious of her, though his suspicion shouldn't bother her as much as it did. Because she'd also had a moment where she'd suspected him. "I don't blame him. At first, I thought he might have done it. You know, to win his way back into your heart the way I now think Deputy Griffin is trying to do with Jenn."

Marissa shifted on her seat.

Tandy leaned forward, resting her chin on her fist to get a better look at the other woman's discomfort. "Wait a minute. Are you back together?" Greg had thought as much.

Marissa eyed her, saying no without words. "We are not together. We are...being friendly. Because he kinda saved my life a couple times recently."

Too bad the two hadn't reconciled. Tandy had hoped something good might have come from the horrific cruise. "He actually thinks I caused the explosion to knock you into the water? Honestly, if I was going to kill you, I had so many other opportunities."

Marissa's eyes widened. "How would you have done it?"

What a question. Tandy had never considered killing anyone before. She thought back through the time they'd known each other. "Well for starters, in the car accident, I could have rammed your side of the car into the hill rather than risking my own life."

Marissa pursed her lips. "That's a good point. Though maybe you were trying to make yourself look innocent before you killed me."

"So much for looking innocent." Tandy shook her head. "Not even getting the firemen to lower the bucket to help prevent your fall made me look innocent."

"Also true." Marissa took a sip. "You are the worst murderer ever."

Tandy grunted. "Connor knows about both of those incidents. How could he still suspect me?"

"He's paranoid like the rest of us. And when he looked you up online and found out you'd been fired from your job, he got worried." Marissa set her cup down with a clink. "Why did you get fired anyway?"

Tandy had hidden that fact for precisely this reason. But perhaps if she'd been honest and humble from the beginning, they never would have gotten here. She stood. "I'll show you. May I use your computer again?"

Marissa motioned toward the corner desk as the doorbell rang. "Probably Connor."

Tandy removed Cocoa's Santa Paws suit so Connor wouldn't take him running then she pulled up her article on the computer. She'd show Connor before he left too. Then he could return to helping her out. Maybe he could even sniff out more clues while downtown.

Marissa studied Connor freely through the peephole. Why did he have to be cute even when dressed like Santa Claus with little wire-rimmed glasses? Of course, last Christmas Eve morning she'd been dressed like Mrs. Claus for the run. And they'd made good use of Billie's mistletoe.

"It's me, Marissa," he called impatiently, ending her moment of hidden reflection.

With a heavy sigh, she swung the door open. She missed the days when she would swing the door open for him with a sigh of contentment.

Before Connor could greet her, Ranger leaped up and smacked her face with his warm, wet tongue.

"Lucky dog."

She pushed Ranger down, and wiped her cheek, though her heart chimed like a church bell. She pictured herself being whipped around by the pull rope when trying to control the ringing. Hadn't a woman at St. Nicholas Church been knocked unconscious that way? Marissa refused to give this St. Nick that kind of control over her again.

Cocoa charged from the kitchen, yipping at the bigger dog. Ranger watched in curiosity.

Connor knelt. "I brought you something." He pulled out a rubber gingerbread man and tossed it.

Cocoa retrieved the toy without prompting then bounced in anticipation of his dog treat.

"Good boy." Connor rewarded him. "Why isn't he in costume?"

Marissa twisted her lips to one side. "Tandy wasn't a fan."

Connor's brows dropped, and he scanned the room. He leaned forward. "Tandy's here?"

Cocoa bent into a crouch and snarled, as if protecting his treat from the bigger dog.

"Cocoa, hush," Tandy's voice called from the other room, answering for Marissa.

Cocoa quit snarling long enough for Ranger to step forward and lower his head to the little dog's level.

Connor did the same to Marissa. "I don't want you alone with her."

Marissa would have stepped back and created space between them if she wasn't trying to avoid Tandy overhearing their conversation. She kept her voice low. "If she'd wanted to kill me, she could have done it already. Remember how she helped you catch me when I fell out of the fireman's bucket?"

Connor's fake beard wiggled as he shifted his jaw side to side. It also hid his lips, which was a good thing. She shouldn't be looking at them anyway. "We still don't know her that well," he warned.

"Greg does," Marissa argued. Though for some reason she was starting to feel like she knew Tandy better than anyone else in town. And she knew everyone. "He wouldn't have volunteered his time to get her out of jail if he thought she was capable of murder."

Connor rocked his weight onto his leg closer to her then looked away before turning back and leveling his gaze. "He knew her as a kid. People change."

What did he say? People change? Like a pot of tea?

Though the pot remained the same, she could dump out the contents and brew more tea? She didn't get rid of the whole pot if the tea was bitter or weak. Such an analogy made more sense than the phrase about throwing out the baby with the bath water.

Did this mean that if Connor messed up, they could get past it and move on? They could learn from their disagreement and get back together? Was it possible for her to trust him again if he'd changed? How would she know for sure whether he'd changed or not?

That scent of fresh cut timber that hung on him everywhere he went hadn't changed. His protective instincts toward her hadn't changed. The power of his cloud gray eyes to cause a storm inside her hadn't changed. Were they growing darker?

"I can hear you, Connor," Tandy's voice called.

Marissa grimaced. Both because Tandy had overheard and because she'd interrupted.

Tandy continued. "You're growling like a Pomeranian. Get in here and see for yourself who I am now."

Connor pinched his eyes shut.

Marissa used the diversion to disappear into the kitchen. The whole idea of change stirred her even more than Connor's heated gaze. If people could change, then it was okay to make mistakes and grow from them. It was okay to not be perfect.

It would be okay that Grandmother wasn't the true Miss Ohio. Had she not been crowned, she could have competed again and won. The fact that she hadn't honestly earned the title in her first attempt didn't mean that she never would have. Didn't mean she was less of a person.

"Look." Tandy pointed at the computer monitor.

It took a moment for Marissa to see through the haze of

her thoughts to focus on the article. Then Connor joined her, and his warmth sent her senses haywire once again.

He leaned forward over Tandy for a better view. "This is the column you wrote?"

Tandy twisted around to look at them. "Yeah, I usually reviewed local coffee shops, but after I interviewed a guy who roasted coffee beans in his garage, I decided I wanted to try it. That's when I started researching how coffee is grown. Did you know it's the second highest traded commodity in the world after oil?"

Marissa shook her head. Normally, she'd want to argue the benefits of tea here, but she had the feeling Tandy was about to say something negative about coffee herself.

"I discovered that because of the high demand, many coffee plantations are getting rid of trees and using more pesticides and fertilizers. This not only causes erosion and contaminates waterways, but it reduces habitat for birds and monkeys. So I wrote about it."

Connor squinted at the screen. "You implored your readers to buy shade-grown coffee only."

Tandy nodded. "Yeah. I didn't realize the paper would lose advertisers, and I'd lose my job. I thought I was doing something good by educating people."

Connor stood straight and folded his arms across the pillow stuffed in his shirt. "You wanted to start over here with your coffee shop."

Tandy held her arms wide. "I did. But I'm not desperate. My only crime is trying to protect animals the way you always try to protect Marissa."

He slid his gaze Marissa's direction. "She needs a lot of protection."

Marissa narrowed her eyes.

Connor lifted his eyebrows above the rim of his silly

glasses.

She looked away. Down to Cocoa waiting with the toy gingerbread man in his mouth. She bent to retrieve it. "Look. Here's the perfect man for me."

Connor shook his head in pretend disapproval. "A gingerbread man? Why? Because he's quiet and sweet and if he gives you any trouble, you can bite his head off?"

He knew her too well. "Exactly." She tossed the toy.

Cocoa bounded after it.

Though she couldn't see any part of Connor except his eyes, their twinkle told her his lips were curling up on one side underneath his beard. "You'd be bored."

"You'd also be fat because you like to bite heads off." Tandy looked past her shoulder. "Marissa, there is no such thing as a perfect man. At least this one isn't a killer like Jenn's ex. Oh my goodness, did Cocoa just fetch?"

Connor blinked. "Who thought I was a killer?"

Tandy gasped and bent over her dog, rubbing him and cooing. She glanced up. "Anyone who's seen your killer smile."

Oh wow. Marissa wasn't expecting that. Maybe Tandy really was interested in Connor. If not before, surely now that he'd taught her dog a trick. Marissa had to get Connor out of there before he decided to pursue another woman in her own home. One who would let herself be caught.

Connor tugged his beard down. "This killer smile?"

His grin was as warm and steamy as her favorite cuppa, but Marissa refused to melt.

"That's the one," Tandy agreed.

"Let's go, big guy." Marissa escaped into the living room then crossed her arms and stared at the ceiling, waiting for him to follow.

"I don't really believe you're guilty, Tandy. I only wish I

knew who was."

"Me too."

Marissa leaned toward the doorway to interrupt. "Come on, Santa. You don't want to miss your race."

Connor strode into the room and almost into her. She jerked upright to avoid the collision. Those other times he'd caught her, they hadn't been alone, but in her living room they would have more privacy. She didn't want to have to reject him again because she didn't know if she could.

He didn't even pause but strode past, snapping for Ranger to follow. "It's nice someone still believes in Santa," he called back.

Tandy grinned at Connor's parting shot. As far as people went, he was at the top of her list. And not her suspect list.

As for suspects... She frowned at her own picture on the computer screen. She should be looking up the people who might possibly have committed the crime, not herself. She'd researched Cross and Randon, but what about the deputy? Would he really have killed Virginia to get Jenn back? How close had the couple been? Were they engaged like Marissa and Connor had been? Or was it nothing more than a few dates when she was in town. With Jenn gone overseas so much, they couldn't have been engaged. Or could they?

She slid her fingers over the keyboard and typed in "Jenn Pierce and Deputy Griffin."

An old article popped up. Too old to be an engagement story. In fact, it was so old Tandy had still been spending summers in Grace Springs at the time. Were Jenn and Luke childhood sweethearts the way she and Greg had been? That would definitely be a hard relationship to give up. And if so, Griffin would have known Jenn's family well. He would have known about Virginia's heart condition.

Tandy clicked to enlarge the article.

Cincinnati Student Has Diamond Stolen

Tandy's heart lurched at the headline. Déjà vu with the stolen diamonds. It couldn't be the same criminal, could it? Is this where Griffin's double life started?

Her eyes devoured the article looking for his name. She'd even accept Cross or Evans.

A sixth-grade student discovered a rare Ohio diamond while on a school field trip to a sand pit. The teacher confirmed her find with the gemology experts at the local university, only to have it stolen from the teacher's classroom during a lunch break. Police Deputy Collins claims they are looking for any leads to the stolen diamond, and a reward is currently being offered by the student's mother, Virginia Pierce.

Virginia Pierce? That meant Jenn had discovered one of the rare Ohio diamonds. Then Jenn had her diamond stolen.

Tandy lifted a hand to her mouth as if holding herself back from making any more accusations until it made more sense. Because this really didn't make any sense at all.

Just because Jenn once found a diamond and had it stolen didn't mean she had anything to do with the current heist. And even if she did, how would that lead to killing her own mother? Had Virginia found out and tried to stop her? If so, Jenn would have known exactly how to kill her.

A warning siren rang in her head. Virginia had changed

her will to give everything in her antique shop to the historic society. If the stolen diamonds were somehow in her shop, the historic society would get them back.

Had Virginia really thought her own daughter might kill her over the diamonds? If Jenn was that dangerous, then there would have to be some kind of past history of her being a criminal.

"Marissa," Tandy called. Either the other woman would talk her out of this crazy idea, or she'd confirm it.

Marissa already looked skeptical as she entered the room. "Tandy, if this is about Connor, then—"

Connor? The beauty queen had a one-track mind. "It's not." Tandy pointed to the computer. "What do you know about Jenn Pierce?"

Chapter Nineteen

MARISSA SQUINTED IN CONFUSION AT THE computer screen. Was Tandy trying to act as if she wasn't interested in Connor? Or perhaps about to make another ridiculous claim in an attempt to direct guilt somewhere else? Because seriously. "Now you think the victim's own daughter killed her?"

Tandy looked up, wide green eyes full of confusion. "I don't know, but it looks like she has a history with diamonds. Do you know the rest of her history?"

The article on the screen claimed Jenn once had a diamond stolen from her. Coincidence? The last story Tandy looked up about the local diamond heist suggested a woman had committed the crime.

Marissa scrolled through her memory. "Jenn was a few years behind me in school, and she left for college as soon as she graduated. Since then, I think she's worked as an English teacher overseas."

Tandy stiffened. "Where?"

How was Marissa supposed to remember? Just because she knew everybody in town... "Beijing." The name of the city popped out. "I remember last year Billie was afraid Jenn wouldn't get much of a Christmas celebration over there, so she sent a package with apple cider and ornaments. I guess Christmas ball ornaments originated from a glassmaker trying to imitate the apples Germans originally used to decorate their trees. You know how Billie loves apples."

"Okay..." Tandy's breath whooshed out as she replaced her fingers over the keyboard. She probably wasn't talking about the apple/ornament connection. Nope. She typed "Beijing jewel heists." A list of articles popped up. Most of them related to some sort of Pink Panther gang of British men.

Marissa twisted her lips to one side at the thought of Jenn in such a gang. Jenn wasn't British, and she wasn't a man. She didn't even drink tea like most Brits, so that couldn't be it.

Skeptically, she pointed to another article outlining the seven biggest heists in Beijing history. "Try this one."

Tandy positioned the arrow icon and clicked. The image flashed to a list of stolen items and the stories behind them. Bit coins? That required hacking skills. Yuan from 1,400 convenience store ATMS? That would take a syndicate of criminals. A vase?

Marissa held her hand to her heart. That vase was the very vase she'd almost knocked over in Virginia's shop. A vase worth over ninety-thousand dollars according to the article. Randon had recognized it but must not have realized it was stolen.

Tandy froze, as well. "This is huge," she whispered.

"What if..." Marissa's eyes bulged at the implication. "What if Jenn became a thief after she had her diamond taken from her? Virginia could have fenced stolen items for her from all over the world."

Tandy sat back. "But she wouldn't be able to fence the diamonds from her very own town."

"You think she told Jenn not to steal them, but Jenn couldn't resist since this is where it all started for her? Perhaps even *why* it started?" The idea was crazier than dressing up a dog like Santa Claus and going for a run. She was simply throwing out ideas. But somehow, this idea made more sense than Lukey or even Lavella being a killer. She scrunched her nose because, man, she'd really wanted Lavella to be the bad guy.

Tandy twisted around. "You think the diamonds are in the shop right now? Virginia could have hidden them so she wouldn't get caught."

Marissa shrugged. That seemed way too easy after all they'd been through. "Can it be that simple? It's not like Virginia could have hidden the diamonds forever."

Tandy ran her fingers through her hair and blew out a breath. "I don't know, but we have to tell the police."

Marissa cringed because that was a big problem. "I'm not sure I believe us, so I know Lukey definitely won't."

Tandy bit her lip and stared out the window at the falling snow. She didn't only want to be proven innocent of the crime in a court of law—she wanted the real criminal locked behind bars. Could it be that all this time Griffin had been investigating her, the woman he loved had been trying to kill them? Would love blind him to that fact? Would he come after Tandy even harder if she made an accusation against Jenn? Was that why Jenn had dated him in the first place?

At least Tandy had Greg on her side. She grabbed her phone and dialed his number. Last time she'd called him, she'd been on a rotary phone with a long cord for twisting around her finger as she listened to it ring on the other end. She wished she had something to nervously fidget with now.

Marissa stood in front of her, hands folded in a pose that would make Tandy think she was praying if not for her wide eyes.

The receiver clicked, and a tinny recording of Greg's

voice played through the earpiece. "You've reached Greg St. James, defense attorney at the Law Office of St. James and Sons. Please leave a message." A bell chimed.

"Uh, Greg, this is Tandy." Should she call him something more formal like Gregory or Attorney St. James? No, that would be weird. "When you get this…"

Marissa's head fell backward. "He's at the Santa run, collecting toys at the finish line for the children's home."

Tandy paused. It bugged her that Marissa knew more about her old friend than she did. But, on the other hand, now they could find him easily.

"I need to talk to you, so Marissa and I are going to head your way. We think we know who killed Virginia." She clicked to end the conversation. Even if her beginning had been weak, the ending would definitely have piqued his interest.

Marissa held up the puppy Santa costume. "It's a good thing I bought this now, huh?"

Cocoa ran for cover underneath the desk.

"No." Tandy squatted and tapped her fingernails on the stone tile floor. "Come here, Cocoa. I won't let the crazy lady dress you in any more clothes."

"But he was so—"

Tandy hushed Marissa with a look. "We're not running in the race, Marissa. We're only looking for Greg."

Cocoa scurried toward her, keeping low to the ground. Tandy scooped his fuzzy little body against her shoulder and stood.

Marissa struck her pursed-lip pose again. She probably got it from the cover of a fashion magazine and perfected it in the mirror. "It'll be good to have Greg on your side, though he's not the one who can arrest Jenn. We need to stop at the police department and talk to Officer Woodward."

Tandy groaned. "I just came from there, and I really don't want to go back. Especially not wearing the same dress from my mugshot."

Marissa's eyes lit up. She grabbed Tandy's hand and pulled her past the desk into her bedroom. "I have a Mrs. Claus—"

"No." Tandy's eyes snapped shut. This was going from bad to worse.

"How about a polar bear onesie?"

Tandy opened her eyes to scowl, but she couldn't keep from chuckling at the image of herself showing up at the police department dressed like an Arctic animal. "Are you kidding me right now?"

"Yes." Marissa giggled then disappeared into her cavernous closet. "But you have to wear something festive." She reappeared with a black baseball cap that read Santa Claus across the front in white stitching. "Here. I won this in a white elephant gift exchange and have been looking for an opportunity to give it away."

Tandy tilted her head. She kind of liked it. Well, she liked that it was black. "Fine."

Once changed into the outfit she'd left at Marissa's the day before, which actually matched the hat, she rode shotgun to the police station. With all the cars lining the streets for the Ho-Ho-Holiday Run, this was probably as close as they could get to the finish line anyway.

Tandy climbed out, carrying Cocoa. His ears perked up at the sight of wave after wave of red and white joggers pouring across the intersection one block over. They were all dressed like Kris Kringle. As small as Grace Springs was, it looked like the whole town had shown up for the event. They probably considered themselves safe since Tandy had been arrested the night before. If they'd known the real killer was still on the loose, they'd more likely be running for their lives.

Marissa joined her on the sidewalk, tossing her hair and almost losing another beanie. Tandy wished she would lose this one. It matched her Fair Isle sweater and made the plain red beanie from the day they met seem appealing. "You'll let me do all the talking?" she asked.

"Gladly." Tandy hadn't met Woodward yet, but if he was anything like Griffin, he wouldn't listen to a word she said. Of course, some of those words had been accusing the deputy of murder...

Marissa paused in front of the doorway. "Do I tell him about the diary?"

Tandy arched an eyebrow. Two days ago Marissa wouldn't even consider it. She'd joined in the investigation to protect her grandma's good name. "You don't have to. Jenn's crime had nothing to do with you."

Marissa looked past her. "Right. Good." She pivoted and marched inside the building, only slipping once in her red Ugg boots with the bows on the back. Ugg was a good name for those boots. "Merry Christmas, Kristin."

Today the blonde receptionist wore a headband with mistletoe attached overhead. What was it with Grace Springs residents and their outrageous headwear?

"Merry Christmas, Marissa." Kristin smiled then frowned at Tandy. Either she'd read her thoughts or wasn't a fan of suspected criminals running loose.

Tandy ducked behind the brim of her hat. Headwear did come in handy occasionally.

"Is Officer Woodward here?"

Tandy peeked up to find Kristin watching her through narrowed eyes. No more friendly interaction like they'd had on her first visit. "Woodward is directing traffic downtown since Main Street is closed for the fun run. Griffin is running, but he's on call. I can get him to come straight to the station if you need anything."

Tandy turned to read Marissa's expression. If it were up to her, they'd track Woodward down rather than drag Griffin back here. He wasn't likely to listen to them in the first place, but if they kept him from winning the race against Connor this year, he'd be even more upset.

"Huh-uh." Marissa tucked her chin as if wanting to avoid the situation. "I'm not getting in the middle of the race between him and Connor again."

They saw eye to eye on the situation. Maybe her experience with competing in pageants made her more competitive than the average person.

"We'll find Woodward." Marissa marched toward the door.

Tandy followed outside then realized they weren't headed toward the Jeep but toward Main Street. She was all for tracking down the police, but she wasn't ready to dive into a sea of Santas. Not only was she still recovering from broken ribs, but it had been years since she'd run. She preferred to take a spinning class where the instructor gave out shots of espresso. "Can't we drive?"

Marissa wrinkled her nose. "We could drive down a couple of blocks, but then we'd have to park and cross to get to the town square, and there's no guarantee we'll even find parking. Walking will be faster."

Tandy grimaced but lowered Cocoa to the ground and wrapped a new red leash around her wrist. Presumably purchased with the Santa Paws costume. The little dog bounded forward. "All right."

But not all was right. Once they reached Main, the tide of jolly bodies carried her along until her feet had to pick up speed, her injured ribs ached, and her cheeks burned with exertion. Maybe that's why Santa's cheeks were always so rosy. He ran 5Ks to work off all those extra milk and cookie calories. If only someone hadn't shoveled the roads and used a bunch of rock salt ice melt, then Marissa would have slipped by now and Tandy wouldn't be racing to keep up.

A Santa with holes in his earlobes jogged by. "Nice costume." The compliment rang with Randon's trademark sarcasm.

"Thanks, Hipster Claus."

A Mrs. Claus in a short skirt and candy cane tights followed. "It'll match the black and white stripes you'll be wearing soon."

"Prisoners wear orange now," Tandy called after Lavella. Though she should have said something about how she wasn't going to be going to prison. Because it kind of sounded like she was burning herself.

"Don't let her get to you." Marissa gave advice she was still learning to take.

Tandy watched Miss Ohio disappear into the crowd. "I'm more offended by her dress than anything else. That's not the same costume you offered me to wear, is it?"

"You could have been twins." Marissa answered without so much as sounding a little out of breath. For being uncoordinated, she certainly had good stamina, while Tandy's lungs began to wheeze.

Even Billie caught up with them, though Tandy didn't recognize her at first in the curly white wig. "Tandy, I heard Greg St. James is representing you. You'll be in good hands."

Billie must not really think her guilty. Either that or Billie offered more grace than anyone she'd ever met. "I know. Greg and I go way back."

"Really?" A GQ Santa, also known as Joseph Cross, jogged with Billie around a storm grate then gazed at Tandy.

"Are you the little girl who used to spend every summer here with him?"

"How'd you know that?" Had Tandy met Cross before in her past life? It had been a while, but Tandy couldn't imagine forgetting someone as wealthy and commanding as Cross.

Cross stroked his beard. "He told me about you when he bought shares in my cruise ships. He said he'd loved the river ever since building a rope swing from his tree house with a friend who visited in the summers."

Tandy's feet slowed. She maneuvered toward the side of the street and onto the sidewalk in front of the old antique shop to hold her side and regroup. This was a lot to take in.

Billie waved. "See you at the finish line."

Tandy waved. Greg would be at the finish line. Could there be more of a future together than that?

What if Jenn Pierce wasn't guilty? What if Tandy still went to prison? Then she'd have no future.

Marissa joined her and continued to jog in place, knees high. "Did you need a break, Tandy?"

Tandy's heartbeat raced but not from physical exercise anymore. She looked down at Cocoa. He gazed up, tiny tongue hanging out, adoration in his dark, trusting eyes. "I'm picking Cocoa up, so he doesn't get trampled." She squatted down. "And actually, I'm worried about—"

Marissa gasped. "Jenn Pierce."

Tandy stood. "Yes, I'm worried about Jenn Pierce."

"No." Marissa pointed through the window of the shop they'd both wanted to buy. "Jenn Pierce is in there."

Chapter Twenty

MARISSA PULLED TANDY TO THE SIDE of the window and pressed her body against the cold, rough bricks to stay out of eyesight. "What is Jenn doing in there?"

Tandy scooted slightly away. Probably so they didn't squish Cocoa between them. "She has to be looking for the diamonds."

If their theory was correct this time, Jenn was going to tear the place apart until she found her stolen gems. She might even take the other things she'd stolen that hadn't been sold yet. Things like the vase. Then what? Would she disappear? She'd have no reason to come back to Grace Springs if her mom was gone. Plus, if she fenced the stolen items, she might not need to work anymore. She could live off the money her thievery brought in.

"How did she get in there?" Marissa spoke the question out loud. When Grandmother passed, the bank had seized her house immediately. If Virginia had willed everything to the museum, then Jenn was trespassing on their property.

"She probably still has a key, though if we're right about her stealing the diamonds, then she *is* an experienced thief." Tandy leaned forward to peek toward the doorway. "It doesn't look like she broke in. At least not through the front entrance."

Marissa's pulse thrummed. "Why now? Why didn't she search for the diamonds earlier? Or at night?"

Tandy looked past her toward all the jogging Santas. "Maybe because she's had to play the grieving daughter.

Maybe because the police have finally cleared the place from being a crime scene. Maybe because now that I've been arrested, she thinks she's free."

Lots of possibilities. Marissa followed her gaze to find a group of runners casting them curious glances as they passed. The two of them probably looked pretty goofy playing Cloak and Dagger in the middle of broad daylight at a public event. Though nobody stopped to talk to them because they had their own goals. The same as Griffin's goal. "Or she knows Griffin is occupied."

Tandy clicked her tongue. "That's it. She doesn't think anyone is going to catch her because the police are busy."

Marissa jerked away from the wall. "We have to go get Griffin right now."

Tandy pulled her back. "You think I can catch up with him? He's like Rudolph, guiding all these Santas on their Christmas run. I can't even keep up with Billie."

Marissa's chest rose and fell with shallow breaths. She was ready to dash away, dash away, dash away all. "You wait here, and—"

"And what? Let you know when Jenn escapes?"

Marissa frowned in confusion. "What do you want to do?"

"You said it yourself." Tandy pulled out her cell phone. Hopefully to call Lukey. "She's here right now because she doesn't think she'll get caught. So we catch her."

How? It wasn't like they could grab a big red sack from one of the Santas trotting by and use it to stuff Jenn inside. Even if they could, then what? Stick a bow on her head? Gift her to the police department? "Tandy, no. If she killed her mom, then she's a killer who may have tried to kill us." Chills formed on her skin, and not only because they'd quit jogging. "During the explosion on the steamboat, you weren't the only one in the bathroom. Though nobody even questioned her."

"That's right." Tandy clenched her jaw. "Not to mention the fact that she was dating the deputy, which meant she would have also known about the kids playing pranks on the road where we ran into the rockslide. She would have known the police wouldn't suspect attempted homicide."

True. But how would Jenn have known they were investigating the murder at that time? Marissa shook her head. "The only people we questioned at the point were Billie and then Mr. Cross at the retirement center, and she wasn't there either of those times."

"Yes, she was." Tandy paused, her gaze flicking to meet Marissa's. "Remember Cross said Jenn's aunt was crying about Virginia's death? Someone must have gone to the retirement center to tell her aunt. And who else would have done that besides Jenn?"

Marissa covered her mouth at the image of Jenn listening in to their conversation. She lowered her fingers to whisper over the thumping of her heart. "Then she also knew about Grandmother's diary."

Tandy's eyes widened. "She must have stolen it since she was at the police station when I discovered it was missing."

The pieces of their puzzle fit together to form a crime scene. Marissa gripped Tandy's arm. She couldn't let her new friend confront the killer. "It's not wise to go in there."

Tandy pushed away from the wall. "Then we'll do what the wise men did when warned about King Herod's murderous intent." She headed around the corner away from the front door. "We'll use a different route."

Marissa pulled out her own phone. The wise man would have had it a lot easier if they'd simply had the use of a little technology. With a little help from Google Maps and Wikipedia, they never would have had to deal with Herod in the first place. "I'm calling Lukey right now."

"Great." Tandy reached the alleyway and poked her head out. "Tell him I'm involved, and you'll get him here with jingle bells on."

Marissa wanted to argue, but Tandy was probably right. That would be why she was so desperate to prove Jenn guilty. It was like she and Marissa had traded places. At first Marissa had been desperate to prove Lavella guilty to keep Grandmother's name out of the news, but now that she'd started to feel a little more confident with who she was, perhaps due to her friendship with Tandy, Tandy had become the desperate one. Of course, she'd wrongly spent a night in jail, so she might have a better reason for her desperation.

Tandy disappeared around the corner. Marissa gasped and scrambled forward. She peeked around in time to see Tandy pull the back door open silently.

Marissa fumbled for her phone and swiped a trembling finger over the screen. What if she didn't call fast enough? What if Jenn led Tandy up to the roof and pushed her off, claiming suicide? What if she cut the cord on the beautiful chandelier so it would crash down on Tandy like they did in the movies? Or worse, what if she got away with the diamonds before Lukey arrived, and Tandy was arrested for trespassing and had to go to jail again?

Marissa held the phone to her mouth and whispered into the device, "Call Lukey."

"Calling Lukey," the automated voice on her phone responded without concern for alerting a killer that she was being reported to law enforcement.

Marissa covered the speaker with her hand and glued her eyes at the back door in case the phone had been overheard and Tandy had to run out before getting crushed by a light fixture. The alley remained eerily calm.

There was plenty of noise behind Marissa though, with most of the out-of-shape Santas huffing and puffing their way toward the finish line. And what was that other sound? The clomping. It couldn't really be reindeer hooves…

She held the phone to her ear, listening to it ring while twisting around to see what was going on. She found Connor's parents' horse drawn carriage bringing up the rear of the run like it always did. Mr. Thomas had the best Santa costume with ruby colored velvet and actual white fur. His belly was authentic too, probably because he frequently dipped into the candy stash he now tossed to children.

Abigail Thomas waved her direction. "Marissa, do you want a ride?"

Oh no. Could Jenn hear her from inside? Marissa shook her head wildly, willing Lukey to pick up.

"Okay, dear. I just thought seeing you would cheer Connor. He messaged me that he lost the race."

Ranger must have needed a potty stop. She would take joy from that fact later when she wasn't worried about being the cause of Tandy getting caught. She pointed to the phone at her ear to indicate she was busy.

Abigail nodded and returned to waving like she was in a parade as the carriage passed.

Marissa sighed in relief. Now if Lukey would only—

"This is Deputy Griffin." Lukey barely got his name out between his heavy breathing. Cheering roared from the background. And Mayor Kensington could be heard over some kind of loudspeaker.

Marissa almost wished he hadn't won his first race, so she wasn't pulling him away from his moment of glory. Hopefully the Ho-Ho-Holiday Trophy would make him feel better when he realized the woman he loved was only using him for his badge. "Lukey, I—"

"What's that? I can't hear you."

Marissa gritted her teeth in frustration. "Lukey, it's Marissa."

"Hi. Or should I say 'ho-ho-ho' now that I'm the champion Santa?"

"Neither, listen…"

More heavy breathing and commotion. "Are you calling to congratulate me on beating your ex? He's going to claim that I only won because Ranger saw a squirrel right before the finish line, but that's a pathetic excuse." Laughter.

"Lukey, this isn't funny."

"It is to me. Maybe now you'll stop calling me Lukey."

Marissa squeezed her fingers around the phone as if it would get his attention. She'd love to scream, but that would draw other unwanted attention. "Detective Griffin," she hissed. "I am at Virginia's shop where Jenn Pierce is currently looking for the diamonds she stole from the museum. She also killed her mother to get them back, and if you don't—"

"Did you say you're with Jenn? Does she know I won the race?"

If only he had ears as large as an elf then he could hear her over his finish line celebration. "Shush and read the text I'm going to send you."

She jabbed at her phone to end the call and seriously considered kicking the wall a couple of times. The kid may have beaten Connor in a race, but he still couldn't beat Marissa in a game of Where in the world is Carmen Sandiego. She scrunched up her face at her phone while angrily typing a text about the woman of his dreams being a homicidal maniac. Then, because she was so furious, she texted Connor too. It would be interesting to see which man was faster when it really mattered.

Now she had to wait. Or did she? She had enough pent up energy to beat Jenn in a foot race. Might as well follow Tandy in to make sure she was still alive.

Tandy held her breath against the stabbing sensation in her side and crawled through the jumble of old furniture and knickknacks, her knees creaking like the rocking horse she'd received for Christmas in preschool. Back before Santa accused her of murder and put her in a jail cell.

Well, she was about to catch Santa's girlfriend red-handed. And not just because the woman knew how to knit festive mittens. No, she wore black gloves as she systematically made her way through the merchandise, running her hands along everything from the backs of mirrors to inside clocks.

Tandy had thought *she* had mommy issues, but her mom had never taken anything from her more than their dog when her parents divorced. Not that Gemma hadn't been priceless, but Tandy wouldn't have killed anyone over her.

She patted Cocoa on the head. He was being good, staying with her and staying quiet. She really should have left him with Marissa. Then it would have been a little easier to get past the vintage sewing machine for a better angle to film Jenn's illegal endeavor.

Sinking down to her belly on the dusty floorboards behind a couple of large paintings tilted against the wall, Tandy opened up her phone's camera app and slid the icon to record. She twisted her wrist to get a better view.

Jenn filled Tandy's screen, ripping open bags that had

been zip tied to cover furniture and delicate items in preparation for delivery. She'd run her hand over each item then wrap them again in a new bag as if it had never been touched.

A noise clattered from the rear of the store. The close-up of Jenn's face showed her freezing and her eyes darting toward the back door.

Tandy bit her lip to keep from moaning. Marissa must have followed her in. Tandy thought she'd been calling the police. With her clumsiness, she should have known better.

Jenn lowered the dishes and scanned the empty street. Where were a thousand Santas when you needed them?

Fur lined boots tromped Tandy's way.

Silently, Tandy edged backward. Cocoa barred his teeth, but she clamped his muzzle shut in time.

The boots continued past. Marissa might be able to hide, but Jenn knew she was there. What would Jenn do when she found her?

Jenn paused at the jewelry cabinet. She pulled a glass door open and reached inside. Had she found the diamonds? How brilliant would that have been if Virginia had hidden them in plain sight?

Jenn pulled out a golden dagger.

Tandy slapped a hand over her mouth. The woman had killed through coffee and then attempted to cause accidents, but she'd never actually spilled blood with her hands. This took it to a whole new level of evil.

Should Tandy call out to warn Marissa? If it was two against one, they might be able to overpower her. But then again, one of them might get hurt. Or worse.

She gauged the distance between herself and the front door. If she could sneak out, she could run for help. The way Marissa had wanted her to do. Hopefully Marissa could hide until the deputy arrived.

Tandy ignored the throbbing pain underneath her rib belt so she and Cocoa could army-crawl forward again, checking over her shoulder to make sure the coast was clear before scurrying next to an armoire and then behind the gold brocade loveseat with scrollwork legs. She came face to face with two vintage cans of gasoline and a brand new lighter. Dear Santa. Those cans weren't full, were they? She poked one to see how easy it would move. It stayed in place, resistance coming from enough liquid inside to torch the building.

Tingles shot through her limbs as she crouched and pulled Cocoa close, listening for any signs that Jenn was still looking for Marissa. She couldn't leave now in case Jenn decided to set the place on fire with Marissa inside.

"Merry Christmas, Marissa." The low, smooth tone spoke of control as well as irritation.

Tandy closed her eyes. Not the sign she'd been hoping for.

"Merry Christmas, Jenn." Marissa's voice squeaked as she tried to lighten it with a little too much cheer. "I'm sure this holiday has to be hard for you with losing your mom and all, and I thought I'd stop by to see how you're doing."

Tandy arched her eyebrows at Marissa's response. Not a bad cover. And really, the squeaky voice could be related to the awkwardness of a beauty queen who'd lost her crown. Tandy wouldn't have thought anything of it when they'd first met. What mattered is that Jenn bought it and put down her weapon.

"Thanks." The word came out dryer than Dad's holiday turkey. "If you're looking for me, then what exactly were you doing behind the bookshelf?"

Oh no. Tandy made the kind of face that would

accompany a wince were she free to express her emotions aloud.

"You know me." High-pitched giggle. "I knocked a book over and had to pick it up. Here."

Marissa must have at least had a book in her hand. That made her story more believable. Tandy held her breath.

"I see." A soft thud as one of them put down the book. "Well, you're right about this holiday being hard. I thought I'd come here to be around some of Mom's old things, but I really don't want to be alone. Won't you join me for a cup of coffee?"

Tandy's mouth fell open. While both women were lying, Jenn could also be plotting her next murder. Of course, Jenn couldn't cause Marissa's heart to go haywire with extra caffeine, but she could add some other kind of poison. Or a sedative that would make her sleep through the shop being burned to the ground.

Was Jenn trying to scare Marissa or bait her? Tandy waited.

"I...um...I don't drink coffee, though I appreciate the offer."

Tandy's shoulders sagged in relief. She'd never before been so glad someone didn't share her passion.

"Cocoa perhaps?"

Tandy's dog's ears perked up at his name. She rubbed his neck to keep him from going where he thought he was called. Jenn didn't know she and Cocoa were there too, did she?

"Uh, sure. Thanks, Jenn."

Footsteps. Why did Marissa follow Jenn in? Why didn't she make up an excuse to leave? Why wasn't there an old-fashioned Red Ryder BB gun handy?

If only she could see, then she'd be able to get a better idea of whether Jenn was feeling threatened and going to hurt anyone or if she was buying Marissa's act. Maybe Tandy could use her phone. Flipping the camera app to selfie mode, Tandy slid it forward around the arm of the loveseat. She had to tilt it a couple times until it focused on the other women in the room, though it wasn't the image she wanted to see.

Jenn held Marissa's hair in a fist so that her neck was exposed to the tip of the dagger. The gold glinted in the sunlight, sending an almost electric shock to Tandy's heart.

"I know you're in here, Tandy. Come out, or I'll kill her and pin it on you the same way I have everything else."

Chapter Twenty-One

UNSHED TEARS CLOGGED MARISSA'S THROAT UNDERNEATH the cold edge of a knife at her neck. She'd wanted to help Tandy, but she'd messed it all up with her klutziness. Would Tandy come out to save her life? Marissa hadn't earned that kind of friendship yet.

Could she even call what they had a friendship? She'd jumped on Tandy every time she thought the other woman was interested in Connor. She'd made her wear a dress when she didn't want to. Called her dog a varmint the last time they were in this building.

The room remained quiet. Should Marissa warn Tandy not to reveal herself or would that embolden Jenn even more? Or perhaps Tandy wasn't there. Maybe she'd snuck out the front when Jenn had been hunting Marissa. She'd been left to die for her failures.

Those failures continued to play through Marissa's mind. It was no wonder she didn't have many friends. She was selfish and controlling. The more she tried to make up for her mistakes and prove herself, the more selfish she became.

Connor was known for coming to her rescue, and he might even be coming now, but she didn't deserve him either. As for Mr. and Mrs. Thomas, they were the kind of parents she'd always wanted, but she'd pushed them away to try to live up to her own parents' standards. Which was stupid — she didn't even like being around her parents. She liked jolly men who ate too much chocolate with no regrets and kind women who drove impractical cars and prayed a lot.

She also liked Tandy. She liked her honesty. Her tenacity. Her wit. The black ball cap she'd chosen to wear instead of something more festive.

That very ball cap rose from behind the ornate trim of a settee, the words Santa Claus implying Tandy considered Marissa to have made the nice list. Wood creaked.

Jenn yanked Marissa in a quarter turn so they both faced the settee, though it was hard to see Tandy with the way Jenn held her head back. What if Jenn hurt her then went after Tandy? Why would she not? Her friend could at least save herself.

Marissa swallowed the lump. "Tandy, don't."

Tandy stepped forward anyway. Willing to risk her life for Marissa. Despite their differences. Despite Marissa's faults. Despite the fact that if something happened to Marissa, the coffee lover would have no competition for the shop of her dreams.

Jenn readjusted the blade against Marissa's skin so that it practically strangled her. "Stop."

Tandy rubbed her hands down her pant legs but didn't come any closer.

"Here's what's going to happen." Jenn's breath rustled Marissa's bangs. "If you want Marissa to live, you're going to grab one of those zip ties on the counter and bind your wrists together."

Tandy's face dipped toward the counter. She wouldn't really do it, would she? Then she'd be at Jenn's mercy, and there was no guarantee the killer would truly let them live.

Tandy picked up a zip tie in slow motion. Of all the people Marissa knew to do as they were ordered, Tandy wasn't one of them. Then what was she doing?

Tandy's head tilted to one side then back.

Marissa ignored the ache in her neck to get a better view.

What had Tandy's head tilt meant?

There it was again. Like she was pointing with the brim of her hat. Marissa followed the direction with her eyes to find the stolen Chinese vase on a pedestal next to her. So? They already knew Jenn had stolen the vase.

"You figured me out from the vase, huh?" Jenn asked. Uh-oh. She'd noticed Tandy's motion as well. "Mom thought it was these diamonds that were going to get us caught, but she hung onto this vase much longer than she was supposed to. I told her to hide it if Billie ever came over. Who would have thought Randon would be the one to recognize it? Thankfully he didn't realize it was stolen."

Again, Marissa didn't care about the vase. And they'd already pieced the rest of the information together. What they needed was a plan. She glanced toward heaven for a Christmas miracle. All she saw was the beautiful chandelier that she'd imagined would make a good weapon. Was it too late for Tandy to somehow cut the cord holding it up? Probably, but even if it was still possible, how would Marissa ever convey such an idea. She could use her eyes. Bug them out then flick them upward so Tandy would follow the direction of her gaze like she'd followed Tandy's motion toward the vase.

Wait. What if the vase was Tandy's plan? It could make a good weapon too—if Jenn ever loosened her hold. Could Tandy possibly cause some kind of distraction?

Tandy held up the zip tie parallel to the floor like she was about to set her opposite wrist against it. "It wasn't the vase that gave you away, Jenn. It was the article in my old newspaper about you as a child. Nobody around here knew that you once found a rare Ohio diamond and had it stolen. I figured it was too much of a coincidence that the collection of diamonds had been lifted while you were in town."

Jenn snorted. "The gemologist from the university took it, but I couldn't prove it because I was only a kid. I'm not a kid anymore. I grew up and took a job overseas as a cover for scouting with the Pink Panthers so I could learn from them. It was all practice to come back here and regain the diamond that rightfully belonged to me. I should have known Mom cared more about the money than her own daughter."

Marissa wished she didn't know that feeling. It was awful, but it didn't justify Jenn's actions. "You must have felt the same way about her to kill her," she pointed out.

Jenn tightened her hold, the blade stabbing deeper into Marissa's flesh. "Like Tandy accused Luke, I hadn't been trying to kill my mom. I only wanted to send her to the hospital for a while so I could get in the shop while she was gone."

Marissa pressed back closer to Jenn to create space between herself and the blade. It still gagged her to talk, but these might be her last words. "Then turn yourself in. Your mom's death was an accident, and you don't even know where the gems are. Lukey would stand by your side. You could do your time and start over fresh."

If only Jenn would accept the town's grace, everyone would be better off.

Jenn tugged her hair tighter. "I'm going to start fresh, but far away from here. Tandy, lock that zip tie with your teeth."

Tandy lifted the zip tie slowly to her mouth. Marissa's heart sank. Though if Tandy was willing to sacrifice herself for Marissa, then Marissa would do the same. She'd wait for Jenn to relax after Tandy tied herself up, then she'd grab the vase and swing.

Her muscles tensed. She prayed for perfect timing. She scrunched her face in concentration as she waited. Would the moment come? Would she be able to get away, or would she still get stabbed?

Tandy flung the zip tie their direction. "Cocoa, fetch," she yelled.

A brown blur shot from underneath the chair, and leaped into the air, headed straight toward Jenn.

The knife slipped. Jenn loosened her hold on Marissa's hair. She didn't wait another moment, but pivoted like a figure skater, gripped the vase with both hands like a baseball bat, and cracked it against Jenn's skull. She flinched in anticipation of Jenn's retribution, but as shards of centuries old porcelain rained down to the floor, an assortment of clear, shiny stones scattered among the debris.

"My diamonds." Jenn dropped to her knees to retrieve the gems.

The front door burst open. Lukey charged in with a gun, Connor with a dog on a leash. Marissa had never been so happy to see her ex, but Tandy was her true hero.

Tandy sank onto the old-fashioned couch she'd shared with Marissa the first time Deputy Griffin had questioned them. At the time she'd wanted to buy the place to run a coffee shop, now she was simply glad to be alive. And she had Cocoa to thank for that. His stocking would be stuffed extra full this year.

"Come here, boy."

The little fluff ball sprang into her arms, warm tongue scrubbing her cheeks. She laughed. Best watch dog ever. And somehow the best Christmas ever. There was nothing in the world that could improve her day. Except maybe a cup of coffee.

"Hey." Greg stepped in front of her, holding a steaming paper cup.

Correction, there were two things in the world that could make her feel better. A cup of coffee and Greg. Even if he had developed an alarming sense of fashion and was currently dressed in a brown leather jacket and houndstooth driver's cap. She'd thought the suit had been bad, but this? Somehow he'd been included in the Grace Springs ridiculous headwear policy. Of course, she'd been a jailbird when they'd reconnected, so she shouldn't complain.

He held out the coffee cup. "With all the excuses you could have come up with for not running the full 5K, you decided to risk your life to catch a killer and discover stolen diamonds."

Tandy sipped, the warm brew working its magic. "I really hate running." She grinned.

Greg smiled back before sinking down next to her. "I thought I was going to get to be your hero by keeping you from going to jail, but I see that once again I've been shown up by your dog."

Tandy hugged Cocoa closer. "It wasn't only Cocoa. I mean, if Connor had never taught him to fetch, he wouldn't have charged Jenn the way he did. If Marissa hadn't smashed the really expensive vase over Jenn's head, she might have killed one or both of us. And, of course, if you hadn't gotten me out of jail, then I never would have been able to put the pieces together."

"I'm glad I could help." Greg sobered, his blue eyes searching hers. "Now that you're free to go, what are you going to do?"

What *was* she going to do? Did she have to decide right now? It was Christmas. All she wanted was a long winter's nap, and maybe a festive dinner with friends. She looked across the room to find Marissa on the phone the same way she had been after Virginia died. Talking to her mom again perhaps, even though Connor was right in front of her. What was it that made Marissa try so hard to impress the people who didn't really care about her?

Her own phone vibrated in her pocket. Dad? Who else would call on Christmas Eve?

"Excuse me," she said, pulling her phone from her pocket. The caller ID revealed her former boss's name and number.

An ache formed in her temples. Why would he want to talk to her now? Had she unknowingly also sabotaged the paper's Christmas ad revenue? She'd meant them no harm, and it hurt that they'd turned on her the way they did, but for the first time she felt sorry. As much as she didn't want to talk to Shawn, she did owe him an apology.

Tandy swiped the screen to answer then took a deep breath and held the device to her ear. "Merry Christmas, Shawn. Before you say anything, can I ask for your forgiveness? I messed up, and I never owned up to it. You were right in letting me go."

Silence.

Tandy eyed Greg. If Shawn didn't have anything else to say, she'd hang up and apologize to her old friend too. For not looking him up sooner. Had she known he was an attorney, she could have asked him for advice from the beginning and most likely stayed out of jail. Wow, this apology stuff was addicting. Kind of freeing to admit she made mistakes. Humbling. In a good way.

"Uh...Merry Christmas to you too, Tandy. I'm calling about exactly that—about how we let you go." Shawn rabbled on as if she hadn't momentarily made him speechless. "I heard from our crime reporter that you solved the missing diamonds case. Is that true?"

Of course. He wanted her story. Might as well give it to him. If she was truly repentant, she wouldn't hold a grudge. "I had a little help." She smiled at Greg then at Marissa who was still on the phone and looking not so merry. She'd finish this conversation and go check on her friend. "You want the scoop?"

"Actually, Candace will be calling you about that. She's doing a whole Heist for the Holidays angle." His voice lowered. "But I was thinking, if you're this good at investigating, we could make you an investigative reporter. There's a position open."

Her lips parted. "Oh." She'd thought she'd burned bridges with her former boss, but here he was, offering her another chance.

She looked around the antique store she'd once imagined to be her coffee shop. She'd only come to Grace Springs because she'd lost everything in Cincinnati. She'd only dreamed of roasting her own coffee beans as revenge for the way she'd lost her job over them. Kind of like how she'd bought a foreign car to show up her ex.

But now that she wasn't holding grudges, and her old boss was inviting her to return, she had to figure out what her heart truly desired. She had to move forward towards the life she wanted rather than running away from what she didn't want. "Thank you for the offer. I'm going to have to think about it, Shawn."

"Yeah, well don't take too long. I've got to get this position filled." Shawn paused. "You know, I was hesitant about offering you the job, but after you apologized, I feel like we could work together even better than before. Which means there's definitely going to be a raise involved."

Tandy laughed, dropping her head back a little too quickly against the wooden frame of the fancy sofa. Now that she had a real reason for her headache, she had too much joy to focus on the pain. Who would have thought admitting she was wrong would ever get her a raise. "I'll keep that in mind, Shawn. Now go home. Spend the day with your family."

Shawn chuckled. "You do the same, Tandy. Merry Christmas."

Tandy lowered the phone and smiled. That was good advice. But first she'd need to figure out where her home was.

She looked up at Greg in his ridiculous hat. Did her own hat count as ridiculous? Could she fit in with the townsfolks who hadn't seemed to want her there at first? "I don't know what I'm going to do yet," she said. But she had an idea.

Marissa listened to her mom as if in a daze. She was being given the gift she'd dreamed about, but somehow it didn't hold the value she'd thought it would.

"The head judge called me and said that since Lavella admitted to tripping you, you can challenge her crown. Then, as first runner up, you'd be the one to step in." Mom sounded as giddy as a teenager.

Marissa scanned the floor, eyeing the area where the diamonds had spilled out. Those diamonds had been the reason she'd had a knife held to her throat only half an hour ago. Shouldn't Mom be more concerned about the threat on her life than a stupid beauty pageant?

Mom laughed. "You're in shock, aren't you? You don't know what to say."

"Kind of." Marissa lifted her gaze to find Connor talking to the police. Perhaps giving his statement. He'd been there for her through the whole thing even though she'd publicly rejected him. But he'd never really cared about appearances, had he?

"Once you get your voice back, you'll need to call the judges right away and—"

"Mom, it's Christmas."

"Marissa, it's the crown."

"So?"

"So if you're going to compete for Miss USA, then we need to get to work right away."

That opportunity had once meant so much to her. She'd felt like a failure having competed every year and never been crowned the way her mother had been and the way she'd thought her grandmother had. In fact, it had been the desire to make sure everyone else still thought her grandmother had won Miss Ohio that had gotten her into this mess in the first place.

That had almost gotten her killed. That had shown her how her mom was a lot like the criminal who *had* been killed.

Had mom known Grandmother hadn't truly won? Marissa hadn't explained the part about Grandmother yet. How would Mom take it?

For the first time, Marissa really didn't care. "Did you know Dad's mom shouldn't have won Miss Ohio?"

"Marissa," Mom hissed. "Don't speak ill of the dead."

"She said it herself, Mom. In her diary." No response. "Mr. Cross rigged the judging to get Grace Springs on the map, and Grandmother was planning to come out with it." In the end, it was the thing Marissa admired the most about her relative.

"Well." Mom's voice tightened. "There's no reason to

come out with it now."

Marissa pursed her lips. Whether Grandmother's secret was revealed or not, it wouldn't affect who she was. Marissa had nothing to prove anymore.

Originally the idea of a starting a teahouse had been just that. Trying to prove her worth despite losing the Miss Ohio title. But now, if she decided to return to a life of pageantry, she'd have to let that desire go.

She looked around the antique shop again. She still would love to make it a teahouse. She truly loved tea. She loved the warmth of it. The way it brought people together. The healing properties when being nursed back to health. The beauty and joy that came from memories of big hats and flowered wallpaper and tiny sandwiches with cucumbers. The refreshment of a break from all the striving that life so often required.

Or did she only think life required striving because that's what she'd been taught? She was like a teapot, constantly pouring out all her energy to impress others. What if she simply let herself be filled up? What if she overflowed like a punch fountain instead?

"Marissa?" Mom checked to make sure she was still there. Or was she checking to make sure Marissa wouldn't reveal their secrets. "You can call the head judge when you get here for dinner tonight."

Oh yeah. Christmas Eve dinner. Where Mom traditionally served Pigs in a Blanket even though Marissa hated them. Where she worked on a jigsaw puzzle with her father as he discussed his latest academic journal articles and how great he was. Then they gave her some gift to imply she wasn't good enough and needed help. Like a gift certificate for Cool Sculpting. How was that a holiday?

She looked around at the people in the room. Connor,

whose parents loved people despite their flaws. And Greg, who had given up his own holiday celebration to help out an old friend. And Tandy. Marissa's new friend. Who might very well be spending her evening alone.

"You know what, Mom?" She was going to let down her parents on purpose this time. And she'd be fine no matter how they responded. "I'm not going to make it tonight. I have a friend here who saved my life today, and I want to take her to see the living nativity. I think that's what a real beauty queen would do." Thoughts of Billie crossed her mind. The way she served. The way she offered grace. She was the kind of grandmother Marissa had always wanted. "Truly great people know how to make other people feel like they are great."

"Truly great people don't abandon their families." Mom huffed. "But as long as this means you're going to claim your rightful crown as Miss Ohio…"

Marissa looked down and shook her head. Not so much at her mother's blindness but at what had been her own. If she did go on to compete for Miss USA, it would only be so that she could share the lesson she'd learned here today. "I don't know what I'm going to do yet, Mom. But I know that whether I mess up this decision or not, the people who truly love me will still love me."

Chapter Twenty-Two

"I LOVE IT." TANDY STARED IN awe at the show a little town like Grace Springs could put on.

Next to the simple brick church with the arched windows and an actual belfry, nestled a stable with a straw roof. It looked like the people dressed up inside also held a live baby, but she wouldn't know for sure until the line they waited in wound closer. First they had to pass the church choir dressed like angels and swaying back and forth on the stairs as they hummed "O Holy Night," then past a couple of "shepherds" with actual smelly sheep. There were even three magi with camels.

"Where did they find camels?"

One of the magi tilted his royal blue turban at them. Connor?

Marissa nodded in return. A big change from how she'd treated him when Tandy had first arrived. "Connor's family has a farm. Their biggest holiday is Halloween with a pumpkin patch, corn maze, and hay rides, but they also keep camels for the Christmas pageant."

"Hm." Tandy considered the word pageant as she strolled forward.

"What?" Marissa waved goodbye to Connor when they passed.

"Both your family and Connor's family really care about pageants."

They stopped at the railing in front of the stable Connor had probably built, watching the woman dressed as Mary rock a real baby in her arms. The baby reached for her face with his tiny hands. Tandy had thought she'd been humbled earlier that day, but it was nothing compared to how the King of the World had humbled himself enough to come to earth as a vulnerable infant. All to forgive her sins. And she hadn't even wanted to apologize for them.

Marissa smiled softly. "This is the pageant that really matters, isn't it?"

The old Tandy would have loved to agree and rip on the Miss Ohio contest, but the new Tandy knew she wasn't any better. She had also put on a show of perfection in refusing to accept her failures as failures. "Yes. It took me coming to Grace Springs to really admit the fact that I need grace."

Marissa's smile turned pensive. "Isn't it interesting how you didn't think you needed it while I thought I had to earn it?"

Tandy lifted a shoulder. "Just another example of how none of us get it right, I guess."

Marissa twisted her lips. "I also need to offer it to others, as well. I'm not good at doing that."

Tandy glanced over her shoulder at Connor. If Marissa offered him grace, it would change his life. Tonight was going to be a night for him to remember.

Marissa continued forward. "I'm not going to contest Lavella's title. She can be Miss Ohio."

Tandy followed, waiting for Marissa to continue on about how she couldn't be Miss Ohio anyway because she wanted to marry Connor.

Marissa tilted her head. "This is huge for me, Tandy. Aren't you going to say anything? I turned down the Miss Ohio crown."

Tandy opened her mouth. *Gah.* What did she say? Did Marissa really not see how she was offering grace to one person, but completely ignorant to the person who needed it the most? Or had she just not gotten that far yet? "What are you going to do now?" Tandy prompted.

Marissa stood up taller. "I'm going to put a bid in on the antique shop and start my teahouse."

Tandy stopped to face her, the crowd pouring around them toward Grandma's Attic where Billie served refreshments after the event. Had Marissa learned nothing at all? She was still choosing to pursue her own goals without regard to others. Others like Tandy.

Tandy pinched her mouth shut. Even if Marissa hadn't learned anything, she had. She'd been planning to offer a partnership to Marissa, but now she'd let Marissa pursue her dream while Tandy returned to Cincinnati. She had a job waiting, and though it wasn't the job she wanted anymore, she hadn't wanted to come here either. Yet, look what God had given her through it. He knew best, didn't He?

The star twinkled from the top of the tree in the town square as if a sign. Whether Randon ever got to hang it or not, it had somehow ended up right where it was supposed to be. She had to trust that God would do the same in her life.

Marissa scrunched her nose. "What?" She challenged. "You're not going to try to compete against me this time?"

Tandy looked down and narrowed her eyes. It sounded like Marissa wanted her to compete. "No... This is your home. You love it here. The people love you. I couldn't contend with that."

Marissa beamed. "Good. Because I don't want to contend. I want to be partners."

Tandy rocked back on her heels. They'd been thinking the same thing. "We do make a good team. You with your intuition. Me with my logic."

Marissa turned her forward and linked arms. Probably so

she wouldn't slip. "I think so."

Tandy matched Marissa's pace toward Billie's shop, mulling over the idea of starting their own. "We still have what Virginia would have called a caffeine conundrum."

Marissa's dark eyes sparkled. "So that's what we'll name our shop. A Caffeine Conundrum. We can make downstairs more urban for you while the upstairs loft can be Victorian for my tea parties. It already has that beautiful chandelier."

Tandy stopped. "You like that chandelier?"

"No."

Tandy sighed in relief.

"I *love* the chandelier." Marissa tugged her forward into Grandma's Attic.

Tandy followed with a surprisingly happy headshake, unsure if her sudden warmth came from the shop or from her heart. She was going to get to start her coffee shop in the town she'd always loved, and she wasn't going to have to do it alone. The partnership was something she never would have considered before, but that's because she hadn't understood grace before. If they were going to work together, they'd definitely need to offer each other a lot of grace. For example… "The chandelier appears to have come from a creepy old gothic monastery."

Marissa's forehead wrinkled. "It's a priceless antique. Granted, the place will need a little work, but with the two of us, we'll get it done twice as fast."

Which brought up a good point. Together they'd have the money needed to remodel. "We can hire Connor."

Marissa pulled away, her nose in the air. "I'm not ready for that. I still need some space to figure things out. I mean, he's a great guy, I'm just…you know…need more time."

Tandy rolled her eyes. If Marissa took too much time, some other woman would realize how great Connor was, and he'd make the healthy choice for himself and move on.

Marissa headed toward the refreshments table. "You want any apples? On Christmas Eve Billie slices them crosswise so you can see the symbol of a Christmas star in the center. I think there's some tradition in Europe that says the better the star, the better year you'll have."

"Sure." Though Tandy was already excited for what the year had to offer.

Billie stepped out from behind her counter, arms wide for a hug. "Did I hear you say you and Marissa are starting a shop together?"

Tandy embraced the little woman, wondering how they ever could have suspected her of killing Virginia. "Yes. I'll sell the good stuff, and she'll sell her boring beverage."

Billie leaned away, a serious look in her eye. "By good stuff, you mean apple cider, right?"

Tandy laughed. "We'll let you have the monopoly on that one, Billie."

Billie's face relaxed then her eyes widened behind her funky glasses. "You know what? I have something for you too. Joseph just told me I won the decorating contest."

Tandy wasn't sure how that was for her. "Congrats."

Billie placed a hand on her hip. "You know what the prize is, right?"

Tandy sniffed in embarrassment. The decorating contest had been one of the reasons Marissa had suspected the older woman of murder. "Yeah, free remodeling by Connor, right?"

"Right." Billie motioned to the beautiful shop. "I can't use his services, but perhaps if you girls are starting your own place, you might be able to use him."

Tandy blinked. Did that mean what she thought it meant? Billie was gifting them her prize? It wasn't only generous, it was perfect. Because whereas Tandy couldn't convince Marissa to hire Connor, her partner wouldn't be able to turn down his free handiwork. "Oh, Billie. You are more of a saint than St. Nick. That is the best present ever. I'll be right back."

She gave Billie one more hug than ran out to pick up the last-minute Christmas gift.

Where had Tandy gone? Marissa bit into one of the juicy apple slices she'd picked up for her new partner and surveyed the crowd. There was Randon in an ugly suit made out of snowman print, chatting it up with Mayor Kensington. Lukey was there too, now wearing a sheriff's badge in the shape of a Christmas star. He didn't seem too upset about finding out his ex had been using him, but of course he'd also won the Ho-Ho-Holiday run on his way to closing a couple cases. And then there was Mr. Cross wooing Billie. She laughed as if fifty years younger. If so, their age would better match the spikey thing he'd done to his hair and the popped collar on his red and green plaid shirt.

Marissa headed over to join them and ask if they'd seen Tandy. "Hey, you two. You seem to be getting along quite well."

Billie blushed. "Joseph has been asking me out for a while, and with knowing his secret about rigging your grandmother's beauty pageant, I couldn't say yes. But now I can. He's a changed man."

"Oh…" Marissa pursed her lips. So that's why Billie had wanted them to talk to Mr. Cross in the first place. "Are you going to tell anyone else about what happened back then?"

Grandmother had been willing to come clean about the beauty contest, but was he? If so, was Marissa ready to let him?

Mr. Cross nodded. "It may affect my business, but it's the right thing to do. I don't want any more criminals thinking they can come to me to ask for help with their crimes."

Marissa's spine didn't stiffen. Her heart didn't pound. Her face didn't burn. She was somehow okay with revealing the fact that Grandmother had been a fraud much like Lavella. Though Mom might not agree, it didn't make Marissa any less of a person. In fact, she felt more whole.

In accepting that she needed grace, her shame had been wiped away. And though she hadn't yet recovered Grandmother's diary from Jenn, it was okay because she had nothing left to hide.

"Billie, you have a good man." Marissa smiled at the sweet couple, though she still didn't understand how Billie could not only forgive Mr. Cross but choose to trust him again. What if he let her down? What if she got hurt?

Marissa hadn't yet admitted to herself that she was truly thinking about Connor when Tandy appeared outside the front door, hauling him behind her. His gray eyes snagged on hers and her breath whooshed out. How could he even make a royal blue turban look good?

"Hi," she said, remembering she'd asked that very thing about how he'd made his Joseph costume look good the year before.

"Hi." Connor looked around in confusion as to why he was there rather than still at the living nativity.

"Billie?" Tandy ignored them both and grinned ridiculously at their hostess. "Do you want to tell these guys what you told me?"

Marissa eyed Connor. He shrugged. They seemed to be

in this together. And for some reason that made her heartrate thrum.

Billie beamed. "I won the holiday decorating contest."

"Congratulations." Truly winning an award had to be so much better than rigging the competition.

"Congrats, Billie," Connor added.

"Thanks." Billie peeked at Tandy. "Though I don't have any need for Connor's handiwork."

Marissa met Connor's gaze again. She loved his handiwork. Her extra bedroom turned into a closet. Her built-in bookshelves. Her gorgeous kitchen. "Maybe not here, but what about remodeling your house? He does good work."

"Nope." Billie's face broke into a grin. "Though I'm glad you like his work because I've decided to pass on my prize to you for your new shop."

Marissa set her last apple slice on a napkin. Tandy knew she didn't want this. But Billie didn't. "Billie." She shook her head. Shook it again. "I don't think Connor would—"

"Wait, Marissa." Billie stopped her.

What? Were they ganging up on her?

Billie pointed. "Before you say anything else, Connor needs to kiss Tandy. They're under the mistletoe."

A numbness started in Marissa's soles and worked its way up her body. She turned slowly to face the pair in the doorway. The very spot she'd stood with Connor twice in the past couple days. The very place she'd refused to honor tradition. Would Tandy turn him down too?

Tandy formed an O with her lips but rather than turn to face Connor, she slid her eyes sideways to look at him.

Marissa bulged her own eyes in warning. Was it to protect Tandy or to protect herself? She wasn't sure, but it didn't matter because Tandy missed it.

Connor shrugged. "I haven't had much luck with

mistletoe lately, but I'll give it one more try." He stepped to Tandy's side. "Will *you* let me kiss you, Tandy?"

Marissa's guts churned. Did Connor want to kiss Tandy? Troy the firefighter had thought he was honestly interested in her.

"All right." Tandy turned and smiled up at him.

No, no, no. This wasn't how Christmas Eve was supposed to end. If only she'd gone to her parents' house. Then she could be miserably putting together a puzzle and wouldn't have to watch this.

Connor moved closer. He tipped from his hips. Marissa imagined it was her he was tipping over. He would smell like a woodshop.

She couldn't handle it anymore. She lunged forward, grabbed Tandy's arm, and yanked her away. But that left Marissa under the mistletoe.

Tandy staggered sideways before straightening. She didn't look upset though. Her grin grew. She'd planned this all along, hadn't she?

Now what?

Connor crossed his arms, as if waiting for Marissa to answer that very question. Except she didn't have an answer.

His jaw hardened. His eyes darkened. His head tilted. "You won't let me kiss you, but I can't kiss anyone else either?"

"Uh..." What were her options here?

One, she could pretend she'd accidentally pushed Tandy out of the way when tripping. That wouldn't be too unbelievable.

Two, she could admit that she didn't want Connor to kiss anybody else. Ever. Though that would require letting him kiss her.

Her toes curled, and she realized she was focusing on his

lips. She blinked and looked back up. "You can kiss me if you want to." Whoa. Had she said that out loud?

Yes. She had. And they were the most delicious words ever.

He unfolded his arms.

Her breath hitched. He was going to reach for her. He was going to wrap her in a warm embrace and never let go and...

His hand rested on a bookshelf beside her head. It was like he was holding himself back.

She rocked, off balance by false expectations. But why were they false? They were standing under mistletoe.

He remained steady. "You'll let me kiss you, but you don't trust me to remodel your shop?"

Now *this* was blackmail. He was so going on Santa's naughty list.

Tandy cleared her throat. Why was she still there? "Who else would you hire, Marissa?" she asked.

Tandy had a point. If there was anybody in town Marissa trusted to do good work, it was Connor. Even if his work was the reason they'd stopped kissing in the first place. "Fine. I accept. You can remodel our shop."

She'd kiss him now and figure out their future later.

One corner of his lips curved in that adorable half smile. He leaned in.

She started to melt, like a candle from his heat. From the way he was going to softly brush his mouth over hers then...

He stopped. Inches away.

He gazed into her eyes, but not with adoration. With challenge. "So you trust me to do your renovations, but you don't trust me enough to go out with me."

Seriously? He was going to make her decide their future now? In front of an audience? Because everybody had turned to watch.

She wrinkled her nose. Probably not the most attractive expression she could make, but this was getting ridiculous. She should have let him kiss Tandy.

Tandy giggled. Did she have a crush on Connor? Marissa had plenty of reasons to suspect so. It would be cruel to both him and Tandy if she led Connor on without plans of dating him.

"Yes, I will go on a date with you." There. She was a new person. The kind that would give new meaning to the title Miss Grace Springs.

Connor gave her his full smile.

Satisfaction warmed like a cup of Chai. She linked her fingers behind her back to keep from reaching for him. "You can kiss me now."

He pushed away from the bookcase. Reached for the doorknob. "Oh no, Marissa. You're not getting me back that easily."

Her jaw dropped.

He shoved the door forward and winked over his shoulder. "I'll pick you up on New Year's Eve. Wear your sequin dress."

He stepped through the exit, leaving nothing behind but a chilly swirl of air. Did she just get snubbed? With everyone watching?

She lifted her chin and spun on her heel to face them. "He'll kiss me on New Year's," she claimed. Her toes curled again.

Tandy lifted her eyebrows. "You have a sequin dress?"

Marissa strolled past to return to her apple slice. "Who doesn't?"

Tandy followed. "Normal people."

Tandy wasn't being snooty because she really did like

Connor, was she? The two women had barely gotten past their caffeine conundrum. They didn't need something new to separate them. Marissa cringed and looked over her shoulder. "You didn't really want to kiss Connor, did you?"

Tandy's small smile eased the tension. "Not as much as you did."

Billie linked herself to Mr. Cross with a hand inside his elbow. "I think there's someone else Tandy wants to kiss."

Marissa lifted her eyes to Tandy, whose cheeks dimpled and eyes sparkled. The sure sign of a crush. Who could Tandy possibly have met in the little time she'd been in town? Marissa had been so busy worrying about Tandy liking Connor that she'd completely missed the blossoming of love. She scrunched her nose. "Who else is there? Randon? Lukey? Jumpsuit George?"

Tandy's face lit up with a mixture of delight and disbelief. "Jumpsuit George? Who in the world is Jumpsuit George?"

"He was our tow truck driver. I guess you didn't meet him." Marissa waved a hand. "So who is this secret boyfriend of yours?"

"You're a horrible detective." Tandy laughed. "How did you ever solve a mystery?"

Marissa smiled and strolled away from the mistletoe to join the group at the counter where Billie poured another round of drinks. "I had a little help with my sleuthing."

"That's the important thing." Tandy picked up the fancy tea cup in front of her and nodded for Marissa to do the same. "We're going to continue to help each other out because we're partners now."

Marissa clinked her cup against Tandy's. "I'll drink to that." She sipped the tangy cider and wrinkled her nose. Too sweet. Too sticky.

Tandy sipped then waited for Billie to turn away before sticking out her tongue in revulsion.

This was what it was like to agree on something. They'd start here and let everything else be an adventure. Though neither of their cups was filled with their favorite brew, they were both filled with good cheer.

AUTHOR NOTE

Dear Reader,

As a fellow reader who grew up on Nancy Drew, I'm excited to share my very first cozy mystery with you. In the past I've written quirky romance and suspense, but now I get to mix my puns with peril, my jokes with jeopardy, and my anecdotes with danger. What could be more fun?

The idea for these mysteries actually came from my editor, Miralee Ferrell, who enjoyed my crazy coffee shop owners in *Finding Love in Big Sky* so much she suggested I give them their own series. I tried, but being that they are thirty years older than me, I didn't feel I could do them justice. Thus I created some younger characters who struggle in areas I can relate to, starting with learning to work together and offering each other grace.

Some of the events in the book were taken from my own life, as well. The part about kids throwing snowballs at cars? That comes from my husband's mischievous childhood. The rides in the back of a police car and in the fireman's bucket are experiences I've personally had through a local safety class—where, thankfully, I learned enough about safety to NOT fall out of the bucket. As for the riverboat setting, I got stuck when writing that chapter and asked my husband if we could immediately drive to the Columbia Gorge to take a cruise. He's more realistic than I am, so my only knowledge of riverboats came through YouTube. The internet is such a handy tool for writers, and it's also where I found the true story that inspired the origin of our sneaky diamond thief.

If you share my infatuation with heist stories, watch for

my next novel *A Cuppa Trouble*. This one incorporates real life events involving car thieves. Of course, all car chase scenes will have to be done carefully so as not to spill tea or coffee.

Now I'd love to hear what you have to say. You can write me from my website or sign up for my newsletter at: www.angelaruthstrong.com.

If you want to have input in future books, join us on my Facebook fan page:

www.facebook.com/groups/1557213161269220/ where I frequently ask for ideas and offer giveaways, follow me on Book Bub to get info on my upcoming releases and sales at https://www.bookbub.com/authors/angela-ruth-strong, and/or if you enjoy my books you can help me by reviewing them at Amazon:

www.amazon.com/Angela-Ruth-Strong/e/B00B8BSHLE.

In the same way Tandy and Marissa need each other, I need you.

Keeping CafFUNated
Angela Ruth Strong

Now — A Sneak Peek at Book Two
A Cuppa Trouble

Chapter One

"I'M TURNING ON THE HEAT, AND I don't mean on the espresso machine." Tandy rubbed her hands together while standing behind the brick counter tucked underneath the loft that would soon hold Marissa's foo-foo tea parties.

Marissa flipped the sign in the bay window from closed to open on the first day at their new shop, A Caffeine Conundrum. "You may get the early crowd with all the Type A personalities to buy your coffee, but this afternoon, the dignified tea drinkers will come in to try my crumpets."

Tandy arched her eyebrows. She hadn't realized she was going into business with an elderly British woman. "You made crumpets? No wonder we don't have any customers yet."

Marissa wrinkled her nose at Tandy before staring out at the falling snow. "It's this weather. Beautiful but dangerous."

Marissa might as well have been describing herself. Her business partner had already spilled water and slipped in it that morning. Tandy refrained from making any jokes because the large wet spot on Marissa's rear pretty much said it all.

"Someone's coming." Marissa turned and dashed straight into a chair. Thankfully she caught herself against a table and was able to join Tandy at the counter without injury.

Tandy bit her lip to keep from laughing as she joined Marissa in peering outside to discern whether their first customer would be a coffee or tea drinker. "Oh..." She pointed toward the tubby man turning the corner. "He's wearing coveralls. He's mine."

Marissa tossed her long blonde waves over a shoulder. "You underestimate my skills as a salesman."

Tandy rolled her eyes. Would the men of Grace Springs really start drinking tea simply because the hostess was gorgeous? She'd like to think more highly of men than that.

The door swung open with a gust of icy air, and the man in question stomped his feet on the mat.

"Jumpsuit George." Marissa greeted him with the energy of all the green tea in the world. "You're our first customer."

The man took off his gloves and looked around at the wood floors, white walls, brick accents, exposed beams, and metal table tops. "The place looks nice. I expected you to make it more girly, Marissa, but I'm glad you didn't. Then it would be awkward for me to stop in for my morning cup of joe."

Tandy smacked her palm on the counter in triumph. "Large black coffee?"

"Yes, ma'am."

Marissa narrowed her eyes at Tandy before beaming up at their first customer. "The ground floor has more of an urban feel to it. Upstairs will be decorated with chandeliers and roses for those who appreciate classic taste. It'll open next week on Valentine's Day."

Tandy would avoid going upstairs at all costs. She

cringed and grabbed a mug. "For here or to go?"

"I need it to go." The man cleared his throat and faced Tandy, his hazel eyes widening in what she assumed to be relief that she'd gotten him out of talking about roses and Valentine's.

Tandy returned the smooth white mug to its tray in favor of the paper cups they'd had designed with their company logo of a coffee bean next to a tea bag. "Headed to work?"

"Yep." The man shook his head. "This weather may be bad for your business, but it keeps me hopping. I already pulled a car out of the snow this morning, and I'm in the middle of towing it to the body shop. I can't believe anybody would try to drive a vintage Corvette in these conditions."

Marissa laughed. "Randon Evans, right?"

Warm steam condensed on Tandy's hand as she poured her favorite brew. From what she remembered of the local hipster's bragging, he'd purchased a vehicle based on it being rated best-in-snow. "I thought he drove a Subaru."

The tow truck driver shrugged. "He does, but it appears he doesn't know what to do with all the money he's making from his phone app software so he started collecting cars. He had me check out this Corvette before he purchased it. Nice ride. A shame he left it stranded on the side of the road when it got stuck."

A timer rang in the kitchen behind them, and Marissa pivoted on the stacked heel of her burgundy boot to check on whatever buttery-scented concoction she had baking. Crumpets couldn't smell that good, could they? "Wait one second, and I'll let you be the first to try my crumpets."

Maybe they were actually tasty, but once Marissa disappeared into the back room, the man rolled his eyes and muttered, "Do I have to try it?"

Tandy fitted a plastic lid to the cup and handed it to him.

"I think I like you. I'm Tandy Brandt, by the way."

The man took the cup and sipped. "I think I *really* like you. I'm George Knibbs."

Marissa's boots click-clacked back into the room, and she held out a shiny new plate with a small, thick, bubbly-looking pancake in the middle. "I call him Jumpsuit George because..." She motioned to his ensemble. "I surprisingly like the color of this jumpsuit. Navy is the new black, you know. Tandy, you should try it sometime."

Tandy clicked her tongue. "Black is the color of coffee. You can't go wrong with black."

George took another sip. Probably fuel to make a quick getaway. If the man didn't want to discuss Valentine's, then he definitely didn't want to discuss fashion. "Marissa, if anyone is going to try something new, you need to try a jumpsuit like I've been telling you. They are comfortable, and also, if you're wearing a jumpsuit, it wouldn't matter if you spill tea on yourself. I've got an extra one out in my truck if you want."

Tandy turned sideways to face her business partner and grinned. "Yeah, Marissa. Try a jumpsuit."

Marissa shot her a pseudo scathing look before pretending to ignore her. "I don't want to keep you any longer, George, as I know you've got work to do. Shall I put this crumpet in a bag?"

George lowered his chin and voice. "Sweetie, I really don't want to try your fancy flapjack any more than you want to wear coveralls."

Marissa blinked. Or could she be fluttering her eyelashes? "But it's good. I know you'll like it if you try it."

"Back at ya."

Marissa stood taller. Her eyelash flutter hadn't worked. "Fine. Get me the jumpsuit, and I'll put the crumpet in a bag."

George tilted his head in what appeared to be confusion. Apparently he'd never thought this day would come. But then, neither had Tandy.

She shooed him into action. "Go, George, go. Before she changes her mind."

George shrugged a shoulder. "A deal's a deal." He set his coffee down and headed out the door to retrieve the coveralls in question.

Marissa leaned closer as soon as he was out of earshot. "Do you think he said that part about spilling tea on my clothes because of the wet spot on my jeans?"

Tandy pressed her lips together to hold back the belly laughs rumbling around inside. "Perhaps. But even if he didn't, you have to consider how much money a jumpsuit could save you in dry cleaning."

Marissa eyed her up and down. "That's really why you always wear black, isn't it?"

Tandy twisted her lips in thought. She'd never considered wearing anything other than black, but if she wore a lighter color, would she suddenly realize she was as messy as Marissa? "You know if the jumpsuit is black, I'm gonna want to wear it myself, right? It'll go with my motorcycle boots and leather choker."

Marissa's cappuccino brown eyes widened in horror.

The bell over the door chimed, and Tandy spun to see what color jumpsuit George had brought Tandy. Only it wasn't George at the door. It was Connor, wearing his tool belt and a hairstyle that either required a lot of hair paste or naturally looked that messy when he rolled out of bed. Knowing Connor, he'd never even heard of hair paste before.

Marissa clapped at the sight of her boyfriend. "This customer is mine." She grabbed a paper cup and opened the mini-fridge for milk. "Connor, I'm going to make you tea the way they make it in Chile. Miss Universe taught me at that pageant I judged last month. I want to know what you think before I add it to the menu."

Connor eyed the milk dubiously then slid a quick glance toward Tandy.

Tandy placed a hand on her hip. "He doesn't count as your customer if he doesn't pay."

"Connor counts double."

Marissa had no idea how true her statement was. Tandy grabbed a paper cup to combine regular coffee with a shot of espresso, knowing the beverage Connor really wanted to drink was called a Black Eye. Once the contractor finished their renovation, he wouldn't have an excuse to use a paper cup anymore, and the two of them wouldn't get away with their secret little exchanges.

Marissa worked beside her, steaming milk. "You giving yourself an extra shot of espresso to keep up with me?"

Tandy fitted the lid to her cup and held it by her heart rather than take a sip. "Everyone needs espresso to keep up with you." Especially Connor.

Marissa filled her cup three-fourths full with milk then added tea from a floral tea pot with a jarringly bright turquoise spout and top. She handed the cup to Connor and stepped back with a smile, her face beaming with pride.

Connor nodded thanks, his gray eyes sparkling at Marissa. It was cute to see how much the man adored his girlfriend despite how different they were. He didn't even have to say a word for his infatuation to show.

Marissa nodded toward his hands. "Aren't you going to try it?"

Connor didn't move. "I don't want to burn my tongue." It was impressive he could come up with such a great excuse while still half asleep, though it could also be true.

Tandy snorted accidentally.

Marissa looked over her shoulder. "What?"

George returned. Saved by the bell.

Tandy pointed to the jumpsuit in George's hand. It was brown, which would almost be worse than black for her business partner. "Connor doesn't know what *you* are trying yet, Marissa."

The other woman's gaze landed on the garment folded in George's hands, and she visibly recoiled. "Connor has work to do in the loft." She stood on tiptoe to give him a quick peck on the cheek. "Go ahead, honey. I'll come up later to find out what you think of my tea."

Connor didn't go anywhere. He looked from person to person, and once George gripped the shoulders of the coveralls to let the legs unfold toward the ground, the confusion on his face melted into curiosity. "I'm in no rush." He leaned against the counter.

Tandy joined him because with Marissa stepping toward George, they were free to switch cups behind her back. They did so with practiced precision then Connor soundlessly clinked his cup of coffee against the tea in Tandy's hand and took a gulp.

His shoulders relaxed. Tandy knew that feeling well.

George held out the jumpsuit.

Marissa pinched the edges gingerly and lifted it away from her body like a dirty diaper.

The bell over the door chimed again, announcing Billie, the older Asian woman who owned the antique store across the street. "Wow, you girls are busy already, and it's barely seven a.m."

"Hi, Billie." Tandy didn't consider one paying customer to be the definition of busy, but Billie was always completely genuine in her optimism, and Tandy loved her for it.

Marissa would love her even more for this distraction. "Yes, we are busy. George, I'll have to try your jumpsuit on later."

"Sure." George sent Tandy a smug smile, saying he didn't believe Marissa for a second. "I've got to get back to work as well. Congrats on the new shop, ladies."

Tandy waved. "Thanks, George. Nice to meet you." She would have preferred he stayed and made Marissa model for them, but as this was the grand opening of A Caffeine Conundrum, she should focus on her job. She rounded the edge of the counter and lifted her cup toward the waste basket to free her hands for taking Billie's order.

"Tandy," Marissa hissed, stopping her in her tracks.

Tandy glanced up, her muscles flexing with a surge of adrenaline. Perhaps residual panic from when their lives were threatened in this very building a couple months before. Though, at the moment, Marissa was likely only horrified by the thought of wearing a jumpsuit. "What?" Tandy asked anyway.

Marissa jutted her chin toward the cup in Tandy's hand, mistaking it for the cup of coffee she'd thought Tandy made for herself. "Are you not going to drink that?"

Oops.

Connor covered his mouth as if hiding a grin and escaped up the stairs. If he let Tandy take the fall like this, she'd be better off giving him a real "black eye" rather than the coffee with an extra shot. But she'd have to deal with him later. Right now she needed to think quickly.

What could she say? "I've already had two coffees this morning, and I'm starting to feel nervous." Completely true. She had anxiety about Marissa finding out what was inside her cup.

Marissa crossed her arms, her new jumpsuit hanging

from one hand. "Do you not remember the rant you went on when I almost threw away a couple of your leftover coffee beans? You said it was wasteful, and we needed to cherish our goods the way we want our customer to cherish them."

Yes, Tandy had said that. But she hadn't been thinking of tea at the time. Of course, Marissa didn't know she was holding tea. "You're right." She pulled the cup back to her chest. Now what?

"What are you going to do with it?"

Tandy paused, but she didn't have a choice. She had to appease this monster to save Connor's soul. "Drink it?" she guessed.

"Only if you think it's worth drinking."

Drat. Tandy was cornered by her own words. Slowly, she raised the cup to her lips.

Would it be suspicious if she plugged her nose while sipping? Possibly.

Connor owed her big time.

With a deep breath, Tandy closed her eyes, curled her toes, and sipped the most...the most...the most satisfying drink she'd ever tasted. Rich. Silky. Liquid pleasure. Like crème brûlée in a cup.

It was that good.

Could Marissa's morning get any worse? First, she'd slipped in a puddle, then she stupidly agreed to try on a jumpsuit that resembled a paper bag, and now, Tandy was acting like their product didn't matter. Granted, Marissa would have thrown away the coffee herself, but Tandy was supposed to be selling the stuff. Would she continue to be this wasteful?

Speaking of waste, Marissa's little white paper bag she'd given to George with a crumpet inside still sat on the counter. She'd agreed to try on the jumpsuit only if he tried the crumpet, but he hadn't kept his end of the bargain.

The bell over the door chimed, and she looked up in hopes George had returned.

Randon trudged in, his thick eyebrows low over dark, brooding eyes. Obviously, he wasn't having a good day either. Oh yeah. The Corvette.

"Hello, Randon." Marissa stuffed the jumpsuit in a basket behind the counter before he could see it and ask questions. She would have preferred not to speak to him at all since he was more likely to order coffee than tea—and also because of their almost fateful date last Christmas. But Tandy was busy trying to talk Billie into ordering a Mexican Mocha under the argument that since Billie liked cinnamon in her apple cider then she'd also enjoy cinnamon with coffee. When Marissa got a second, she'd brew a cup of orange spice tea for Billie, and the woman would vow her allegiance forever. But at the moment, she had to make a similar offer to Randon. "Can I get you anything?"

Randon scraped a chair against the wood floors then landed in it with a thunk. "Can you get my car back?"

Marissa frowned. Why was he asking her about his car? "I can't, but Jumpsuit George can."

Randon studied her out of the corner of his eyes. "Why do you think that?"

Marissa scratched her head. Maybe Randon didn't know George had found his car. "Because that's what George does when people get their cars stuck in snow."

Randon swiveled to face her fully. "My car isn't stuck in snow. My car was stolen."

Stolen. The word and its implications echoed through Marissa's mind. Her lips parted. "Oh." Her heart trilled. Did this mean what she thought it meant? "Jumpsuit George just stopped in for coffee after picking up your Corvette. He thought you abandoned it."

Randon jumped to his feet. "George was here? With my car? Is it okay?"

Marissa blinked, shook her head, and pointed out the window. "He parked around the corner. You didn't see him?"

Randon sprinted toward the door. "I came in the other way—from the police station."

Wow. Marissa had helped crack another crime. On her first day of business. She could see the headline now, Tea Shop Owner Serves Solved Mysteries. It could really boost her sales.

"I'm coming too." She grabbed the bag holding her crumpet from the counter and ran outside after him. She needed to be there when the news reporters showed up. Maybe they'd even get a photo of George eating her pastry. "Wait, Randon." Running in snow was not one of her talents.

Thankfully, he paused at the corner.

Her foot slipped twice, but she caught up to him without further incident...until she followed his gaze. Then her heart plummeted.

Not only was Randon's Corvette missing from the back of the tow truck, but George lay lifeless in a mound of bloody snow. And somehow, she knew it wasn't because he'd slipped.

Their very first customer had been murdered.